ENDORSEMENTS

An Ode to Poison is an absolute pleasure to read—a journey full of twists and turns. I love how the author continually develops the characters so that by the last chapter you have feelings for every one of them. I especially appreciate how so many questions Christians face are woven into this story—questions about integrity, honesty, honor, submission, prayer, faith—things believers wrestle with in our walk with Jesus every day. Betz finds a way to include biblical truth in an easily understood and practical manner. I found my faith being encouraged as I cheered on the heroine and her posse. I highly recommend it!

Rick Taylor,
Pastor of Care and Administration, Hopewell Church

Lisa Betz masterfully weaves together equal parts suspense, intrigue, and lighthearted humor to portray a stunning story set in the first century culture of ancient Rome. I found myself passionately rooting for the character Livia on her quest to uncover the mystery in *An Ode to Poison*. The plot unfurls with unexpected twists and turns, keeping you riveted until the very last page.

Anna Moore Bradfield,
award-winning and bestselling author of
The Lambswool Chronicles *series*

A captivating glimpse into the life and mysteries of ancient Rome. Strong characters and a highly engaging story-line make for a powerful read. Highly recommended.

Davis Bunn, NY Times bestselling author

Intriguing and suspenseful, *An Ode to Poison* is a masterful blend of historical intrigue and nail-biting mystery. Livia Aemilia emerges as a formidable heroine, navigating the treacherous waters of Roman politics and lethal secrets with intelligence and bravery—qualities of a bravehearted woman! The unexpected twists and richly detailed settings make this book a captivating read, especially if you love historical mysteries!

***Dawn Damon, Author of* The Making of a BraveHearted Woman: Courage, Confidence, and Vision in Midlife**

An Ode to Poison. If only I could write a worthy ode to Lisa. She brilliantly crafted a page-turning book with so many attributes of poison I stayed hooked, not just from the mystery but the complexity of how it can be used. Like the characters who are wise and brilliant, Betz is too. Written with a clearly superior imagination, her beautiful prose fed my mind ingredients with such clarity that I see scenes and characters that seem real long after the book is done. I love novels and movies that follow brilliant lines of logic to conclusions. This one kept me on the edge!

Deborah M. Maxey PhD,
***award-winning author of* The Endling**

A delightful read, full of suspicious characters and clues for an exceptional amateur sleuth. A great mystery readers will enjoy.

Darlene L. Turner, Publishers Weekly bestselling author

This series has everything I love in historical fiction--a feisty heroine, a fascinating setting, and mysterious goings-on. Betz's story is an intriguing journey into ancient Rome, with a character facing challenges similar to our own. Recommended.

Tracy Higley, historical fiction author of **The Incense Road**

A LIVIA AEMILIA MYSTERY

AN ODE to POISON

LISA E. BETZ

BREAKTHROUGH
CHRISTIAN PUBLISHING

An Ode to Poison
©2024 Lisa E. Betz

All rights reserved.

This book is a work of historical fiction. Names, characters, places and incidents are products of the author's imagination and are used fictitiously to depict a period of early Christian History within the Roman Empire, and with the exception of public figures, any resemblance to any persons is coincidental.

No part of this pubication may be reproduced, stored in a retrieval system, or transmitted in any way by any means – electronic, mechanical, photocopy, recording, or otherwise – without the prior permission of the copyright holder, except as provided by USA copyright law.

ISBN 979-8-9907557-0-3 Paperback
ISBN 979-8-9907557-1-0 Ebook
LOC 1-13889859301

Published by Breakthrough Christian Publishing
PO Box 1011, Ketchum, OK 74349
www.breakthroughchristianpublishing.com

DEDICATION

In memory of Beth Ellis. She introduced me to the world of books and instilled a profound respect for the power of Story to touch hearts and change lives.

DRAMATIS PERSONAE

Livia's Household
    Livia—spunky, determined, courageous.
    Avitus—Livia's husband, determined to protect his household.
    Roxana—Livia's enthusiastic maidservant.
    Grim—Livia's pessimistic bodyguard.
    Brisa—the housekeeper, at war with dirt, cats, and her mistress.
    Momus—the doorkeeper. Fond of dogs.
    Nissa—a young slave who might be good at cooking.
    Sorex—Avitus's servant. The big, silent one.
    Timon—Avitus's secretary. He knows people who know things.
    Fumo—a (mostly) well-trained dog.
    Nemesis—a grouchy pregnant cat.

Livia's Friends and Relations
    Publius (Senator)—Avitus's older brother.
    Hortensia—Livia's oh-so-sophisticated sister-in-law.
    Brother Titus—a kindhearted physician and follower of Christ.
    Tirzah—Brother Titus's wife.
    Calida—Salvia's sister. She wants justice.
    Merenda (Senator)—Calida's husband. A friend of Gracchus—or is he?
    Auntie Livilla—Livia's wise and well-connected aunt.
    Pansa and Placida—a wise baker and his wife.
    Curio—Livia's brother.
    Dap—a missing messenger boy.
    Elpis—Livia's friend, a perfumer.
    Fortis—Publius's handsome slave.

AN ODE to POISON

Senator Gracchus and His Household
>Gracchus (Senator)—He always gets even.
>Salvia—Gracchus's disgruntled wife.
>Rutilia—Gracchus's bitter ex-wife.
>Iris—Salvia's accident-prone maid.
>Melancton—Gracchus's secretive servant.
>Zoe—a flirtatious kitchen maid.
>(Plus a doorkeeper, steward, cook, and several dozen others.)

Other Residents of Rome
>Dioges—a grouchy physician.
>Leto—Dioges's deceased sister, missed by many.
>Nerilla—a mysterious healer.
>Brassicus—a suspicious herb seller.
>Drash—an even more suspicious herb seller.
>Equitius—a widower with a grudge.
>Fausta—she died under mysterious circumstances.
>Abru—a grieving nursemaid.
>Big Marcus—a helpful bargeman.
>Lucius Calidius (Senator)—Calida's brother.
>Lollia Paulina—a wealthy celebrity.
>One-Legged Lurco—a grouchy landlord.
>Valeria—a fictitious second cousin from Marruvium.

PROLOGUE

Attempting to win the favor of capricious gods was enough to drive anyone crazy, especially a man of logic and reason. Yet Aulus Memmius Avitus felt it prudent to thank Rome's esteemed gods for protecting his wife from kidnappers. Livia had almost fallen into the clutches of his longtime enemy Gracchus, but she'd been rescued in time, thank the gods.

But which gods? Avitus didn't know whose supernatural hands had guided the rescue efforts that fateful night. Thus he was forced to bring offerings to every god who might have played a part. He'd begun with the grand temples to Jupiter, Juno, and Saturn before working his way through lesser gods. Today's final stop was the temple of Neptune, the sea god. Although his wife had been attacked on land, the underlying troubles had involved water.

Better safe than sorry.

Avitus adjusted the drape of his toga on his narrow shoulders, rubbed an itch on his scarred left cheek, and settled in to watch the priestly rites. Part of Avitus's mind followed the ceremony lest he inadvertently speak or move incorrectly and nullify the proceedings. Another part of his brain wondered if the sacrifice would win him the god's protection against Gracchus's retaliation.

Avitus and Livia had been on the side of justice, risking their lives to uncover crimes against the emperor. The gods ought to reward them for it. But when had Rome's gods cared about fairness? Even if he spent every last *sestertius* to beg their favor, would it be enough?

The ceremony came to a close. One more god honored. Avitus beckoned his bodyguard Sorex, a towering ex-gladiator. Together, they turned their weary feet eastward toward the Quirinal Hill and home.

They turned a corner and found their way blocked by a group of burly men. Although clad in togas, the men carried themselves like soldiers, staring at Avitus with immobile faces and cold, hard eyes.

Sorex was immediately at his elbow. He was a head taller than his master and in top fighting shape, but the odds were not in his favor. Especially when two more men stepped into the road behind them.

Trapped!

The men surrounding Avitus tensed as if expecting him to flee. An impractical choice. Like his adversaries, Avitus wore a toga, not a garment designed for athletic activity of any kind. Instead, he raised his chin and looked his attackers in the eyes. "What do you want with me?"

In reply, a broad-shouldered man with a sneering aristocratic face pushed through the throng. Senator Tiberius Sempronius Gracchus.

The biggest thug of them all.

"Greetings, Avitus." Gracchus infused the words with enough venom to kill an ox.

In contrast, Avitus kept his voice neutral and his face bland. "Greetings, Senator Gracchus. You've fallen on hard times if you have nothing better to do than ambush a harmless citizen like me."

"Harmless is right. Your little victory last month is like a mosquito that has drawn a single drop of blood. In return, I will completely ruin you and your brother. Your wealth, your reputation, your families—everything you care about will be utterly destroyed. Before I'm finished, your family name will become a curse."

Gracchus's cruel smile sent prickles up Avitus's neck.

"You have been warned." Gracchus spun on his heel and strode away. His henchmen followed like a flock of geese, their togas flapping in their haste.

Pollux! If that was how the gods protected Avitus after all his sacrifices, why had he even bothered?

CHAPTER ONE

An Ode to Poison

O silent death, stealthy and bitter,
Waiting in patience for unwitting victims.
All who taste will die.
Innocent or guilty, both succumb.

Without blade or blood, you slay your foe,
No need to face them as they breathe their last.
A cup, bowl, or dish,
Disguised by clever herbs or honey sweet.

Yet poison of a different sort
Appears in vivid black on pale sheets.
The pen of man
Is deadly as the juice of hemlock.

By Livia Aemilia
(who doesn't pretend to be a poet, and only wrote this because her sister-in-law insisted. She would appreciate it if you kept your unkind remarks to yourself).

AN ODE to POISON

Livia was not fond of poetry. Let that be stated from the start. She was not looking forward to tonight's celebration of stuffy poetry in flowery language recited by snooty women and hosted by a friend of her sister-in-law, Hortensia, the snootiest of them all. Worse yet, their hostess had insisted every attendee pen at least one brief ode or epigram. Even Livia.

"You like flowers," Hortensia had said when she'd invited Livia. "You can write a nice ode to a rosebush."

Like that was going to happen.

But Livia had married into this exalted stratum of society and the sooner she got to know these women the better. She couldn't afford to miss this opportunity to mingle with Hortensia's peers at a function where no men were present, providing a rare opportunity to observe these women when their husbands weren't watching.

So Livia had written the stupid poem. It wasn't an ode to a rosebush. Or a marigold. Or a butterfly. Since poetry was a deadly bore, she'd written an ode to deadly poison (a topic intended to disqualify her from the "honor" of reciting her literary masterpiece).

An ode to poison had seemed brilliant at the time, but as the litter jostled and swayed its way to the party, Livia prepared for the worst. Would Hortensia cluck her tongue at Livia's lack of poetic sensibilities or find the poem offensive? If so, Livia would fall from Hortensia's good graces. But since she didn't care two figs for Hortensia's graces (good or otherwise), Livia decided not to fret over it.

The swaying litter came to a stop outside the front door of a grand house. Torches flanked the open doorway, creating a warm glow of welcome that did nothing to dispel the tension in Livia's gut. Clambering from the litter, she allowed her maidservant

Roxana to adjust the drape of her sleeveless *stola* so it fell in perfect folds over her ankle-length tunic of sunny yellow.

After a few tugs, the maid stood back, her dark brown eyes assessing her mistress. "You look gorgeous, my lady. The equal of any lady in Rome."

It was almost true. Roxana had worked long and hard to create the complex braids of hair that adorned Livia's head this evening, and she'd transformed Livia's plain face into a woman of elegance. Which was important because tonight she must hold her own with some of the elite of Rome.

Roxana gave Livia's hand a squeeze. "Promise me you'll enjoy yourself, my lady."

"I'll do my best."

As Livia headed for the door, she sent a quick prayer to heaven. *Lord Jesus, help me hold my tongue and be patient with these women even when they look down their long patrician noses at me. Help me find the few who care about something more important than the latest scandal or the contents of their jewelry chests.*

Livia pasted a confident smile on her face and strode into the house. Passing through the front atrium and into the large central courtyard, or *peristyle*, where the guests were gathered, she stopped under the colonnaded walkway that framed the peristyle to size up the situation. This home's peristyle boasted a central fountain with a scallop-shell basin made from imported pink marble. Radiating from the fountain were paved pathways bordered by shrubbery manicured into rigid symmetry. These were accented by a selection of statues featuring the family's notable ancestors and the most important Roman gods and goddesses.

AN ODE to POISON

Livia smirked at a statue of the goddess Minerva. What a scandal she could cause if she told these women she no longer worshiped the Roman pantheon. But that wasn't what Livia wanted to accomplish. She was here to figure out who among these women might be worth befriending.

Wandering the perimeter of the peristyle, Livia studied the clumps of well-dressed strangers to determine who the leaders were. In any group no matter how exalted, there were one or two who held sway over the rest. They weren't always the ones with the most powerful husbands or the longest list of famous ancestors, but they were the women who mattered.

The nearest group contained five women. Four of them tittered and repeated innocuous platitudes, agreeing with every statement made by a willowy woman with a severe chin and understated jewelry. She would be one to get to know. Livia fixed the woman's face in her memory and moved on to the next group.

After circling half the peristyle, Livia spotted her sister-in-law. Hortensia's face and figure were too angular to be called beautiful, but she had the poise and presence of a queen. Speaking of queens, Hortensia was deep in conversation with none other than Lollia Paulina, who'd briefly been married to their previous emperor, the mad Caligula.

The fabulously wealthy Lollia was this evening's guest of honor. Hortensia had been bragging about it for days.

Livia drifted nearer. Noticing her, Hortensia deigned to introduce Livia to the esteemed guest, smiling with something approaching warmth. Well, well! Perhaps mixing with this crowd had thawed Hortensia enough to smile without cracking her brittle mask of Roman perfection.

After exchanging pleasantries with the ex-empress, Hortensia excused herself and led Livia away. As they walked, Hortensia murmured into Livia's ear, "There's someone I need you to befriend. This may be our best chance, so I want you to learn as much as you can."

If Hortensia thought Livia was willing to become a pawn in her social scheming, she was dead wrong! Livia was composing an oh-so-polite rebuttal when they stopped beside two women whose faces hinted at a shared lineage.

"May I present my old friend Calida, wife of Senator Merenda, the city's latest Urban Praetor. This is my new sister-in-law, Livia Aemilia."

Calida and Livia exchanged polite greetings. The Urban Praetor was one of the most important magistrates in Rome. Did Hortensia think Livia would ingratiate herself to this woman in order to gain favor with her husband?

Wrong!

Hortensia turned to the second woman. "And this is Calida's sister Salvia, wife of Senator Gracchus."

Livia barely managed to hide her shock. Gracchus was her husband's bitterest enemy. She gave Salvia a gracious smile. "Good to make your acquaintance."

"We've been looking forward to meeting you," Calida said, laughter sparkling in her eyes. "Although I doubt our husbands would approve."

"Fortunately, they aren't here, and we shan't tell them." Hortensia smiled benevolently at Livia. "If you'll excuse me?"

Her sister-in-law sailed across the peristyle to greet a newcomer, leaving the three women assessing each other. While the sisters' features and coloring were similar, their demeanors were not. Calida was relaxed with a quick smile and warm brown eyes. Salvia was wary and withdrawn. Livia sensed deep emotions behind her gaze. Anger. Bitterness. Determination. This was a woman who was profoundly discontented with life.

After several seconds of silent scrutiny, Salvia said, "Are you one of Hortensia's sycophants?"

Livia gave a derisive laugh. "Hardly."

"Be nice." Calida waggled a finger at her sister. "You're here to enjoy yourself for once."

"No, I'm not. I'm here to accomplish something."

Calida rolled her eyes. "My younger sister is not fond of the chattering magpies who normally flock to events like this hoping for a chance to enhance their standing by claiming they dined with a Vestal Virgin or the ex-wife of an emperor. Hortensia assures me you are not that type."

"I'm not." Livia said. "I was dreading a tedious evening of dull poetry, inane small talk, and insults couched as compliments. Are you offering something more interesting?"

"We are."

Livia gave her first sincere smile of the evening. "It appears I may enjoy myself after all."

Instead of returning the smile, Salvia frowned. "If you hate inane small talk, why are you here?"

Her sister tsked, but Livia wasn't offended by Salvia's blunt question. She preferred bluntness to the cattiness of most women. She flicked a hand at the clusters of bejeweled women. "I've married into this world. The sooner I learn who to watch out for and who I can ignore, the better. And you? Do you and your sister often attend events hosted by wives of your husbands' rivals?"

"Only when it's worth our while," Salvia replied. "Hortensia assured us it would be to my benefit to meet you."

Uh oh! What had Hortensia promised them? "Why me?"

"Hortensia told us you hate Gracchus and that you'll help me find a way to see him suffer."

"Wouldn't Hortensia make a better choice?"

"No. She's ambitious. She weighs every action, always considering what's best for her husband's career. I'm told your husband has no such ambitions, and with your background, you aren't mired in generations of competing political sympathies."

That was the most courteous insult regarding her provincial origins that Livia had ever heard. Salvia almost made her lack of illustrious ancestors sound like an asset.

Almost.

"I'm looking for an ally without any competing political considerations that could get in the way." Salvia raised an eyebrow. "Are you that woman?"

"I might be. Tell me more."

"I married Gracchus because I was led to believe the alliance would be beneficial to my brother and my brother-in-law. Unfortunately, my husband has proved to be as shameless in his alliances as he is in his dalliances." Salvia wrinkled her face as if she'd bitten into an unripe quince. "I did not expect his affections, but I did expect him to honor my family's reputation. I can no longer turn a blind eye to my husband's corrupt and perfidious activities, and I won't stand idly by while he drags my family's honor through the muck. Thus, I'm searching for means to take revenge."

Livia was taken aback by the woman's vitriol. She must tread with care.

"How do you suppose I can be the instrument of your revenge?"

"I know more than my husband realizes regarding his illicit dealings. I can bring you information your husband can use to build a case against him."

Exactly what Avitus and his brother had been seeking! And this woman was offering to drop it in her lap.

But Gracchus must not be underestimated.

"How would you bring me this information without your husband becoming aware of it?"

Before Salvia could elaborate, the hostess gathered the women and started the recital with a brief ode to Erato, the muse whose inspiration the poets relied upon tonight (although Erato might deny responsibility for some of the poems that were offered).

The poetry was as tedious as Livia had anticipated, but Calida supplied an irreverent whispered commentary that had Livia stifling chuckles. Between poems, Salvia and Livia worked out an arrangement for communicating without their husbands' knowledge. By evening's end, they had a plan and a budding friendship.

The hours spent composing the deadly ode hadn't been wasted after all.

CHAPTER TWO

While his wife enjoyed her party, Avitus closed himself in his study and pondered how he would protect his household from Gracchus and his threats. He imagined Gracchus would toy with him, setting him on edge with small incidents before striking the final blow. It would start with Avitus's slaves suffering suspicious accidents. Then someone would break into his house and damage his precious scrolls. Next, a legal case would be lost through a bribed judge.

The troubles would escalate until Avitus found himself accused of treason on trumped-up charges. No matter how adeptly he argued the case, he would be found guilty. With Avitus gone, Gracchus would turn his attention to Livia. She would be helpless to protect herself from his…

No! Avitus would not let that happen. Not ever.

But how was he going to stop his enemy?

His brooding was interrupted by three taps on the study door, followed by Sorex's voice. "Sir? Your brother has arrived."

Publius (husband of Hortensia) was Avitus's older brother. He'd upheld the family's honor by becoming a senator, a role for which he was far better suited than Avitus. Publius was more charming, more jovial, and better looking. His skin was not marred by burn scars as Avitus's was, and his heart hadn't been warped by their father's rejection.

Avitus found his brother standing in the peristyle, grinning like a fool. Beside him was a pale gray dog who seemed to be grinning as widely as Publius.

"Good evening. You didn't tell me you were bringing Fumo."

Hearing his name, the dog wagged his tail.

"I thought you'd enjoy a surprise. Go on, Fumo. Say hello." At Publius's command, the dog trotted to Avitus, tongue lolling happily and his whole backside wiggling in anticipation.

Avitus knelt and welcomed the dog with open arms. "Hello, my friend."

Seeing the dog sent grief twisting through his chest. Fumo had belonged to Jonas, a trusted friend who'd been foully murdered a month ago. Did Fumo miss Jonas as much as Avitus did? Or were dogs blessed to live in the present, untroubled by memories and old wounds?

Fumo rolled onto his back. Avitus gave him belly rubs. Then he got to his feet. "That's enough. Fumo, sit."

The dog obediently sat on his haunches, ears perked, staring up at Avitus.

"See how well he heeds you," Publius said.

Avitus looked sharply at his brother. He knew that tone of voice. "What are you up to?"

"Finding Fumo a new home."

"I thought you were keeping him."

Publius shook his head ruefully. "Hortensia says otherwise. The children have been spoiling the dog rotten and rampaging around the house like barbarians. Two days ago, one of Hortensia's favorite vases was toppled and smashed to bits. It was the final straw. She's turned deaf to the children's pleas. The dog must go."

"And you think I want him?"

"Yes." Publius held up an imperious finger. "I know what you're going to say, and I don't want to hear it. Forget all your logical reasons why a dog isn't practical and listen to your heart for once. You'll realize how much you want this dog."

A low blow! Publius knew Avitus loved dogs.

But Livia did not.

"I don't think a dog is a good idea. Livia won't like it."

"Who's the master of this household, you or your wife?"

"You're one to talk."

"Hortensia has the children to consider. You don't. Besides, how do you know Livia won't be happy for a pet?"

"She likes cats."

In particular, a malevolent black cat with the all-too-apt name of Nemesis. The beast was an inveterate thief and all-around nuisance who was forever sneaking into the house no matter how often Avitus complained. Worse, the infernal cat was expecting offspring—and Livia had been hinting that the kittens would need to be coddled.

But if he owned a dog ...?

He ruffled Fumo's head. "Do you hate cats?"

The dog's ears perked, and his head darted back and forth.

"Despises them," Publius said, chuckling. "The children have been setting him after the mangy creatures who inhabit the refuse pile in the alley behind the house. Cleared them right off."

Interesting.

"I'll give it a try."

Publius gave him a hearty slap on the shoulder. "That's the spirit. Jonas used to say that if anything happened to him, he hoped you would take Fumo."

But could Avitus bear to have this poignant reminder of Jonas living in his house? He scratched Fumo's ears. Maybe the dog would serve as healing balm on his grieving heart. He could hope so.

"Sorex!"

The big man stepped from the shadows.

"We're adopting Fumo. Find him a place to sleep."

"Yes, sir." Sorex hunkered down to let the dog lick his face. "How's my boy? Want to go for a walk?" Grinning, he led the dog away.

When they were gone, Publius sat on a bench and leaned his elbows on his knees. "Now that's settled, we can get down to business. Any developments in our search to stop Gracchus?"

The brothers had brought Gracchus's illegal water supply scheme to the attention of the authorities last month. Since then, they'd been searching for a legal way to stop Gracchus before he retaliated. They had yet to find one.

And now it might be too late.

"Gracchus ambushed me earlier today outside the temple of Neptune. He and a group of toga-clad thugs. Must have followed me there." Avitus found himself rubbing the burn scars on his arm. The scars were a reminder of how much he hated Gracchus.

"What did Gracchus want?"

"To scare me. He promised to ruin our careers, trample our family name in the mud, and see our wives and children begging for mercy."

This was no idle threat. Six years ago, a brave soul had taken Gracchus to court over a defamation suit. Before the case had come to trial, the man's wife had been mugged and his mother's house burned to the ground. Most alarming of all, the protective amulets had been stolen from the necks of the man's small daughters while they slept.

The thought made the hair on Avitus's neck stand on end. This was the man who threatened Livia's safety. They must stop him!

"I have good news," Publius said. "Hortensia may have led us to a breakthrough."

Uh oh! Hortensia and politics were a dangerous mix. "What kind of breakthrough? Did she overhear a juicy rumor while soaking in the warm pool with other senators' wives?"

Grinning, Publius shook his head. "Better than that. Guess who she's introducing Livia to at tonight's party."

Avitus ran through the possibilities. Who might … oh!

"Please tell me you don't mean Lollia Paulina."

Publius gave him a look of mock horror. "Olympus, no! Although inviting her was a touch of genius. With everyone fawning over Lollia Paulina, no one will notice Livia befriending a less important guest—Salvia."

Jupiter, Best and Greatest!

"Are you telling me Hortensia is scheming with Gracchus's wife? With your knowledge? Have you gone mad?"

"It's brilliance, not madness. Apparently, Calida and Hortensia were once friends. Calida contacted my wife because Salvia is looking for an ally. They decided Livia would be perfect."

Avitus groaned and rubbed his temples. There were so many ways this could go wrong.

"How do you know Salvia isn't planning to use Livia to spy on us?"

"Pshaw." Publius waved his hand dismissively. "I've seen the loathing looks she darts at Gracchus. He's driven her to hate him, and Hortensia thinks she's ripe to get even by spying for us. If Hortensia can make it work, this could be our chance."

Or it could be a disaster.

CHAPTER THREE

Livia opened her eyes, staring at the ceiling as vestiges of a dream floated through her mind. Last night's droning recitation of dull verse faded away, but an incessant noise continued. Was that ...?

She sat up. "Do I hear a dog barking?"

Avitus didn't answer. He stood with his back to her, his well-toned muscles rippling as he rinsed his face in a washbasin. He wasn't handsome in the classic sense. His face was too narrow, and his cheek, chest, and left arm were marred by old scars. When they'd married, she'd felt awkward looking at his scarred face, but after he'd told her the story behind the scars, she saw them as his badge of courage and character. Plus, they reminded her to count herself lucky she was married to a healthy, good-natured man instead of a fifty-year-old with no teeth, bad breath, and a vicious temper.

The dog barked again. Avitus smoothed his short hair and dried his face with a towel before turning to her. "His name is Fumo, and he'll make an excellent watchdog."

Uh oh! Had yesterday's run-in with Gracchus frightened Avitus more than he'd let on? Was that why he'd suddenly acquired a dog?

"We have Momus, Sorex, and Grim to protect us. We don't need a watchdog."

"Fumo isn't just any watchdog. He was Jonas's dog, and Jonas told Publius that if he were killed, I should keep the dog for him."

Oh, fish pickle! There was no way she could refuse the wishes of man who'd been like a father to Avitus.

But a dog!

Their small household had enough problems without adding a noisy, energetic creature. "You might have warned me."

"I didn't know about it until Publius brought the dog last night. I'm pretty sure he wanted to keep Fumo for himself, but Hortensia put her foot down so he was forced to own up to Jonas's wishes."

Livia was tempted to put her foot down, but gentle persuasion worked better than a direct attack (or so her mentors told her). Gentleness was not one of her strengths, but she took a breath and curbed her impatience.

"I assume you've assigned someone to care for the dog. Who? Momus?" Their aging doorkeeper was fond of animals and would dote on the beast.

"Actually, the whole household has fallen in love with him."

Wasn't that a jolly thought! Next thing she knew, her bodyguard Grim would be begging to take the dog with them on outings. That was one thing Livia had the authority to prevent!

Someone gave three taps on the door in the particular rhythm that told Livia it was Sorex. (Avitus and his slave utilized a host of secret signals between them, which they had not bothered to explain to her. At least she'd figured this one out.)

"Enter," Avitus said.

Sorex opened the door, and a pale, furry creature bounded into the room. It was a smallish dog with short hair, upright ears, and a pale gray coat that matched his name—Fumo meant smoke. Thank God it wasn't one of those huge, shaggy beasts that slobbered and shed everywhere.

"Good morning, Fumo." Avitus knelt. The dog put its paws on his chest, its rump waggling in joy. Then the beast slurped its tongue across Avitus's face.

Her staid, unemotional husband laughed.

Yes! He laughed.

Livia stared, open-mouthed, as her husband, grinning from ear to ear, ruffled the dog's head and then pushed it away.

"Enough of that. Let's show your mistress what a good dog you are." Avitus stood and raised a peremptory finger. "Fumo, sit!"

To Livia's surprise, the dog obeyed, plopping his hindquarters on the floor and looking up at Avitus with an eager alertness that hinted at intelligence and good training.

"Fumo, let me introduce your new mistress, Livia." He turned to her. "Will you say hello to him?"

Avitus gave her a pleading look. It seemed the dog had turned her normally unflappable husband into a puddle of sentimental mush. Fascinating.

Livia got out of bed and offered a hand for the dog to sniff. "Good morning, Fumo. Pleased to make your acquaintance."

Avitus smiled. "Thank you. I was hoping you'd find it in your heart to love our new family member."

Sigh. It wasn't that she hated dogs, but she could foresee so many problems. However, as a follower of Christ, Livia was encouraged to show love to everyone. She doubted the Lord Jesus had dogs in mind when he'd commanded his followers to love others, but it seemed the appropriate response.

Within reasonable limits. She knelt and looked the dog in the eyes. "If you are to be part of this household, then we should make some things clear from the start. Your master and his menservants are entirely responsible for your care. They will walk you, clean up after you, and find you a suitable place to sleep, where you will be expected to remain until morning. Most importantly, you may not under any circumstances chase Nemesis. Is that clear?"

Fumo wagged his tail, happily agreeing with his new mistress.

"Good boy." Livia gave the dog's ears a scratch, then stood and quirked an eyebrow at Avitus.

"You agree with my terms?"

"I agree," Avitus said. "No dogs in the bedroom. And since the cat isn't allowed in the house, Fumo won't be tempted to chase her."

"Then so long as Fumo keeps on Brisa's good side, I suppose we'll manage."

Brisa was their housekeeper, a petite, stern woman who viewed dirt and disorder as a personal insult. If Fumo was obedient enough to please the exacting Brisa, Livia would find little to complain about.

Avitus gave Fumo a final scratch and shooed the dog from the room. Then he sat down on the bed and his smile disappeared. "Publius told me Hortensia introduced you to Salvia last night. Is that true?"

"Yes. Salvia and her sister Calida hate poetry as much as I do, so we spent most of the evening talking about more important subjects. She's come to despise Gracchus. She says he's brought dishonor to her family, and she's looking for a way to punish him. Since we were brave enough to thwart Gracchus over the water fraud, she's decided we're her best choice for allies."

Instead of congratulating her on her cleverness, Avitus frowned. "Gracchus's wife sought you out mere hours after he ambushed me and threatened to destroy me. Doesn't that strike you as too much of a coincidence? How do you know Salvia hasn't won your trust in order to assist her husband?"

"Don't be absurd. First of all, Salvia wasn't feigning her bitterness. She's profoundly unhappy with her husband. Secondly, she isn't asking me for information. She's offering to provide us with information on her husband's dealings. I thought you'd be overjoyed to find a reliable source for evidence you're not likely to get any other way. Isn't this what you've been hoping for?"

"What if she brings us false information to draw us into a trap?"

Livia gave him an exasperated look. "I'm sure you'll check the facts before acting, so there's no reason to fear."

"Yes, there is. How many times must I warn you how dangerous our enemy can be? Have you forgotten that Gracchus was behind the thugs who kidnapped you?"

"I'm aware how dangerous Gracchus is. That's why I agreed to cooperate with Salvia. We've devised a plan for communicating without Gracchus knowing."

"It won't work. Sooner or later, Gracchus will find out what Salvia is doing."

"What if he does? He's already threatened to ruin you. The time for caution is over. I've been praying that God would protect us from Gracchus and give us the ability to fight back. Do you not see how this could be his answer?"

Avitus harrumphed. "A whispered plan made by two bored women at a poetry soirée. Is that the best your god can do?"

Oh, how ignorant he was about God and his power! But saying so wouldn't help matters, and before she could come up with a tactful way to correct Avitus's assumptions, Roxana interrupted them.

"Mistress? A message for you."

"Come in."

Roxana entered, bearing a wax tablet. She bowed to Avitus, then handed the tablet to Livia. "Sorry to intrude, but the Lady Hortensia's messenger boy said it was urgent you receive this at once."

Hortensia? Livia exchanged puzzled glances with Avitus, then unfolded the hinged wooden leaves to reveal the message scratched on the wax-covered wood.

Hortensia Prima,

To Livia Aemilia,

Greetings.

An emergency has arisen with Calida's sister. We need your counsel immediately. Please come.

P.S. Inform Avitus he has nothing to fear.

Hortensia was asking for Livia's counsel. What was the world coming to? Livia handed the tablet to her husband and ordered Roxana to help her dress.

Frowning, Avitus read the message. "What did I tell you? Your clever little plan has already gone awry. I bet Gracchus found out Salvia was plotting with you. He's enraged over it, and now he's sent threats to both Hortensia and Calida. This is what comes of women interfering in the affairs of their husbands."

Livia rolled her eyes. "Really, Avitus. Can't you consider the positive possibilities for once instead of always imagining the worst possible outcome?"

Avitus tapped the tablet. "Hortensia refers to an emergency. What else am I supposed to think?"

"Don't let her melodrama frighten you. It's not really an emergency, and she said you have nothing to fear. If it will comfort you, I'll ask God to grant me protection."

He didn't object, so she held up her hands and closed her eyes. "Dear heavenly Father, please give me wisdom and protection for all that will happen today. Amen."

Livia opened her eyes and gave her husband a reassuring smile. "Please don't worry. Whatever has occurred, I'm sure I'll be able to figure it out. If not, I'll send you word. I promise."

CHAPTER FOUR

Livia set a brisk pace through the busy streets of the awakening city. She loved the throbbing energy of Rome, its streets filled with men and women from every corner of the empire and every social class from beggar to magistrate. Some hawked their wares in a multitude of accents while others hurried past, heading to an important meeting or rushing to the market to get the best produce and the freshest meat.

Grim, Livia's bodyguard, strode along at her side with his usual somber expression, alert eyes constantly scanning for danger. Grim had once been a gladiator until he'd lost three fingers on his right hand and could no longer wield a sword. Somewhere in his past, he'd also lost his ability to see the positive side of life.

Roxana, Livia's maid, made up for Grim's pessimism with her bubbling exuberance. She loved solving a mystery as much as Livia did and was eager to reach Hortensia's and find out what "emergency" awaited them. (Livia had allowed Roxana to read the message and was proud of her for sounding out the entire thing on her own. She'd come a long way since their first reading lesson last spring.)

As they wended their way through the streets, Livia briefed Grim on what had transpired at last night's party and the contents of Hortensia's message. He wasn't delighted by the news.

Before he could start a litany of dire outcomes, Livia changed the subject. "Let's discuss the dog."

Roxana pulled a face. "That obnoxious beast woke me up with its barking. It's going to be nothing but trouble."

"Fumo won't be trouble," Grim said. "He's well-trained and intelligent, unlike that gluttonous, thieving cat of yours."

"Nemesis is not gluttonous."

"She's fat and lazy."

"She's not fat! She's pregnant, you dolt!"

"At least with Fumo in the house, the cat won't be stealing any more sausages."

"Ha! Dogs steal food too, you know. Can't we get rid of him, Mistress?"

"No," Livia said firmly. "Fumo was Jonas's dog, and he wanted Avitus to have him. We will honor Jonas's memory by accepting the dog into our household. Is that clear?"

"Yes, my lady," Roxana said in an obedient monotone.

"However, Fumo isn't allowed to harass the cat. Is that clear?"

"Yes, my lady," Grim said in an equally flat tone.

Livia could feel Grim and Roxana glaring at each other behind her. Cats and dogs. One more thing that brought division to her household.

Sigh.

They arrived at Hortensia's house to find her dressed and pacing the peristyle, eyes dark with worry. "You're here. Calida is in the dining room. We'll talk there."

She stalked away. Exchanging eye rolls at Hortensia's brusqueness, Livia and Roxana followed. Calida was dozing on one of the dining couches. She sat up when they arrived. Her face was taut and pale, her eyes hollow with anguish. So different from the warm, friendly woman of last night.

Hortensia took a seat beside Calida and motioned Livia to sit opposite. "There's been a tragedy. Salvia has been poisoned. She died early this morning after hours of agony."

For two heartbeats, Livia's brain refused to accept what she'd heard. Then anger surged through her chest. Hadn't Salvia suffered enough? Why did she have to die on the night she'd found a friend and ally? It wasn't fair!

"How can I help?"

"Gracchus must have killed her," Calida said through tight jaws. "Hortensia says you can help me figure out how to prove it."

Why on earth would Calida ask Livia for help instead of taking the crime to her husband? Was Calida afraid to enlist him lest he discover who his wife had been plotting with last night? That might be part of it, but Livia sensed there was more. What were they not telling her?

"How did it happen?"

"Salvia was feeling fine when we left the party, but sometime in the middle of the night she became ill. She grew rapidly worse. Her maid called the steward, who sent for the doctor and for me. I arrived first, so I was there when the doctor stepped into Salvia's room. I watched his face when he saw her. He was horrified. He—" Calida's voice broke as sobs wracked her body.

While Hortensia squeezed her friend's hand and whispered kind words, Livia said a silent prayer. *Dear Father God, please comfort Calida and her family. Please protect the rest of Salvia's household from death. And please show me how I may help Calida find justice for her sister.*

After a long pause, Calida gathered her emotions and continued her story. "Until the doctor arrived, I'd assumed Salvia would get better, but when I saw how he reacted…"

She paused, squeezing her eyes shut to hold back the tears. "Dioges tried every remedy he could think of. To no avail. Salvia died a few hours later. I held her hand until the end."

Swiping the tears from her cheeks, Calida turned to Livia, determination and anger hardening her face. "After my sister breathed her last, I ordered Iris, her loyal maid, to keep everyone out of the room until I returned. Then I came here to ask Hortensia's help. I suspect Gracchus will say his wife was poisoned by someone at the party. We know that's not true, so we must find a way to prove it. Hortensia says you can help us."

Livia studied her sister-in-law from the corner of her eye. Did Hortensia respect Livia's sleuthing skills, or did she consider investigating a murder beneath a senator's wife?

Did it matter? Livia was good at solving murders, and she enjoyed the challenge of it. Who cared about her sister-in-law's snobbish views?

"If you want my advice, you should start by proving your sister wasn't poisoned at the party." Livia turned to Hortensia. "If Salvia's food was poisoned, traces of it would be found in the leftovers. Send to the hostess and ask her to check every slave who served, cleaned up, or tasted the food or wine left over from last night's party. Has anyone become ill?"

Calida raised her eyebrows. "Clever."

While Hortensia dictated the message, Livia considered what else she could do. Without access to Gracchus's household, what facts could she investigate? She turned to Calida.

"You're absolutely sure it was poison?"

"Yes."

"Is it possible Salvia took her own life? Maybe she felt guilty for agreeing to betray her husband?"

"No," Calida said vehemently. "You don't know Salvia like I do. Our plan to spy on her husband gave her new purpose. She was happier last night than I've seen her in months."

And now she was dead. Why?

"Could her maid have tattled to Gracchus about who her mistress was talking to last night?"

"No. Iris doesn't know who her mistress talked to. Plus, she has her own reasons for hating Gracchus. Whatever happened, Iris is above suspicion."

And yet, Salvia was killed the very night she'd secretly plotted with the wife of her husband's enemy. It was too big a coincidence to ignore.

"Why would Gracchus want to kill her?"

"They had a violent argument last week. Salvia refused to say what about, although I can guess. Regardless, the argument is what made Salvia decide to approach you. Only while she was plotting with you to uncover her husband's crimes, Gracchus was apparently plotting to murder her. We must prove it and make him pay."

"That is where your expertise comes in," Hortensia said. "We need you to accompany Calida to Salvia's home and look for clues."

Had Hortensia gone delusional? Livia enter Gracchus's house? Avitus would have apoplexy at the mere thought of it.

"Impossible."

"You must help us," Calida said. "Last night when Gracchus was told his wife was gravely ill, he didn't bother to check on her. He was sick with stomach pains and couldn't be bothered to get up. Shows how little he cares. The mongrel."

Gracchus was a mongrel, and Salvia deserved justice. But Livia remembered Avitus's grave face when he'd told her about the ambush outside the Temple of Neptune. "Gracchus is already looking for a reason to attack Avitus. I can't afford to give him one."

"We can't afford to lose this chance," Hortensia said. "Even Gracchus can't bribe himself out of a murder charge, but we must be able to convince the judge. And that means you must go to the house before the evidence of his guilt is tidied away or the slaves who know something are bullied into silence."

"You'll have to find somebody else. I've been kidnapped once for prying into Gracchus and his crimes. I'm not going to tempt fate a second time. And Avitus would never agree to it."

"I will personally guarantee your safety," Calida said. "When Gracchus has a bout of stomach pains, he's usually in bed for hours. I've already asked for full authority to oversee the funeral arrangements, so the entire staff will cooperate. They trust me and they hate him, so they'll take Salvia's side in this affair. Believe me, they'll be glad to assist us in finding her murderer."

Livia shook her head. "You can't guarantee that every single slave in the household will keep my visit a secret. Sooner or later, Gracchus will learn I was there."

"Slaves can't tell what they don't know," Hortensia said primly. "Neither Gracchus nor his staff have met you, therefore you can use a false name. No one will be the wiser."

Calida nodded. "That could work. I'll say you're Valeria, a second cousin from Marruvium who's come to see the big city. Please help me. If you don't, Gracchus will get away with killing Salvia. My sister deserves better, and I want justice!"

The idea was beginning to sound plausible. If Gracchus was sick in bed and she used a false name, surely she'd be safe long enough to find what proof she could. Fortune favored the bold. If Livia could uncover proof of Gracchus's guilt, then Avitus would finally have an opportunity to be rid of their enemy for good. Either seize the opportunity or forever regret it.

However, bold action didn't mean reckless action. "I'm not going without Roxana, and I want Avitus to know where I've gone just in case things go wrong."

"A wise precaution," Hortensia said. "I'll send Avitus a message at once, and I'll have disguises brought for you and your maid." She beckoned Roxana. "Can you turn your mistress into a country woman who's trying to fit in with the elegant women of Rome?"

"Yes, my lady."

Hortensia shooed them to a guest room to complete their disguise. Roxana brushed out Livia's hair and pinned it into a lopsided mound set too far back and slightly off-center. As a final touch, she plucked a few strands loose to hang over Livia's forehead.

Next, she applied a few quick strokes of kohl around Livia's eyes, then licked a finger and smudged them. A couple of dabs with lip color and Roxana stood back. "Will this do?"

Livia studied the result in a polished bronze mirror and was shocked to see a frumpy woman peering back at her. She looked exactly like an unsophisticated provincial woman attempting (unsuccessfully) to compete with the fashionable ladies of Rome.

Next came a tunic that had once been beautiful but now bore faint marks of wine stains and a bit of fraying at the embroidered hems. Probably one of Hortensia's castoffs that had been given to a maid. Livia's skin prickled at the idea of wearing her sister-in-law's old clothes, but the outfit gave the perfect impression of a woman pretending to be wealthier and more elegant than she was.

The sacrifice would be worth it.

While they donned their disguises, Roxana whispered to Livia, "Are you sure we should do this, my lady?"

"I don't sense any warning in my spirit that we're headed for danger. Do you?"

"My head tells me this is crazy, but my heart is eager to see what we can do for the poor dead woman."

"Mine, too. Join me in prayer. Lord God, if this is an unwise choice, please show me. If not, protect us as we enter the enemy's house."

"Amen," whispered Roxana.

CHAPTER FIVE

After his wife left the house, Avitus retreated to his study, his gut taut with worry. If there was an emergency at Hortensia's, then Gracchus was sure to be the cause of it. Which meant Livia could be in danger.

Avitus was sick of constantly worrying over how Gracchus might harm his household. He was sick of watching Gracchus prosper at the expense of honest men. He was sick of seeing Gracchus cheat justice through bribes and intimidation. He was sick of the churning fear in his heart and the effort it took to conceal it.

He yearned for peace and safety, and there was only one way to find it—by ridding Rome of Gracchus once and for all. Avitus and Publius had spent years waiting for Gracchus to make a mistake so they could drag him to court and expose his crimes. The opportunity had never materialized, and he doubted Livia could learn anything via Salvia that would change their luck.

Therefore, it was time to switch tactics. He called his trusted servants to join him for a council of war. Sorex and Timon were two of the finest men in Rome, although few recognized the fact. Others saw in Sorex only a battered barbarian giant, a brutal fighter with no brains and a funny accent. Others took one look at Timon and saw only the unsightly "F" (short for *fugitivus*, a runaway slave) branded on his forehead. Thus they assumed Timon was nothing but a troublesome clerk who was bound to run away again.

Avitus knew otherwise—and he trusted these men with his life.

"It's time to do something about Gracchus. You know how he threatened me yesterday."

They nodded somberly.

"We must attack him before he attacks us, but Publius and I aren't powerful enough to destroy Gracchus on our own. Therefore, we need allies."

Unfortunately, Avitus had long been disillusioned with Rome's men of power, with their hypocrisy, backbiting, and constant maneuvering for political gain. He preferred dealing with men who earned an honest living rather than those born into the highest circles. This left him few friends among the powerful.

He looked at Timon. "Suggestions?"

Not only did his secretary have a knack for rhetoric and a good head for numbers, he also cultivated a vast network of clerks and functionaries in useful places.

"Sorry, sir. I've tried all my contacts within the imperial service. A private feud doesn't interest them." Timon gave an apologetic shrug. "Unless we dig up proof of treason, we'll get no help from that quarter."

An accusation of *majestas*—treason against the emperor—was an oft-abused means of destroying a wealthy man. If found guilty, even a senator could be condemned like a common criminal and his estate seized. Unfortunately, so far as Avitus knew, Gracchus had not been foolish enough to dabble in treason.

"I will not lower myself to Gracchus's methods of lies and false accusations. That's not the way a Memmius wages war."

"Good," Sorex said in a rumbling voice that bore a hint of his Germanic origins. "What kind of allies are we looking for?"

"What if we gathered men who have suffered at Gracchus's hands? Angry victims who are willing to join forces and provide testimony regarding how Gracchus has wronged them? If we collect enough allies, he won't be able to bribe or intimidate them all into silence. We're looking for men he has blackmailed. Men whose wives have been seduced by him. Men who have lost cases due to Gracchus's bribes. Can we find such men?"

"I know someone who may be willing to help you collect your band of allies," Timon said. "You're not going to like it, but I think she's our best bet."

"Who?"

"Rutilia."

Avitus's jaw tightened. Rutilia had been Gracchus's first wife. She was as scheming as Cleopatra and as seductive as a Siren. A dangerous combination.

"You're right, I don't like it. I don't want to insult my wife by associating with a woman as notorious as Rutilia."

Rutilia's current husband was out of the country, serving as chief financial officer for the proconsul of Crete. Instead of spending the year living in Crete with her husband, Rutilia had elected to remain in Rome. The forum was filled with salubrious rumors regarding her reasons. Many said she regularly entertained men, whom she enticed with promises (and other favors) into doing her bidding.

"Ignore the rumors, sir." Timon waved a hand to brush them away. "I've yet to hear a single fact that supports them. Rutilia stayed in Rome to remain close to her sons. They are her weakness. When Gracchus divorced her, he banned her from visiting or even communicating with their two young boys. I've heard he was afraid she would turn them against him, but more likely it was his way of punishing her."

Not surprising. In Roman law, children belonged to the father. When Gracchus divorced Rutilia, the children (his heirs carrying his family name) remained with him. Avitus sympathized with her plight, but what could he do about it?

"What makes you think she'll give me the time of day?"

"Hear me out, sir. Rutilia cannot abide being banned from her own children. It's a power struggle, and she'll stop at nothing to thwart Gracchus's will. Since the divorce, she's found ways to see her sons in secret. That tells me she must have informants among Gracchus's staff. However, my source told me Rutilia's situation has become difficult lately. Therefore, I submit she may be open to working with you. Combine her contacts in Gracchus's household, her current husband's influence, and your legal skills, and you may have a chance."

Intriguing. A woman as intelligent and conniving as Rutilia was sure to know men who had reasons to hate Gracchus. Avitus raised an eyebrow at Sorex.

"It's a move Gracchus won't expect," the big man said. "Worth the risk."

So be it. Avitus sent Timon to deliver a request asking Rutilia for an audience.

However, an alliance with Rutilia wouldn't help Avitus deal with whatever Livia and Hortensia were up to today. Livia was confident her god would protect her. But would he? It was time he learned more about this strange religion his wife had adopted.

CHAPTER SIX

"You're sure Gracchus's staff will cooperate?" Livia asked Calida while they were traveling to Salvia's house in a litter.

"Yes," Calida said. "I have it all figured out."

Those words set Livia's teeth on edge, especially when Livia wasn't privy to the planning. "Do fill me in."

"The servants despise Gracchus. In particular, his steward. He was promised his freedom seven years ago, but Gracchus hasn't kept the promise. The steward is furious at Gracchus and desperate to earn the money he needs to purchase his freedom, one way or another. I've promised him enough money to win his full cooperation."

Hmm. A bribable steward. That was useful news.

"As for the rest of the household," Calida continued, "I'll tell them my husband forced me to let you tag along. I resent your being here, and I think you're an incompetent busybody, so I'm using you to run useless errands while I do the important work."

AN ODE to POISON

Livia opened her mouth to argue. Then she saw the brilliance of Calida's plan. It would give Livia freedom to snoop without Gracchus's household wondering why she wasn't helping Calida prepare the body. If acting like an incompetent busybody was what it took to find their enemy guilty of murder, then so be it.

Calida stopped the litter outside the house and sent her maid inside to make sure Gracchus was still sick in bed. While they waited, doubts whispered in the back of Livia's mind. She pushed them aside. She'd done all she could to minimize the risks, and they'd never have a better opportunity than this.

How grand it would be if Livia arrived home and gave her husband proof that Gracchus was a murderer. He'd be speechless with admiration. And since she'd had the foresight to inform Avitus of her plan, he couldn't accuse her of acting behind his back. Thus, he'd have to admit Livia's decision to investigate had been the correct choice.

Slaves emerged from Gracchus's doorway carrying boughs of cypress, the traditional symbol that someone in the house had died. Seeing the cypress hardened Livia's resolve. Salvia had chosen to trust her as a friend. Now she'd been cruelly murdered. It was up to Livia to find the clues that would identify her killer.

Returning, Calida's maid reported that Gracchus was still abed, and it was safe to enter. So they did. Gracchus's atrium was as grand as Livia had expected. This formal entryway was intended to show all who entered that Gracchus was a man of wealth and power. The atrium boasted imported marble on the floor and surrounding the shallow pool under the atrium's central roof opening. The display of wealth continued to the vivid frescoes on the walls and the glint of gold and silver enhancing the wall niche where the household gods were displayed.

The atrium was large (much larger than Avitus's) as befitted a powerful man who was *patronus* to many *clientes*. In Rome's age-old system of patronage, the patronus offered legal help and useful connections to his clientes in exchange for their support of his civic and political activities. In an ideal situation, the patronus-clientes relationship was mutually beneficial. In Gracchus's case, did his clientes feel more like flies caught in the sticky web of his personal ambition? Probably.

A stiff-backed man with thinning hair and a jutting chin approached Calida. Gracchus's steward (the bribable one). He gave them a formal bow.

"Welcome, my lady," he said in a voice loud enough to carry to the doorkeeper and other nearby slaves. "My lord Gracchus remains ill. He hopes to be well enough to sit with his wife's body by late afternoon. In the meantime, he has granted you full authority to make the funeral arrangements."

"Thank you," Calida said. "I have brought my cousin Valeria. She's visiting from her hometown of Marruvium. She and her maid have graciously volunteered to assist me in this time of tragedy."

The steward bowed to Livia. "Welcome, my lady."

Livia murmured her thanks. Roxana gave him an awkward curtsy. She was doing an admirable job of acting like a timid provincial girl, gawking at the room as if she'd never seen such finery.

Calida lowered her voice. "I would appreciate it if you kept the rest of the household from Salvia's room while we work."

"That won't be a problem," the steward murmured. "Everyone is eager to avoid the mistress's chambers for fear they might be associated with this tragedy."

"Keep it that way. And don't mention my cousin to your master."

"As you wish."

Calida dismissed him with a wave.

"Wait," Livia whispered. "I need to question him."

"Let me do it." Calida raised her voice. "Do you have any idea who has done this dreadful thing?"

The steward turned back, eyes wide in alarm. "No, my lady."

"Then I expect you and everyone else in this house to help me find the truth."

He dipped his head in silent agreement.

"You can start by telling me who was awake last night."

Good work, Calida.

"Most of us were in bed by dark, my lady," the steward said. "Since the master and mistress were both away for the evening, the household retired early."

"Who returned first?"

"The master."

"Was Gracchus still awake when Salvia returned?"

"I doubt it," the steward said. "I was informed the master was not feeling well and went directly to his bed."

As was common in wealthy homes, Gracchus and Salvia had separate bedchambers. Livia's home was not large enough to afford that luxury. But for many arranged marriages like Salvia's, keeping separate spaces made things more bearable. Even so, poor

Salvia must have suffered living in this house under Gracchus's hostile scrutiny and volatile temper.

"If the household had retired and Gracchus was in bed, who would have been awake when your mistress returned?" Calida asked.

"No one besides the doorkeeper. I was asleep until Iris roused me, saying the mistress was sick. I sent for the doctor straightaway. Then I woke the cook to heat water and sent a boy to inform you."

"I see. Thank you." Calida shot a questioning glance at Livia. She'd done a commendable job, but there was more Livia wanted to know before the steward disappeared. She winkled her brow into an anxious frown and adopted a provincial accent.

"My dear cousin told me Gracchus was too ill to see his wife last night. I hope he isn't suffering from poison as well. Weren't you alarmed when he couldn't be roused last night?"

"No, my lady. His servant Melancton told me he'd given the master poppy tears."

"Why didn't you tell me this last night?" Calida asked sharply.

The steward adopted the deadpan face of a servant reporting unpleasant news. "My lord Gracchus refuses to take medications prepared by anyone other than Dioges, who has been the family's physician for years. However, the master's stomach pains have grown more severe, and Dioges's remedies have ceased to be effective. In desperation, Melancton has been adding ground poppy to Dioges's tonic."

The steward grimaced. "I didn't want the doctor to know about the poppy. Neither he nor the master would react kindly to that knowledge."

Very interesting! Livia clicked her tongue sympathetically. "I sometimes suffer from a painfully sour stomach. How long has your master been afflicted with this ailment?"

"For many years, although the pains have grown worse of late. He blames the cook, but no one else in the household is bothered, so..." The steward shrugged.

Was Gracchus suffering under the weight of guilt from his many crimes? A satisfying thought.

But Livia must remain focused. "What did your master eat last night?"

"Roasted fish with vegetables."

"Aha." Livia opened her eyes wide. "What kind of fish?"

The steward shrugged. "The cook didn't say."

"I have found that eels turn my stomach sour, but milder fish are not a problem. Perhaps your cook should be told."

"I'll bear that in mind."

Livia beamed at him. "I'm glad to be of help to someone as important as your master."

His jaw twitched, and Livia smirked inwardly. He thought her an annoying nitwit. Perfect.

With a look of grave dignity that silently implied he had more important tasks than discussing digestive ailments with strange women, the steward turned to Calida. "Anything else, my lady?"

"No," Calida said. "You can oversee the construction of the bier while my cousin and I attend to my sister's body."

The steward bowed and left. Calida led Livia and Roxana into the peristyle. As with the atrium, this space was designed to impress visitors. A grand fountain tiled in bright blues filled one short side of the space. The peristyle was oddly deserted other than a lone woman standing like a sentinel at a closed door. The rest of the household must be staying out of sight.

Calida wandered to the fountain. "Why did you ask about Gracchus's meal?" she murmured to Livia.

With the fountain's gentle burble and the space empty of slaves, they weren't likely to be overheard. But to be safe, Livia matched Calida's quiet tone. "Just part of my act to appear stupid. The more the servants think me naive and harmless, the better."

Calida gave a half-hearted smile. "In that case, you're off to a good start. Did we learn anything important?"

"Possibly. The steward said Gracchus was given poppy tears. What if he took them so he'd have an excuse for sleeping through his wife's death? That way he wouldn't have to pretend he was shocked to see her suffer."

Calida's eyebrows rose. "I would never have thought of that. I could tell last night that you were an unusually clever woman, so when Hortensia suggested you this morning, I agreed immediately. Thank you for joining me."

"You're welcome."

They stood in silence for a moment. Calida ran her hands idly through the water, then shook them dry and straightened her shoulders. "We can't put it off any longer. Are you ready to see Salvia's body?"

Calida led Livia and Roxana across the peristyle to the doorway guarded by a middle-aged woman with a bovine face and large, sad eyes. When they drew near, the woman clasped her hands together. "Thank the gods you've come back, my lady. I've been so frightened."

"Why? Has anyone tried to enter your mistress's room?"

The woman shook her head. "The household is terrified of being poisoned. They're avoiding the room like it's cursed."

"Don't let them frighten you," Calida said gently as if speaking to a small child. "Thank you for watching over your mistress while I was gone. I'll take over now."

Dipping her head, the woman moved away from the door in obvious relief.

"Valeria, this is Iris, Salvia's maid. Iris, this is my cousin Valeria from Marruvium. She's come to help me."

The maid dipped her head to Livia. "Greetings, my lady. It's kind of you to help us."

"You will remember my cousin's name if someone asks?" Calida said.

"Yes, my lady," Iris intoned. "Valeria from Marruvium."

Then her forehead crinkled. "I don't remember Mistress Salvia ever mentioning cousins from Marruvium."

"Valeria is related to my husband."

"Oh." The furrows disappeared, replaced by the placid, vacant face of a woman used to a life of following orders.

Calida turned to the door, took a deep breath, and pushed it open.

The sleeping chamber smelled of vomit, vinegar, and acrid herbs. A lamp stand holding three bronze lamps shaped like birds provided sufficient light to see every detail of the small room. Along one wall sat a clothes chest featuring panels decorated with an ivy motif. Opposite was the bed where Salvia's body lay, draped with a sheet.

Livia's stomach twisted at the sight. Her unease with dead bodies was an embarrassing weakness. *There won't be any blood this time. You'll be fine.* She forced an expression of calm, detached interest on her face and pulled back the sheet.

Salvia's anguished face and matted hair showed she hadn't died peacefully. She was dressed in a simple night shift as one would expect. No wounds. Livia replaced the sheet (slowly and without shuddering) and considered the rest of the room. Beside the bed was a silver cup on a tripod table of inlaid wood.

Livia beckoned Iris, who was hovering in the doorway. "Is that the tonic you gave your mistress last night?"

Iris nodded nervously. "I must have forgotten about it in all the confusion. I'd better return it to the kitchen before the cook scolds me."

Livia picked it up. "Not yet."

The cup still held some liquid. Livia raised it to her nose and took a tentative sniff. A pungent odor, bitter with overtones of rue and something else. Willow, perhaps? The liquid in the cup looked like ordinary wine. Still, if you could recognize poison by sight, it wouldn't be a very effective way of killing someone, would it?

"When did your mistress drink this?"

"Right after we returned home," Iris said. "Her head hurt, so she sent me to mix her a cup of headache tonic. I did as she asked." Iris stared forlornly at the cup. "It wasn't my fault. I mixed the tonic just like always. I didn't kill her."

"No one is saying you did," Calida said.

"The doctor seemed to think so, the way he questioned me. He was very cross."

"Dioges was frightened," Calida said. "He couldn't prevent Salvia from dying, and it made him gruffer than usual. That doesn't mean he thinks you could possibly have killed your mistress."

Iris gave the cup another worried glance. "You're sure he doesn't blame me?"

"Yes. Unless you gave your mistress something else you aren't telling us?'

Iris shook her head. "The tonic was the only thing she took last night. I swear it."

"I believe you. Go fetch a basin of water, then inform the housekeeper it's time to help me prepare the body."

"Yes, my lady." Iris bowed and hurried from the room.

Calida sighed. "Poor Iris. She gets flustered when people yell at her. She's timid as a lamb."

"Who can blame her," Livia said. "It must have been terrifying watching her mistress die. I remember Dioges. My father hired him when my mother was ill. I can imagine him frightening Iris by barking orders in that harsh voice of his."

"And he was worse than usual last night." Calida looked down at Salvia's body, and a tear trickled down her cheek. "The moment Dioges arrived and saw how sick Salvia was, he went pale. I could tell right away he feared she was going to die. I'm sure he's worried that Gracchus will blame him for Salvia's death."

She huffed a cynical laugh. "But you and I know Gracchus isn't upset over his wife's death, so Dioges has nothing to fear."

And this cup might be the key evidence they needed to prove Gracchus was guilty. "It was quick thinking to keep servants out of this room. If you hadn't, I'm sure someone would have tidied this cup away before we had a chance to test the remaining wine to see if it contains poison."

Calida looked at the cup in alarm. "You're not going to make someone drink that?"

"Heavens, no. We'll use a mouse. Pansa the baker has been plagued with the vermin lately. I'm sure he'd be happy to catch one for us."

Livia turned to Roxana. "Take this to Pansa's."

The cheeky maid dropped her timid servant act and grinned. "You want me see if it kills a mouse, my lady?"

"Yes, and then come straight back."

Roxana took the cup and hurried off. Calida gave Livia a questioning look. "You trust your maid to handle the task alone?"

"Yes. Roxana is clever and resourceful. Besides, she'll have Pansa to assist her. I grew up next door to the bakery, and I trust Pansa like a father. The poison is in good hands."

Livia scanned the room again. "Speaking of trust, tell me more about Iris. You say she's loyal, but how far can we trust her?"

CHAPTER SEVEN

While he waited for Rutilia to respond, Avitus went to talk with his wife's religious mentor, Asyncritus (whom Livia referred to as Brother Titus for reasons Avitus did not fathom). According to Livia, Asyncritus was a retired legionary *medicus* who now worked as a doctor for the poorer citizens of Rome. He lived one block off Long Street, the busy main street that ran up the valley between the Quirinal and Viminal Hills.

The doctor's ground floor apartment had a small front room set up as a waiting area for patients with benches flanking the entryway. The walls featured simple frescoes of twining ivy and flowers. No pictures of gods, not even Aesculapius, the god of medicine and healing. That was to be expected since Livia claimed these people worshiped only one god.

Having a single god would simplify life. You'd always know which god to placate with ritual prayers and offerings. But how could a single god take the place of the entire pantheon? It seemed preposterous.

AN ODE to POISON

A compact man of perhaps forty emerged from a curtained doorway. "I'm Asyncritus. How may I help you?"

The doctor appeared weary and preoccupied, but his warm smile instantly made Avitus feel welcome. This man appeared sincere, compassionate, and unpretentious, but first impressions could be misleading. Avitus must not allow feelings to cloud his judgment.

"I am Avitus, husband to Livia."

The doctor's smiled widened. "Greetings. I've been eager to meet you. I imagine you wish to know more about our faith?"

"Yes."

"What would you like to know?"

Everything, but to begin with ...

"Livia believes your god protects her, yet she says you have no temple and no altar. How can you win your god's protection without offerings or sacrifices?"

"An excellent question. We Romans have been taught that we can win a god's favor if we make a large enough offering. In contrast, the God whom I worship promises his favor unconditionally. He grants provision, protection, and peace to all who worship him."

"Then Livia is correct? Your god will protect you from all harm?"

"No. God doesn't promise to keep us from facing trials. Rather, he promises that in his perfect wisdom he will lead us through each trouble and use every circumstance to accomplish his perfect will. He controls the cosmos; therefore I can trust him to control my life. When I trust him to guide me through each day instead of trying to take care of everything myself, I find peace in my soul even when I face challenges."

"Isn't it risky to put all your trust in a single god?"

The doctor gave a wry smile. "I spent many months wondering just that. To explain, I must back up to an earlier part of my story. I used to be a very different man. I had a quick temper and a sharp tongue. I was overly proud of my success as a medicus with the Twelfth Thunderbolt legion, stationed in the province of Syria. One awful night after I had drunk too many cups of wine, a wealthy merchant who was a friend of my commanding officer called me to tend his daughter. In my muddled state, I made a mistake mixing a medicine. By the time I realized my error, she was dying.

"I couldn't save her. Nor could I save myself. When her father found out I had poisoned his daughter in my drunken incompetence, my reputation and career would be ruined. To preserve my honor, I was about to drink the rest of the deadly medicine myself. Just then, a maidservant gently took the woman's hand. She prayed to someone named Jesus. Almost immediately, my patient began to breathe easier. A few moments later, she sat up and smiled at me, completely healed. It was the hand of God. There was no other explanation."

Humph. "Sounds more like sorcery to me," Avitus said.

The doctor shook his head. "The woman didn't recite an incantation or invoke secret names of power. She merely spoke a simple plea, asking God to heal her mistress. And he did. I was both terrified and thrilled. What if I learned to harness his power to heal? I would be the most successful medicus in the legions."

Obviously, that hadn't happened.

AN ODE to POISON

"A few days later, my patient invited me to hear more about this God. The men and women at the meeting were mostly poor and powerless, yet their faces showed a peace I only dreamed of. They explained that the Lord Jesus is not an angry deity waiting to punish our misdeeds. Nor is he a god who could be manipulated with offerings. He is a God of love and mercy. He demands but one thing of those who worship him. He wants sole place as Lord and Master of their lives."

"A heavy demand."

"But one I have come to accept. The Jews write in their scriptures that God is like a shepherd, tenderly nurturing and protecting his sheep. I would rather be a helpless sheep tended by my benevolent shepherd than a lone wolf fighting for survival under the capricious rule of selfish and vengeful gods."

Hot anger flared in Avitus's gut. *Lone Wolf* was a derogatory nickname Avitus's peers used behind his back. Time to change the subject. "Why does Livia call you Brother Titus instead of Asyncritus?"

"I've taken that name to remind my flock that I am not a priest or a rabbi. I'm a fellow believer, adopted into God's household the same as everyone else. We see our God as our *paterfamilias*, and we are all members of his household. Thus, I am on equal standing with all my brothers and sisters in Christ."

What an odd religion. No temples, no sacrifices, and a leader who refused to take the role of priest. It didn't fit Avitus's conception of religion.

What were they really up to?

The door banged open. A man with a bandaged arm marched through the door and up to the doctor without a glance at Avitus. "You told me the pain would be gone by now, and it's not!"

He shook his injured arm at the doctor. Instead of bristling, Brother Titus gave the man a look of sympathy. "I'm sorry you're still in pain, but I warned you that if you kept on working, your bones won't knit properly. I told you to rest your arm and give the bones time to heal."

"And I told you I can't sit around doing nothing. My family has to eat."

"As I offered before, I can pray that God will heal you."

"Keep that heathen god of yours to yourself and give me more of your pain tonic."

Disappearing to the adjoining room, Brother Titus returned with a small cloth pouch. The man grabbed it and stomped out, slamming the door behind him.

The doctor heaved a sigh and turned back to Avitus. "Sorry about that. He can be difficult."

That was putting it mildly.

"I would have turned the man out on his ear," Avitus said. "He didn't deserve your kindness, let alone more medicine."

"Our Lord says we must not return evil for evil or insult for insult. Instead, we should forgive those who mistreat us even when they don't deserve it for that is how our God treats us."

How could a man who'd served in the legions be so naive?

"Only an impotent god would turn a blind eye on injustice. Mercy is weakness, and wrongdoing must be punished."

"Forgiveness doesn't mean pretending the offense didn't happen," Brother Titus said. "Rather, it means letting go of grudges and the need to get even. God knows the truth of everything that happens. One day, we will all face judgment for our choices. My job is not to judge others but to extend them the kindness and love my God had given me. I don't understand why an all-powerful God would want to love a weak and corrupt man like me, but I'm thankful he does. I fall on my knees daily in gratitude that the almighty creator of the heavens cares for me and my family."

He looked Avitus straight in the eye. "He cares for you, too."

"Thank you for your time." Avitus bid the doctor a good day and returned home, pondering Brother Titus's strange ideas. Mercy and forgiveness weren't qualities a self-respecting Roman man saw as virtues. And yet, there was an inner strength and confidence in Brother Titus that Avitus couldn't deny. He didn't strive after dignitas, and yet he radiated it. He wielded little power, and yet he had more confidence than many who did. He spent his time serving those of low status, and yet he was neither weak nor pathetic.

How was that possible?

By tacit agreement, Livia and Calida turned their backs on the bed where Salvia's body lay. "What do you want to know about Iris?" Calida asked.

"You speak to her as if she's a bit slow," Livia said. "Is it safe to trust her?"

"Yes. It doesn't occur to Iris to doubt the truth of anything Salvia or I tell her. That's why Salvia has kept Iris as her primary maid all these years. Everyone knows Iris is incapable of lying convincingly, so they believe what she says without suspicion. She was told you are my cousin Valeria. As far as she is aware, that's the truth, and she'll tell it to anyone who asks."

"If Iris is too innocent and transparent to have perpetrated a crime, tell me about the others who were awake last night."

"There was the messenger boy who came to fetch me. I sent him right back to bed. You've met the steward. That leaves the cook. The only other person I can think of is Melancton, who was tending to Gracchus. He's Gracchus's favorite slave. You should avoid him."

Good to know.

"Describe him."

"He has a crooked nose and small beady eyes in a thuggish face with an attitude to match, although he behaves impeccably in public."

This Melancton sounded like his master, a thug who could charm or kill as the need arose.

"Tell me about Gracchus's cook."

"He's the slave I trust most after Iris. He was the assistant cook in our father's household. Salvia took him with her when she married Gracchus. He's as loyal as Iris but smarter and able to keep secrets. More importantly, we pay him well. He's the one Salvia uses to send me messages without Gracchus knowing it. He would have been the one to deliver messages to you if Salvia hadn't …" Calida swallowed. Took a breath.

"I want to talk to him. Will he cooperate with me?"

"I vouch for Cook, but I'm not sure about his assistant. She hates Gracchus as much as Cook does, but I don't know if she can keep secrets."

In that case, Livia would need to find a way to get the cook alone.

Iris returned to the bedchamber along with two other women, who brought a basin, towels, and scented oils to prepare Salvia's body. Time for Livia to get to work.

"May I borrow Iris?" Livia asked.

"Yes, take as long as you need."

Once outside the room, Livia gave the maid a sheepish look. "I need to use the latrine, but I was too embarrassed to ask Calida where it was. Can you show me?"

"Yes, my lady. This way."

Livia oohed and aahed as they passed by one opulently decorated room after another. "We don't have any houses this grand where I live. You must be lucky to live here."

Iris murmured her agreement.

"I'm sorry about your mistress. How long have you served her?"

"Ever since she was fourteen, my lady."

"Was she a good mistress? She treated you well?"

A nod.

"Was she feeling ill last night?"

"No, my lady. She was in good spirits, happier than she'd been in weeks."

"Then why did you give her a tonic?"

The maid stiffened at the question. "She asked for it. She had a headache from drinking too much wine."

"Ooh." Livia slapped her hands to her forehead and grimaced dramatically. "I have that problem, too. Does she get headaches frequently?"

"Yes. That's why old Dioges makes her a special tonic."

"Dioges? Is he the doctor who was yelling at you?"

Another nod.

"Sounds like a real grouch. Is he old and bald with beady eyes and hair sticking out of his ears?"

That coaxed a faint smile from Iris. "You're funny."

She pointed at a corridor. "The latrine is down this hallway past the kitchen."

Livia thanked the maid and made use of the facilities (might as well, since she was there). When she emerged, she gave Iris her friendliest smile. "I feel much better now. Traveling always affects my bowels, if you know what I mean?"

Iris bit her lip and blushed (too well trained to discuss bodily functions with her betters, apparently).

"Speaking of unpleasant substances, Calida told me Salvia had been sick all over the floor. I expected a big mess, and the stink…" Livia wrinkled her nose.

Iris scowled and crossed her arms. "That's not what happened. I made sure there wasn't a mess on the floor."

"Oh?"

"I heard the mistress moaning and thrashing around, so I got up to check on her. By the time I had a lamp lit, she was clutching her stomach, and her eyes were huge. I ran for a basin just in time. I thought she'd feel better after that, but soon she was retching again. Then she began panting and moaning, so I woke the steward. He sent for the doctor, and I begged him to send for the Lady Calida, too."

"Smart of you to send for Calida."

Iris's eyebrows rose. "Do you think so? I wasn't sure I should have asked, but I was so frightened."

"It was the right thing to do," Livia said. "We all need someone to help us face scary situations. What happened after Calida arrived?"

"The doctor came at the same time. He took one look at the mistress and said she'd been poisoned. Then he went to the kitchen to make an antidote. A nasty concoction that smelled worse than his usual medicines." Iris grimaced. "He forced the mistress to drink it, but she retched it back up. That's when he got mad and started shouting at me like it was my fault."

She clenched her fingers. "But I didn't kill her! I didn't!"

"Of course you didn't," Livia said soothingly. "Calida and I know you wouldn't hurt your mistress."

The maid's shoulders sagged in relief. She was worried about something, but Livia had probed enough for the moment. "Just one more question. Where do you keep your mistress's headache tonic?"

"All the medicines are kept in a locked chest in the kitchen."

Hmm, that opened possibilities. Perhaps Gracchus had tampered with the headache tonic when nobody was looking.

CHAPTER EIGHT

Iris and Livia returned to Salvia's bedchamber where servants were bathing Salvia's body and combing out her sweat-matted hair. Calida watched them, arms crossed and jaw clenched.

"There you are, Valeria," Calida said in a patronizing tone that curled Livia's toes. "Would you mind going to the kitchen and seeing how Cook is handling the preparations for the funeral rites tomorrow?"

He was the next logical witness to question, so Livia gave Calida a sappy smile. "I'd be happy to, cousin dear."

The cook was a jowly man who reminded Livia of a camel. He was gutting chickens while a willowy woman with large eyes and reddish-brown hair rubbed a hunk of hard cheese to powder on a grater. They both stopped working and dipped their heads when Livia appeared.

"Good morning, my lady," the cook said. "What can I do for you?"

"I'm Calida's cousin Valeria, here to help with the funeral arrangements. My cousin is weary and in need of food. I will wait while you prepare something."

The cook pursed his lips, his eyes darting around the kitchen. "Will some hard-boiled eggs do?"

"Yes, thank you." Livia dropped her voice to a conspiratorial whisper. "My poor cousin is heartbroken over this tragedy. I can't understand why anyone would want to kill your mistress. Can you?"

The cook shook his head. His assistant stepped forward, eyes pleading. "Your cousin won't let Gracchus blame the mistress's death on Iris, will she?"

Her question earned her a cuff from the cook. "Hush girl! Please forgive Zoe, my lady. She doesn't know how to behave properly. That's why she's kept in the kitchen." He glared at her.

"You're as scared as I am," Zoe retorted. "You know what will happen to the rest of us if Iris is blamed for killing her mistress."

Fish pickle! Livia hadn't considered the terror these slaves must be facing. Roman law decreed every slave in the household could be executed if one of them was found guilty of murdering his master. A ridiculously unfair law created by stern old Romans who were secretly terrified their slaves hated them enough to kill them in their sleep.

"How frightened you must be," Livia said, wide-eyed. "Forgive me for being stupid, but why would Iris be blamed? Doesn't everyone know how much she loves her mistress?"

Zoe scowled. "Gracchus doesn't care. He'll find out Iris gave the mistress headache tonic, and he'll blame her."

And how did Zoe know about the tonic?

"Was it the tonic that killed her?"

"Must have been," Zoe said. "Iris told me the mistress didn't eat or drink anything else."

"If Iris didn't poison your mistress, who did?"

The cook and Zoe exchanged glances.

"We think somebody snuck into the house last night and poisoned the tonic," the cook said.

Interesting. That wasn't a possibility Livia had considered. "What makes you think so?"

Instead of answering, the cook ordered Zoe back to work. Once she picked up the cheese, he turned back to Livia. "When I was sent to the kitchen last night, I noticed the back door was unbarred. I check the door every evening, and I'm sure it was locked when I went to bed."

Livia crinkled her forehead. "I'm confused. Why were you in the kitchen checking the doors?"

"The steward woke me to heat water for the mistress."

"What was the water for?"

"Don't know. The steward was so upset I didn't ask, just did as he bid me. By the time I had the fire going and a pot of water warming, Dioges showed up. He's the master's doctor, Dioges is. He demanded I help him mix an antidote. He took some herbs from his medical bag and sent me to fetch a few things from the pantry."

So far, his story matched what the steward and Calida had reported.

"At what point did you notice the door was unbarred?"

"When I went to look for the dog."

This time Livia was genuinely confused. The cook saw it and hastily apologized. "Sorry, I'm not making sense, am I?"

He took a breath and rubbed his forehead. "Let me start over. The steward woke me. I heated water. Dioges mixed an antidote. Then later, he came back to the kitchen. He was worried someone had tampered with his medicines and he would get blamed for the mistress's death. He had the steward unlock the medicine chest, and I helped him mix a spoonful of each medicine in separate bowls of warm water. He sniffed each one, and then he tasted it."

Had she heard him correctly?

"Dioges tested potentially poisonous substances on *himself*?"

A nod. "Just one drop on the tip of his finger. He didn't taste poison in any of them. But the steward wasn't satisfied. To be extra sure, Dioges ordered me to crumble some old bread in each bowl and set them out in the alley. There's a stray dog been hanging around. He gobbled up the bread in moments."

"You fed all the medicines to the same dog?"

"One after the other. Not a one made him sick."

"Your mistress didn't sicken until an hour or two after she'd taken the headache tonic. Why would you expect the dog to show symptoms immediately?"

The cook's eyes widened. "I hadn't thought of that. Excuse me."

He hurried out of the kitchen. Livia followed him down a hallway to the back door. He whistled. A scrawny dog appeared from behind a pile of rubbish and trotted over, gazing up at the cook, eyes bright with anticipation.

"You're still alive, you mangy cur. Thank the gods!" The cook patted the dog's head. "If he'd eaten poison, wouldn't he be showing symptoms by now?"

"I imagine so."

The cook blew out his cheeks. "Had me worried for a moment."

"While we're here," Livia said, "let's speak privately. Calida is determined to find out who killed your mistress. She trusts you to be discreet, but can we trust Zoe? We don't want Gracchus to know that Calida and I were asking questions about how his wife died."

"Zoe understands we must help you and Lady Calida figure out what happened if we don't want to be blamed for it. She'll keep her mouth shut."

That was as good a guarantee as Livia was likely to get. So back to work. She studied the narrow street. "When you called the dog last night, did you see anything suspicious?"

He shrugged. "It was dark. I couldn't see much."

"Did you notice anything besides the unbarred door that would indicate an intruder?"

"I heard noises like maybe somebody was out there. And I wasn't the only one who heard something. Zoe did, too."

"Oh? Was she helping you in the kitchen last night?"

"Not exactly. I'd better let her explain."

They returned to the kitchen, where Zoe was industriously grating her cheese.

"Tell her what you saw," Cook said to her.

Zoe shook her head.

"Tell her, or they'll accuse Iris for sure."

AN ODE to POISON

Zoe slammed the cheese onto the table and turned to Livia, her jaw tight and her hands clenched at her sides. "I was in the kitchen last night. I was on my way to the latrine when I heard footsteps. I was afraid it was the steward, so I hid in the storeroom."

Zoe pointed at two curtained doorways in the back wall of the kitchen. An obvious place to hide, but why? Even in this household, a slave wouldn't fear a reprimand for using the latrine.

What had Zoe been doing that she feared being discovered? Pilfering the pantry? Enjoying a stealthy rendezvous with a lover? Sneaking from the house? Whatever she'd been up to, a direct accusation would only put her on the defensive. Livia let it slide (for now).

"What did you hear while you were hiding?"

"Iris came in, unlocked the medicine chest, and mixed a cup of tonic. Only she used the wrong jar by mistake, the dolt. She can't tell a cat from a cabbage at twenty paces."

The cook drew a sharp breath. "You let her mix the wrong medicine? You should have stopped her."

Zoe scowled at him. "If I had, she would have told the mistress I was in the kitchen, and then I'd get in trouble. Besides, I thought it would serve Iris right if she got caught using the master's love tonic."

"It's not a love tonic," the cook said quickly, turning to Livia. "It helps the master balance his humors when his choler gets too high."

Zoe rolled her eyes. "I'm not stupid. I've seen Melancton mixing that tonic and pouring it into a jug when the master goes to visit his mistress. He takes it to enhance his, you know…" She waggled her eyebrows suggestively.

68

"Ooh." Livia opened her eyes wide. "Is it an aphrodisiac?"

Zoe nodded gleefully. The cook snapped his fingers at her. "Tell her what else Iris did."

"After Iris mixed tonic into the wine, she left her cup on the worktable and went out. While she was gone, I heard someone else come into the kitchen." Zoe flicked a glance at the cook. "We think somebody crept into the house and added poison to the cup when Iris wasn't looking."

Ah, they were finally getting to the mysterious intruder. "Which direction did the footsteps come from?"

"The back door, I think."

"Did you see this person?"

"No. I was huddled in the back of the storage room so whoever it was wouldn't realize I was there."

Her story was starting to sound a bit fishy. Time to try a different approach.

"Can you show me the medicines?"

Both shook their heads.

"We don't have a key," the cook said. "You'll have to ask Iris or the steward."

Livia returned to Salvia's bedchamber, where she found the body washed, perfumed, and dressed in a fine tunic of pale green with silver embroidery along the cuffs and neckline. Iris was arranging Salvia's hair so she would look regal as she lay on her funeral pyre. The other servants tidied the room.

"Look cousin," Livia said in a sickeningly cheerful voice. "I've brought you something to eat. I'm terribly sorry it took so long, and I wasn't here to help you with your poor sister."

"We managed without you." Calida's voice dripped with sarcasm. The serving women exchanged smirks. Obviously, Calida had been complaining to them about her "annoying cousin."

Good. Livia would play the interfering busybody to the hilts. "The cook seems to have everything under control, and he actually told me I was in his way. I don't know about you city folks, but in Marruvium we don't allow servants to behave like that."

Calida tsked. The maids hid smiles.

Giving her best imitation of Brisa's most outraged sniff, Livia handed the plate of hard-boiled eggs to a servant. Now to let Calida know who Livia wanted to talk to. "How can I help you *and Iris*?" She stressed the maid's name, hoping Calida would get the hint.

"Let me think," Calida said.

Iris inserted a final hairpin and stood up. Calida assessed the results, then dismissed the extra servants. She beckoned Livia closer. "What have you learned?"

"The cook told me that Dioges tested every medicine in the chest and none of them contained poison. Which means somebody must have added the poison directly to the cup." Livia looked pointedly at Iris.

The maid paled. "I didn't do it! I would never hurt my mistress."

"I believe you," Calida said. "However, if you don't want to be blamed, you had better help us figure out how that cup was poisoned."

"Which means we need the whole story this time," Livia said. "Tell us everything that happened from the moment you entered the kitchen to the moment you brought your mistress the cup."

Iris screwed her face into a look of concentration. "I went to the kitchen. I got an empty cup and filled it halfway with wine from the jug."

"Was anyone else in the kitchen when you entered?" Livia asked.

Iris shook her head. "Next, I unlocked the medicine chest and got out the headache tonic. I mixed one spoonful of tonic into the cup like I always do, then put the jar back and locked the chest."

"And then what? Did you bring the cup to your mistress immediately?"

Iris shook her head.

"Why not?"

"The mistress knew the kitchen would be empty, so she told me to leave a sack of food for Nerilla. The master watches over the mistress's money like a hawk, so she pays Nerilla with food. The cook looks the other way, and the master is none the wiser."

"Who is Nerilla, and why does your mistress need to pay her?"

Iris glanced at Calida, who huffed in annoyance.

"It's a long story, but I suppose you need to know," Calida said. "Nerilla is an eccentric midwife and healer woman. But before we get to her, I need to explain my sister's situation. When Gracchus divorced his former wife, he forbade her from visiting their sons. Salvia saw how much this hurt Rutilia. She vowed she wouldn't allow herself to get pregnant so Gracchus couldn't have that kind of leverage on her. She purchased a salve from Nerilla to prevent her from conceiving."

Calida crinkled her nose. "Nerilla isn't someone I would trust, but Salvia didn't have much choice. She needed someone who would keep her secrets since obviously she couldn't let Gracchus find out."

Hmm. Secret dealings with a midwife. Could Nerilla be blamed for Salvia's death? It seemed unlikely, but Livia had learned not to make assumptions.

"Let me see if I understand. You say you mixed the tonic and left it in the kitchen while you took a sack of food to the back door. Did you meet Nerilla?"

"No."

"Did you speak to or see anyone while you were at the back door?"

"No."

"Did you retrieve anything that Nerilla left for your mistress?"

"No. Nerilla left us a new jar of salve three days ago. Last night, I left food in payment of it."

"Has your mistress used the salve?"

"Not yet."

Then Livia couldn't see how Nerilla might be guilty.

"Where is the salve?" Calida asked. "I ought to take it away before Gracchus discovers it."

The maid went to the clothes chest and dug out a little clay jar with a cork top.

Once the pot of salve was in Calida's keeping, Livia turned her attention back to Iris. "What happened after you left the food sack at the back door?"

"When I came back, Melancton was in the kitchen."

Livia's heart thumped. Gracchus's servant had been alone with the cup. Could the crime be that simple?

"What was Melancton doing? Did you see him near Salvia's cup? How long were you gone?"

Iris blinked rapidly. "I … he… What was your question?"

Livia took a deep breath and forced herself to slow down. "What was Melancton doing?"

"He was mixing a cup of something for the master. Only instead of using the normal medicines, he was grinding something with a mortar and pestle. And I saw a little sack on the table beside the cup."

"What was in the sack?"

"I don't know. I've never seen it before."

"How far was he from your mistress's cup?"

"The two cups were side by side."

Aha! Livia's stomach did a cartwheel.

"What did Melancton say when you appeared?" Calida asked.

"He yelled at me for leaving the cup there. I told him I'd gone to the latrine, but that just made him crosser, so I took my lady's cup and left."

"You're sure you took the correct cup?"

"Oh yes. The master has a special goblet he always uses. There's no mistaking it."

Livia exchanged looks with Calida. Melancton had been grinding an unidentified substance right next to Salvia's unattended cup. It didn't take a genius to put those pieces together. But there was still one more detail Livia needed to check out—Zoe's claim that Iris had used the wrong tonic.

AN ODE to POISON

"Thank you for your honesty. Could you please come with me to the kitchen and open the medicine chest? I want to look for that sack."

CHAPTER NINE

Avitus returned home late morning to find Fumo sitting beside Momus, the doorkeeper. Fumo jumped up and barked a greeting, tail wagging furiously. Avitus gave the dog's ears a good scratch. How nice to come home to a happy face (two happy faces, actually). Momus was delighted to have a dog to keep him company. The garrulous old man had probably been talking Fumo's ears off.

"Good morning, sir." Dipping his head, Momus offered Avitus two wax tablets. "Mistress Livia is still out, but I have some messages for you."

"Thank you." Avitus took the tablets and wandered into the peristyle. The sunny courtyard had been his wife's first improvement project after their marriage three months ago. What had been a serene expanse of grass with a crisscrossing of paving stones was now a vibrant garden filled with color and texture. He still marveled at how different the space felt—peaceful but also invigorating.

Avitus sat down and let the quiet restore him after the bustle of the city. Then he flipped open the wooden leaf on one of the tablets to view the message scribed into the wax inside. It was a brief missive from his sister-in-law informing him that Livia would be with her the rest of the day.

That didn't bode well. What would keep Livia in company with Hortensia any longer than necessary? He might guess they were involved in women-only religious rites except Livia's new religion wouldn't allow it.

What else did women do?

Olympus! What if Hortensia had coerced Livia into joining one of her all-day shopping excursions? Avitus cringed, imagining a procession of porters arriving at his door bearing large pieces of inlaid furniture and waist-high marble statuettes of lovelorn nymphs. Dreadful!

He blinked the image away. Livia was too sensible to cram their modest home with showy furniture.

But if not shopping, then what?

He had no idea, so he pushed aside his misgivings and opened the second tablet. This one bore better news. Rutilia had agreed to his request for a visit.

Excellent!

He glanced at the sun. More than an hour before he was expected at Rutilia's. He whistled for Fumo. "Come, boy. Let's go for a walk."

Sorex tied a piece of rope to Fumo's collar, and they headed out the door. They'd not taken two steps when Roxana's black cat leapt from the shadows and raced away. The next thing Avitus knew, Fumo had pulled the leash from his hand (leaving a rope burn across Avitus's palm) and was chasing the cat down the street, barking his head off.

Pollux!

He turned to Sorex. "You'd better catch him before he mauls that confounded cat."

"Yes, sir."

Instead of racing after the dog, Sorex gave two sharp whistles. To Avitus's surprise, Fumo turned and trotted back to them. The dog sat down at Sorex's feet, looking up with a doggy grin and a lolling tongue.

"How did you do that?"

Ruffling the dog's ears, Sorex broke into a grin. "While you and your brother discussed legal cases, Jonas taught me how he'd trained the dog. A combination of whistles and commands."

"Teach me."

They spent a pleasant half-hour going over the basic commands: come, go, sit, stay. Avitus marveled at how willingly the dog followed orders. Jonas had been proud of Fumo, but until now Avitus hadn't realized how intelligent the dog was.

If only they could train Roxana's infernal cat half so well. (Ha!)

Speaking of cats, when they neared the house Nemesis was sitting on the bench outside the door, eyes half-closed. Avitus immediately whistled the command to sit, then grabbed Fumo's leash and wrapped it around his hand. Twice.

"Now listen closely, Fumo," Avitus said loud enough for Momus and Sorex to hear. "If you want to win Livia's love, you can't chase that cat. I dislike the beast as much as you do, but we must respect the mistress and treat it kindly. And when the kittens come, you must promise not to terrorize them. Agreed?"

Fumo wagged his tail. The dog didn't understand, of course, but Avitus hoped the point had taken root in the others. The cat was greedy, thieving, disobedient, and self-absorbed, but his wife was fond of it. Therefore, it was not to be chased.

"As you wish, sir." Sorex shooed Nemesis from the bench (gently) and the trio entered the house without incident.

The medicine chest was kept on a shelf in the kitchen. At Livia's request, Iris set the chest on the worktable, unlocked it, and lifted the lid. Alas, the chest didn't contain any sacks of mysterious substances. Instead, Livia found five identical clay jars with labels painted in heavy black letters. The labels read Cough, Stomach, Fever, Headache, and Vitality. (The last one must be Gracchus's love tonic. Did he think he was fooling anyone using a euphemism like Vitality to disguise its true purpose?)

It was easy to imagine Iris mistaking one jar for another. Since Dioges had wisely tested every jar, Livia knew none of them contained poison. Even if Iris had used the wrong tonic, it shouldn't matter, but Livia wanted to be thorough. "Show me which medicine you gave your mistress last night."

Iris tapped the last jar, the one labeled Vitality.

"You're sure that's the correct one?"

"Yes, my lady. The medicines are kept in order, and the headache tonic is the one farthest to the right."

Except it wasn't.

Livia pulled the jars labeled Headache and Vitality from the chest. She uncorked them and sniffed each. The one marked Vitality had the same musky acrid odor as the residue in Salvia's cup. Livia sniffed both jars several times to be sure.

It seemed Zoe was correct. Iris had used Gracchus's love tonic last night by mistake. Salvia must had been too tipsy to notice the difference.

Livia returned the jars in the order she'd found them and beckoned the cook. "When you helped the doctor test these medicines last night, did you take note of the order they were in?"

He nodded.

"Is this the same order?"

The cook twisted each jar to study the labels before answering. "Yes, my lady. I'm certain of it because I took pains to put them back in the same place. The steward is very fussy about it."

"Is something wrong with the medicines, my lady?" Iris said, glancing anxiously at the chest.

In reply, Livia held up the love tonic. "What does this label say?"

Iris shrugged. "I can't read, my lady." Her gaze flicked from the jar in Livia's hand to the others. "Did I do something wrong?"

"The medicine you gave to your mistress last night wasn't her headache tonic."

The maid went deathly white. "What have I done? Is it my fault the mistress is dead?"

"No. Your mistake didn't kill her."

But it meant somebody else had been in that chest. Why?

Livia sent Iris back to Calida. Then she crossed her arms and stared at Zoe.

"Iris told me it was Melancton who entered the kitchen while she was gone."

Zoe went pale. The cook muttered a curse and spun to face her. "Why didn't you tell me, you foolish girl? What else haven't you told us?"

"Nothing, I swear it."

"Did you know it was Melancton?" Livia asked.

Zoe nodded.

"Did he have time to add poison to the mistress's cup before Iris returned?"

Both slaves stared at her, open-mouthed.

"Is that what happened?" the cook asked. "Melancton poisoned the mistress?"

"That's what I think. Do you agree, Zoe?"

"Maybe. I didn't see him touch the cup, but I heard him give Iris an earful for leaving it unwatched. The master is always worried about poison. Insists everything he eats or drinks is guarded every second, so Melancton let Iris have it."

If Gracchus was paranoid about poison, he'd be cautious about who had access to his medicines. "Who besides your mistress has a key to the medicine chest?"

"Melancton and the steward," Zoe said.

"And which of them do you think rearranged the jars?"

No answer.

Livia let the silence stretch. Sometimes silence was the best way to coax people to talk. Sure enough, after several long moments Zoe huffed a sigh.

"Everybody knows the mistress keeps her key to the medicine chest on a hook in her room. She was out of the house last night. Maybe someone helped themselves to a bit of the mistress's headache medicine while she was gone."

And maybe that "somebody" had been forced to hide in the storeroom to avoid being caught pilfering. Before Livia could press Zoe to admit her guilt, a burly man with a brutish face, small piggy eyes, and a prominent forehead strode into the kitchen.

Uh oh! Was this Melancton, the one Calida had warned her to avoid?

Zoe was instantly engrossed with her grating. The cook shot the man a venomous look before going stiff and subservient.

"What's going on here?" the man snarled.

The cook held up a chicken. "Just doing our work. What do you want, Melancton?"

Fish pickle! It *was* Gracchus's trusted slave. (The potential poisoner.)

He turned his scowling face to her. "Who are you?"

Livia opened her eyes wide and did her best impression of a simple country girl who couldn't tell a potential killer from a vegetable farmer. "I'm Calida's cousin," she said in a mousy voice.

He crossed his arms and glared at her. "What business do you have in the kitchen?"

"My cousin is hungry after all she's done for her poor sister. Salvia looks so peaceful now with that lovely tunic and her hair all washed and pinned. You should have seen the body when we got here. Ugh!" Livia wrinkled her face and gave a dramatic shudder. "I offered to help with the hair, but Calida said I could be more useful coming to the kitchen to ask the cook to prepare some food, so here I am."

Melancton's piggy eyes narrowed menacingly. "The master doesn't approve of guests in his kitchen. Get out."

It took all Livia's resolve to refrain from slapping the insolent man. But she forced her hands to remain at her side—unclenched—and kept a meek expression on her face.

"While you're at it," the rude slave said, "tell your cousin that my lord Gracchus is awake and she is expected to report to him."

CHAPTER TEN

Back in the sleeping chamber, Calida was weeping as she held her dead sister's hand. Livia paused on the threshold, asking God to comfort her new friend. Then she quietly entered the room.

"Sorry to interrupt, but I've been informed that Gracchus is awake. I must leave. If he finds me here, we're both in trouble."

"Did you find the poison?"

"No, but I learned a few more details." Livia told Calida about Iris mixing the wrong tonic by mistake and about Zoe confirming she'd seen Melancton alone with Salvia's cup.

Calida's eyes blazed. "What did I tell you? Melancton is the culprit, following his master's orders."

A tempting conclusion but not the only possible one. "Why are you so sure Gracchus wanted to killed Salvia?"

"She was acting behind his back to help his former wife Rutilia stay in contact with her sons. When Salvia married Gracchus, Rutilia approached her and begged her assistance. The two made a pact. Salvia vowed she would help Rutilia see her sons from time to time. She has kept that vow, and I fear it may have been her downfall. Four months ago, Gracchus saw the two women together. He was apoplectic with fury and forbade Salvia from speaking to Rutilia ever again. My sister ignored him, and I think Gracchus found out. Her defiance has driven him to kill her."

Defying a husband might be grounds for divorce but not murder. If Gracchus were guilty of murdering his wife, he must have had a more compelling reason. Unfortunately, Livia would have to discover the motive some other way.

"I must leave. Since Roxana isn't back yet, may I borrow the kitchen maid to escort me to Pansa's bakery?"

Calida nodded. "Before you go, let's plan our next meeting. I'll be busy with the funeral rites all day tomorrow. The day after, will you come to my house and tell me the results of the poison test along with anything else you learn?"

"I will."

"Also, would you speak with Dioges?"

"Why?"

"We need him to swear that Salvia's death couldn't have been caused by his medicines even if Iris made a mistake. And we'd better talk to Dioges before Gracchus threatens him into silence."

"Do you think he'll cooperate?"

"Yes. You should have seen how devastated Dioges was over Salvia's death. He tried everything he could to save her. He's always taken pains to serve Gracchus well, bending over backwards to keep him happy. I'm sure Dioges sees Salvia's death as a personal insult and he wants justice for her death as much as we do."

Livia took Calida's hands in hers. "Then I promise I'll talk to Dioges and do everything else I can to see this through."

"One last thing." Calida pulled a folded piece of papyrus from her belt. "I've composed a message for your husband, thanking him for all you've done. I'm aware of the risks you took. I hope this helps you make it up to him."

"Thank you." Livia tucked the note into the wraps of her cloth belt, gave Calida a quick hug, and headed for the kitchen. As she crossed the peristyle for the final time, she considered her plan. Her disguise had worked so far, but she didn't want anyone in this household to know her connection to Pansa and Placida. It would be safer if she headed to a different destination. Hmm …

What about Naso's perfume shop? Yes, that could work. She could pretend Calida was sending her to purchase perfume to anoint Salvia's body.

When Livia entered the kitchen, the cook shot a sideways glance at Zoe and silently beckoned Livia to the pantry. "I have something to show you," he murmured. "Look what I found hidden under a pile of onions." He held up a small sack.

Livia opened the sack to find some whitish shriveled things. "Are these dried mushrooms?"

"I think so, but they aren't any kind of edible mushroom I'm familiar with. I wouldn't touch them."

Livia's skin prickled. Was this what Melancton had been grinding last night? Was she holding a sack of death?

"Nobody knows I've found these," the cook murmured. "Take them. Maybe they can help you find the killer."

Clenching his fists, he looked her in the eyes. "You and your cousin are the only hope we have, my lady. Prove it wasn't one of us who killed our mistress and bring the true killer to justice."

"My cousin and I will do our best. In the meantime, Calida has asked me to visit a perfumer named Naso. Do you know where that is?"

He nodded.

"Calida said I could borrow Zoe to escort me there."

The cook dipped his head. "As you wish, my lady."

He gave Zoe a stern look. "Take this lady to Naso's perfume shop, and don't dawdle on the way back, hear?"

Efficient slaves welcomed Avitus to Rutilia's house and led him to a pleasant peristyle with flower-filled borders and a central arch covered in climbing roses. It was a welcoming place, one that Livia would like. Avitus mentally rolled his eyes. How marriage changes a man! Before taking a wife, he wouldn't have noticed the flowers, let alone been able to identify them.

However, compliments on the landscaping weren't likely to impress Rutilia. He arranged his features and posture to exude confidence and silently rehearsed his speech.

Which suddenly seemed pathetic.

If Rutilia had wanted to destroy her ex-husband, she would have done so before now. If she needed legal assistance, she could ask anyone in Rome. Why did he think she'd bother with a nobody like him?

You should leave now before you make an ass of yourself.

Too late.

Rutilia sailed into the peristyle with her customary grace and poise. She'd been graced by the gods with a powerful force of personality, the likes of which Avitus could only dream of. Her glossy black hair was bound in an elaborate mound highlighted with silver threads that glinted in the sunlight. Silver also gleamed at her throat, wrists, and ankles. Two maids and a muscled youth followed in her wake, arraying themselves behind their mistress.

"Greetings, Aulus Memmius Avitus," Rutilia said in formal tones. "On behalf of my husband, I welcome you to his house."

After thanking her with the same formal dignity, Avitus took a seat opposite Rutilia. She snapped her fingers. The young man stepped forward and deftly filled a cup. Avitus took a sip. "An excellent vintage."

"Thank you. My husband is an avid connoisseur of wine."

"To your husband. May the gods prosper him."

"May they indeed."

Avitus took another slow sip. He dreaded small talk. Why must important business be preceded by inane discussions of the weather and other irrelevancies?

Rutilia set her cup on the table and folded her arms in her lap. "Your message said you wished to discuss something of mutual benefit?"

Praise be to the gods! A woman who got right to the point.

"Correct. We share a common enemy."

"More than one, I imagine. To which do you refer?"

"Gracchus."

A series of emotions flitted across Rutilia's face. One manicured eyebrow quirked in surprised appraisal. "You've piqued my curiosity. Why are you suddenly interested in discussing an enemy you've had for years?"

Avitus explained how he and his brother had exposed Gracchus's scheme to provide illegal water rights in exchange for promises of loyalty.

"That was your doing?" Rutilia favored him with a smile. "Well done! Gracchus's clientes are mad as hornets over the fines they've been forced to pay. You've hurt him more than he's letting on."

"Which is why he ambushed me yesterday and threatened to destroy me. My brother and I are hoping we might join forces with you and defeat him permanently."

"A tall order."

"I'm aware of that, but Publius and I see no other way to protect our families. We hope to collect enough men to join forces that Gracchus won't be able to intimidate them into silence. Will you help us?"

Rutilia took another sip of wine, studying Avitus over the rim of her cup.

Here it comes. She'll give me a pitying smile and send me on my way.

No. She's listened this long. There's hope.

Avitus silenced his fears, met her gaze, and waited.

At last, she set her cup aside and raised her chin. "You've come at a most propitious time. If you'd asked me yesterday, I would have wished you success and bid you farewell. Today, however, the goddess *Fortuna* has given us a rare opportunity."

She paused, ratcheting the tension as deftly as a trained orator. "Last night, Gracchus's wife was poisoned. Prove he's behind her death, and I'll win us the cooperation of Salvia's family. Together, we can bring him down."

CHAPTER ELEVEN

Avitus could barely contain his excitement as he bid Rutilia good day. He and his brother had been waiting years for an opportunity to drag Gracchus into court and see him condemned.

Murder would do nicely.

All they had to do was prove it. They'd need an inside source to find out what had occurred. Hadn't Publius said one of his slaves had a lover in Gracchus's house? They could use him to seek answers to vital questions. How was Salvia poisoned? When? Who was awake? What precipitated Gracchus's decision to kill his wife? Why now?

Hades! Avitus's gut clenched as the implication hit him. Salvia was dead mere hours after plotting with Livia. Had Gracchus discovered that Salvia had been plotting with Livia and killed her for betraying him? If so, what if he claimed Salvia had been poisoned by Livia at the poetry soiree?

Jupiter Best and Greatest!

Avitus looked down to see his hands were clenched. Relaxing them, he shook the thoughts from his head. No point entertaining alarmist notions over nothing.

Gut churning, Avitus hurried to his brother's house to find out if his worst fears had come to pass. He found Publius in the sunny peristyle, composing a speech. No sign of the women.

"Where is Livia? Does she know about Salvia's death?"

"Yes, but how did you hear about it?" Publius asked. "Has word begun spreading around the forum?"

"It's true? Salvia's dead? Where's Livia?"

Publius ran a hand through his thinning hair. "I'll get to that, but first tell me how you heard about the murder."

Avitus related his visit to Rutilia and her promise to win Salvia's family as allies.

"That was gutsy of you."

"Thank you. For once the gods were on our side, but we must prove Gracchus is guilty."

"We're already working on it. Calida came to see Hortensia early this morning, all in a panic. She'd been with her sister through the night and watched her die. She was convinced Gracchus murdered Salvia, and she begged Hortensia to help her prove it. Hortensia apparently offered Livia's services as an expert sleuth."

That sounded ominous. "What kind of services?"

"I only discovered their plan after Livia and Calida were gone. I've lectured Hortensia about it. She stepped outside the bounds and owes you an apology."

"For what?"

Publius wouldn't meet his eyes. "Hortensia sent Livia with Calida to question Gracchus's household."

Beard of Hercules! This was worse than anything he'd imagined. Livia was in the house of the man who had threatened to destroy them all. If Gracchus found Livia prying into his wife's death… It was too horrible to contemplate.

Avitus sunk to a bench and dropped his head to his hands. "How could you let this happen? He'll hold her for ransom and ruin us both."

"No, he won't. He's sick in bed, and your wife took the precaution of a disguise. He'll never know she was there."

"A disguise is supposed to allay my fears?"

"Yes, actually. This is Livia I'm talking about. The woman who kept her head when she was kidnapped and managed to escape. I think you can trust her to take care of herself."

Avitus wanted to grab his brother by the throat and shake him. Instead, he took a deep breath and forced himself to think rationally.

"How long has she been gone? Who is with her?"

"She took her maid, and we expect her back soon. How about a game of Brigands to pass the time?"

Avitus wasn't in the mood for games, but it was better than staring at the fountain and counting the seconds.

"Fine."

Publius set out a polished wooden playing board and a sack of stone markers. "Do you want light or dark?"

"Dark." Like his mood.

Livia followed Zoe out the back door, glad for a chance to question the woman when no one else was listening. She adopted the conspiratorial tone women used to exchange juicy gossip. "Now that Cook isn't here to overhear us, tell me who hates your mistress enough to kill her."

"The master," Zoe replied immediately.

"Ooh! Do they argue a lot? Does Gracchus threaten her?"

"He did the other day. I was cleaning the dining room and overheard them arguing. He accused her of seeing some man, only I didn't hear the name. The mistress denied it, but the master said things I won't repeat. He didn't strike her, but his voice sent shivers down my spine. They've glared daggers at each other ever since."

An accusation of infidelity? That could be enough to push a vengeful man like Gracchus into murder. If so, the supposed paramour was probably in danger as well. He ought to be warned. Unfortunately, Zoe had no idea who the mystery lover might be.

They came to an intersection. Zoe turned left onto a cross street. Livia was about to correct her for taking a roundabout route when she remembered her disguise.

Fish pickle! She'd almost blown it. Pulling her shawl close around her face, Livia trudged behind Zoe until the perfume shop came into sight. Uh oh! Another flaw in her plan. Livia couldn't risk Naso or his talkative daughter Elpis blurting out her real name in front of Zoe.

"Is that the shop?" Livia pointed.

"Yes, my lady."

"Thank you for your help. You may go."

Zoe dipped her head and turned for home. Entering the perfume shop, Livia inhaled the wonderful aroma, a mixture of lavender, roses, frankincense, balsam, and other scents.

Elpis was dusting a shelf filled with delicate glass vials. The young woman looked up when Livia entered and broke into a grin. "Good to see you, my friend."

Livia drew her into a hug and whispered in her ear. "Shh. I'd rather nobody knows I'm here."

Elpis's eyes lit up. "Have you found another mystery to solve?"

"Yes, but I can't tell you about it today."

Livia loitered in the perfume shop until Zoe was out of sight. Then she took her leave, promising to tell Elpis about the murder some other time.

A block and a half later, Livia entered Pansa's bakery. The bakery, located around the corner from her parents' home, had been her refuge since childhood. Entering the shop always brought a sense of peace. She'd been rushing from one thing to the next all morning, and she needed the reminder to slow down a little.

Livia took three deliberate, slow breaths, savoring the warm, yeasty aroma before continuing through the front room into the workroom. It was midday, and the bulk of the day's bread baking was completed. Pansa was pulling golden loaves from the large ovens that filled the back of the room. His wife Placida was putting the finishing touches on a tray of almond pastries that would soon have their turn in the oven.

"Livia, dear, you're safe." Placida wiped her hands on her apron, then wrapped Livia in a warm embrace. "I was worried when Roxana told me where you'd gone. Why did you set foot in the house of that man after the violence his minions committed last month? The Lord Jesus teaches us to forgive our enemies, but that doesn't mean we're to trust them blindly."

"Thank you for your concern, but as you can see, I'm fine." Livia gave her mentor's back a loving pat, then pulled from the embrace. "Where is Roxana and the wine?"

"Pansa and I didn't like the idea of poison near the bread, so I sent her into our apartment." Placida shuddered. "I don't like you messing with poison, although I won't complain about a few less thieving rodents. Since Nemesis left us, we've been overrun by the filthy pests."

Nemesis was an excellent mouser. She'd kept the bakery's mouse population in check before Livia had married and moved away from the neighborhood.

"When Nemesis has her kittens, you and Pansa will have the pick of the litter. We think they'll be born in a week or two."

"The sooner the better."

Pansa joined them. He gave Livia a fatherly kiss on the cheek, then studied her with concern. "You look tense. Why has this woman's death become your concern?"

"I got involved at the request of my sister-in-law." Livia told them about Gracchus's threats to Avitus and about her discussion with Salvia at the poetry recital.

"Salvia and I could have become friends, and now she's been murdered. I've promised her sister Calida I'll do all I can to help her find out who did it. Otherwise, Gracchus will blame Salvia's maid for the death and the whole household will be executed."

"Surely that old law wouldn't apply here," Placida said.

"I hope not, but the easiest way to protect them is to prove someone else is guilty."

"Then you have a heavy load on your shoulders," Pansa said. "How can we help?"

"I need to hear the results of the poison test, and then I'd like to talk over what I've learned."

The three entered the couple's living quarters, where they found Roxana and Grim hunched over a basket.

What was Grim doing here? The plan had been for him to wait at Hortensia's until Livia's return.

"How did you get here, Grim?"

"I found him lurking on the street outside Gracchus's house," Roxana said. "I talked him into helping me with the mouse." She pointed at a dead mouse lying in the bottom of the basket next to the silver cup.

"The mouse gobbled the breadcrumbs we soaked in the dregs of wine. At first nothing happened. I was beginning to think we were wrong about the poison, but then it started acting funny. First it started squeaking, then it threw up. After that it lay, twitching and dribbling frothy spittle before—"

"Thank you," Livia broke in. Placida had gone pale at the unnecessarily vivid description. "In summary, the mouse died?"

"Yes, my lady."

"Then your test confirms the poison was in the cup, which means the most likely murderer is Gracchus's servant, Melancton." Livia gave them a quick summary of what she'd learned about Iris mixing the tonic and leaving it unattended.

"Does this mean we've solved the crime?" Roxana asked.

"Not yet, but we have some strong clues. As I was leaving Gracchus's house, the cook gave me another one." Pulling the sack of dried mushrooms from her belt, Livia told them what the cook had said about the contents.

Roxana's eyes lit up. She opened the sack. "Look, this one is broken. I bet the missing chunk is what the killer used to poison Salvia's wine. Makes me dizzy, thinking how dangerous these might be."

She made to dump them into her hand. Grim grabbed her arm.

"Stop! Don't you know mushrooms can kill on contact? I heard a story about someone who died from using a poisoned ointment."

Roxana rolled her eyes. "Sure, you did."

"Grim's right," Placida said. "Touching poisonous plants can be dangerous."

Roxana hastily set the sack on the table.

Livia turned to Pansa. "May we catch another mouse and test a sample of the mushrooms?"

"No. I can't allow you to continue contaminating my bakery with poison."

Livia's stomach knotted. "Forgive me. I hadn't thought about the potential hazards. I'm sorry we imposed on you."

"What's done is done," Pansa said gravely. "But I must ask that you take these deadly things from our house, and I counsel you to consider the risks before dabbling with poison a second time."

"We'll be careful," Livia said. "Grim, you take the sack of mushrooms while Roxana takes Salvia's cup."

As her servants gathered the items, Livia turned to Placida. "Before we leave, can you tell me where to find Dioges the physician? I promised Calida I'd speak with him."

"You'll find his shop two streets over from Naso's perfume shop and four blocks east," Placida replied. "You've found the correct building when you see a balcony overrun with plants of all descriptions."

"But he may not be home," she added. "It used to be his sister could tell you where to find him if he was out, but she died five months ago. Poor Dioges took the loss hard." Placida shook her head. "He was always an impatient man, but his grief over losing his sister has made him gruffer than ever."

She gave Livia a stern frown. "You must remember to be patient with his brusqueness. He is a man in much pain."

"I'll keep it in mind," Livia promised.

How lovely. A grumpy old man to test her patience after all she'd been through today.

Sigh.

CHAPTER TWELVE

Livia and her servants found the doctor's apartment just as Placida had described. Dioges answered at the third knock, yanking the door open and thrusting his head out. With his thin face, long neck, and humped shoulders, he looked like a vulture.

"Good afternoon," he said, his tone anything but welcoming. "What do you want?"

He's grieving, Livia reminded herself. *Have patience.*

She forced a pleasant smile. "I understand you were called to tend Salvia last night, and—"

"Begone with you! I won't be party to trading gossip with busybodies." Dioges started to shut the door.

"Wait, please! Calida sent me."

His hand jerked to a stop.

"She told me how valiantly you worked to save dear Salvia last night. I know you must be as heartbroken as we are over her death."

Dioges hunched into an even more vulture-like pose, eyes narrowed to slits. "Who are you?"

"I'm Calida's cousin Valeria. Calida would like your professional opinion to set her mind at ease. She suspects that Salvia's maid may have mixed the wrong dosage of her headache tonic. Could that be what killed her?"

"Absolutely not. The headache tonic wouldn't hurt her even if she took a triple dose."

"What about the other medicines?"

"All perfectly safe. I checked them myself."

"Even the one labeled Vitality?"

Dioges looked up sharply. "Why do you ask about that one?"

Livia gave him a knowing smile. "I understand you make it specially for Gracchus, so we wondered what ... er, effect it might have on a woman."

"It affects men and women the same. It wasn't what killed Salvia. I'm certain of it."

Livia placed a hand over her heart. "Thank you. Calida will be relieved to hear it. She promised me we could count on you to give testimony when this foul murder goes to trial. Will you?"

The doctor's face darkened, and his voice grew hoarse. "Tell Calida if she wants to know what killed her sister, she should ask the steward to have the house searched for poison. Furthermore, let me give you a piece of advice. Murder is not a subject women should meddle in. Good day."

He slammed the door in Livia's face.

"Charming man," Roxana said.

"I don't trust him," muttered Grim.

Roxana rolled her eyes. "You don't trust anyone."

He crossed his arms and glared at her. "That's what's kept me alive."

The maid copied his pose and scrunched her face into a scowl. "You're as charming as the doctor."

"Humph. Charm doesn't protect you from swords. Or poison."

Roxana huffed and turned to Livia. "What do you think, my lady?"

"I think Dioges is utterly lacking in charm, but we got what we came for. Iris's mistake can't be the cause of Salvia's death, which means Melancton is the culprit."

Livia couldn't wait to tell Hortensia the news.

It was the slowest game of Brigands Avitus had ever played. His thoughts kept straying to Livia, and he made one strategic mistake after another. Instead of beating him quickly, Publius strung him along, forcing him to mount a desperate but futile defense.

Publius was two moves from winning when Livia finally arrived. Avitus wanted to rush to her and wrap his arms around her. But the servants were watching, so instead he remained seated as a dignified man should. He studied his wife, searching for any indication she'd been harmed. For a moment, he thought her ill-fitting tunic was the result of a struggle, then he remembered she'd been wearing green when she'd left home. The faded pink tunic and lopsided hairdo must be part of her disguise.

Livia approached him. "I'm sorry I had to make the decision without you, but as you can see, all is well." She did a pirouette.

AN ODE to POISON

Avitus was both relieved and alarmed. She was safe, but he recognized the flush of excitement in her face. She'd scented a mystery.

Jupiter help them all!

Hortensia glided into the peristyle, looking serenely pleased with herself. In contrast to Livia, she was immaculately attired and coiffed, and her slippered feet were unmarred by street grime.

"Welcome back, my dear Livia," Hortensia said. "What have you learned? Is Gracchus guilty?"

Publius harrumphed. "Really, Hortensia. Give her a moment to collect herself. I'm hungry, and I imagine Livia is as well. We shall adjourn to the dining room."

They sat on the dining couches. Publius and Hortensia on one side with Avitus and Livia facing them. A tray of fruit, cheese, and olives was hastily brought.

"That's better. Now then, Livia, please tell us what you've learned."

"First, this." Livia turned to Avitus and handed him a folded piece of papyrus "Calida extends her deepest gratitude to you for allowing me to assist her."

Avitus opened the note.

> *Calida Claudia*
>
> *To A. Memmius Avitus*
>
> *Greetings.*
>
> *Please accept my apologies for bringing your wife to this house. I was desperate, and Hortensia assured me Livia was to be trusted. I'm convinced she and Salvia could have become good friends if circumstances had been different, and I am sure*

my dead sister's shade is grateful for Livia's help bringing justice to this tragedy.

An odd epistle. What possible importance did a lost friendship have with the situation? Avitus would never understand women.

"Please tell us what you've discovered," Hortensia said. "Is Gracchus guilty or not?"

"We think so. Calida and I believe Gracchus ordered his slave Melancton to poison Salvia."

In between bites of cheese and figs, Livia delivered a lucid account of the events leading up to Salvia's death. She ended her account by describing the test Roxana had conducted with the dregs of wine in Salvia's cup. Avitus was impressed at all she'd learned in the past few hours.

Publius was too for he beamed at Livia. "Excellent work."

Hortensia looked smug. "I told you we knew what we were doing."

"Indeed you did, my dear." Publius patted her hand. Then he gave Avitus a wolfish grin. "I think we have the proof we require."

Avitus shook his head. "We have a plausible theory, but we must eliminate all other possibilities before we move on. The cook, his assistant, and the doctor must all be considered possible suspects."

"Dioges couldn't have done it," Livia said. "He wasn't in the house until after Salvia was ill."

"That still leaves the two kitchen slaves."

"The cook wasn't in the kitchen when Iris mixed the tonic, so it can't be him either."

"That leaves the kitchen girl. How do we know she's telling the truth? It's possible she poisoned the cup herself."

"Maybe." Livia frowned. "It's been bothering me that she never gave a good reason for being in the kitchen."

"I may have an answer for that," Publius said. "My servant Fortis has become the kitchen girl's lover, and I believe he was with her last night. Let's hear his version of the story."

Fortis was perhaps twenty-five with a solid physique, good skin, and winning smile. He walked with a hint of swagger—a man who liked attention and was used to getting it.

"Were you with your lover last night?" Publius asked him.

"Yes, sir."

"Tell us everything you saw or heard."

"Zoe asked me to visit her because Gracchus and his wife were supposed to be away until late. Ha! No sooner had I come in the back door then we heard footsteps. We hid in the kitchen storeroom with the curtain left open a crack so I could watch. It was Melancton, Gracchus's manservant. He mixed a cup of stomach tonic and left. A while later, we were interrupted again. This time it was Iris. She mixed a cup of medicine too, only she used the master's love potion by mistake. We're sure she got the wrong jar because she set it right next to her oil lamp and we could plainly see the label. Zoe recognized the shape of the letters. She says the medicine Iris used is a love potion. The doctor makes it to enhance Gracchus's powers in bed. Smells awful, but it's full of exotic ingredients like mandrake root, nutmeg, and ground beetles."

Publius flicked his fingers. "We're not interested in the contents of this potion. What did Iris do next?"

"She left the cup on the table and rummaged through the food storage baskets. Then she left the kitchen, carrying something in a sack. While she was gone, Melancton came into the kitchen. He ground something in a mortar, then filled a cup with wine. After he'd mixed what he'd ground into the cup, he shouted for Iris."

"How did he know Iris was there?" Avitus said.

Fortis shrugged. "Maybe he recognized the oil lamp? It was shaped like a bird. Very dainty. Iris came back, and Melancton scolded her for leaving a cup unattended. He slapped her too. She ran off, whimpering. Melancton finished what he was doing and left a few moments later. That was too many close calls for one night. As soon as it was quiet, I came home."

Livia could keep quiet no longer. "Might this be the sack you saw Melancton using?"

She pulled the small pouch of mushrooms from her belt and set it on the table with a flourish. Four sets of eyes settled on the sack. Avitus and Publius studied it with detached curiosity. Hortensia curled her lip in disgust. Fortis's eyes widened in horrified fascination.

"It could be, my lady," the slave said. "It's the right size. What's in it?"

Publius frowned at him. "Thank you, Fortis. That will be all."

Fortis shot a longing look at the sack, then turned and left. When they were alone, Livia answered the question in everyone's face.

"As I was leaving Gracchus's house, the cook gave me this pouch. He said he'd found it hidden in the pantry. It's filled with dried mushrooms but not any edible type he knows about."

Hortensia shrank from the sack. "Why did you bring those horrid things into our house?"

"We need to test them to see if they're poisonous. Can I ask Grim to catch us a mouse?"

"No." Hortensia drew herself up. "You don't imagine you can test them in my house!"

"Why not? I thought you wanted proof of Gracchus's guilt."

"We thank you for all you've uncovered," Publius said soothingly. "Your courage and cleverness have admirably achieved the hopes my wife harbored when she sent you into danger this morning."

He gave his wife a pointed look. She assumed a mask of contrition and turned to Avitus. "Forgive me for insisting Livia go with Calida."

Nobody was fooled. Hortensia wasn't the least bit sorry. Still, Avitus graciously murmured an acknowledgment of the apology.

"Now we've cleared that up," Publius said, "allow me to summarize what we know. With Fortis's testimony to substantiate the others, I think we all agree that Melancton is our primary suspect. Furthermore, we assume he was acting under his master's orders."

Nods all around.

"Then we must consider motive. What drove Gracchus to order his wife's death?"

"Calida thinks it has to do with Salvia befriending Rutilia." Livia explained the situation. "However, that didn't seem like a good enough reason for murder, so I questioned Zoe. She told me she'd overheard Gracchus accusing Salvia of infidelity."

Publius's eyes lit up at that. "Love is at the root of many a crime. Hortensia, you must ask your friends if they know anything about Salvia having a lover."

Hortensia murmured her assent.

"Meanwhile, I will ask certain trusted friends the same questions. In addition, I'll whisper our suspicions of Gracchus's ill deeds in certain ears. By the time Salvia's ashes have cooled enough for Gracchus to collect them, the forum will be filled with talk of Gracchus poisoning his wife. If we sway the public to our theory of Gracchus's guilt before he has time to spread a false story, we'll have the battle half-won already."

Publius rubbed his hands as if anticipating victory. He turned to Avitus. "You must return to Rutilia and tell her all we've learned. Ask her to convince Salvia's family to cooperate with us. Her brother should register this accusation with the praetor of the murder court, but we offer him our assistance in prosecuting the case."

To Livia's surprise, Avitus nodded agreement without protest. Since when was he on friendly terms with Gracchus's ex-wife? Livia would need to hear more about this arrangement.

Lastly, Publius turned to Livia. "You may conduct the test on the suspicious mushrooms. However, it won't be prudent to do so here."

Hortensia curled her lip. "Ugh! Why bother with those nasty mushrooms when we already know who killed Salvia?"

"Because it may be important," Avitus said. "When building a case, every bit of evidence is useful. If we can show that poisonous mushrooms were found in Gracchus's pantry, it will help us refute any claims that Salvia was poisoned at the poetry party."

AN ODE to POISON

Livia sent her husband a smile of thanks for defending her. How pleasant it was to be working together on this case.

CHAPTER THIRTEEN

Outside his brother's house, Avitus and his wife parted ways. As he watched Livia head down the street, the pain of what she'd done settled like a lump of lead in his stomach. His wife had gone behind his back. Again.

After a near disaster a few weeks ago, Livia had tearfully promised she'd never investigate suspicious activities without his blessing. Yet here she was showing no remorse for the appalling risk she'd taken. He'd thought he could trust her. He'd thought she had listened to his warnings about the need to avoid Gracchus's attention. He'd thought she respected him enough to keep her word.

But no.

Although this time she wasn't the only one at fault. Hortensia had urged Livia to action, callously sending her into danger. Publius wasn't innocent either. He'd known and done nothing. How would Publius feel if their positions had been reversed and Hortensia had gone into their enemy's house to look for a killer?

Hades! Avitus strode from his brother's house, jaw clenched and stomach roiling. His emotions were too raw to think straight, so he headed to his favorite bathing complex. A strenuous bout of exercise eased the turmoil in his gut. Then a soak followed with a pummeling by a masseuse worked the tension from his muscles.

Clearheaded and relaxed enough to act rationally, he was ready to face Rutilia. This time his reception wasn't as warm.

"You were not expected, sir." The doorkeeper gave a little huff of censure, the one perfected by important slaves in wealthy households who looked down their self-important noses at unwelcome visitors. "I will inquire if the mistress is receiving guests."

The haughty slave's tone made it clear he expected the mistress was not.

"Tell her I have information on a propitious death."

"As you wish, sir. Please wait here."

Much to the doorkeeper's chagrin, Avitus was invited in. But then Rutilia made him wait before gracing him with her presence, a subtle reminder of who was the more powerful.

Avitus didn't mind. He used the time to review the information and prioritize their requests. Flowery rhetoric wouldn't win her cooperation. He must be direct, but he must also choose his words with care.

Rutilia finally deigned to join him. This time he was not so dazzled by her elegant apparel, and he noticed subtle signs of weariness in her face and demeanor. Was it the burden of running a household while her husband was absent, or were there other worries?

"I wasn't expecting you back so soon." Rutilia's tone betrayed her curiosity. Good.

"I have information on Salvia's death. I thought you'd like to know as soon as possible."

"Excellent. You have proof Gracchus is guilty?"

As before she got right to the point. Avitus walked her through the facts and how the evidence pointed to Melancton. "We assume he acted on his master's orders."

"But can you prove it?"

Avitus drew a breath. He raised his chin and imbued his voice with confidence. "You are a woman who appreciates a direct answer so let me be blunt. Short of forcing Melancton to confess, I don't see how we can obtain irrefutable proof. However, my brother and I are convinced Gracchus is guilty. Will you go to Salvia's family and ask their cooperation?"

She nodded. "When the time is right. What do you need to build a case?"

"We need character witnesses who will expose Gracchus's dishonorable soul. In the past, no one has been willing to testify against him for fear of reprisals. We can use Salvia's murder as a rallying cry to convince them to join forces. Together, we can crush his reputation and destroy his power. Will you compile a list of men who might be willing to testify? You know more than we do about the men he's cheated, bullied, or betrayed."

She gave a bitter laugh. "I do indeed. Much more than Gracchus realizes. I'll send you a list tomorrow morning."

"Thank you." Now came the trickiest part.

"If we hope to convince the court of Gracchus's guilt, we need a compelling motive. Calida thought the issue that caused this tragedy was Salvia's pact with you. Could this be so?"

Rutilia didn't answer immediately. She tilted her head and pursed her lips. Then she shook her head. "I don't think so. He's known about Salvia's agreement with me for months and done nothing more than mutter threats."

"Another possibility. A kitchen slave claims she overheard Gracchus accusing Salvia of infidelity. Could that be true?"

"Unlikely. Salvia is far too smart and too careful to make that kind of mistake."

"Then it's imperative we uncover the reason for this murder. You have spies in Gracchus's household. Ask them for anything Gracchus or Salvia said that could imply motive. Also ask them to report everything Gracchus says or does in response to his wife's death."

"That won't be a problem," Rutilia said. "I've already ordered my contact to keep an eye on Gracchus, especially during the funeral ceremony tomorrow. I want to know how convincingly he mourns for his dear departed wife."

She shifted in her seat and met his gaze directly. Her eyes challenged him from across the room. "Now I have a question for you. How did you discover so much so quickly?"

Because my wife can't resist nosing into murder even when it means betraying her husband's trust and walking into the lair of a ravenous jackal like Gracchus.

He didn't trust Rutilia enough to admit the truth, however, so he told her of Publius's slave. "We were fortunate. Fortis happened to be in the kitchen at the right time."

Rutilia's eyebrows rose in admiration. "Your brother is braver than I thought. I hope he rewards his informant handsomely for this information."

"I'm sure he will."

Livia, however, did not deserve a reward. Not at all.

On the way home from Hortensia's house, Livia told Roxana and Grim the latest news. "While Avitus and Publius seek information about other matters, our task is to test the mushrooms. My dear sister-in-law was horrified at the idea of poisonous mushrooms in her house, so we'll do it at home."

"Brisa will be just as horrified," Roxana said with a smirk. "She'll have a conniption when she discovers we've brought a deadly fungus and a filthy mouse into her immaculate house. I can already hear her moans over using her mortar and pestle to grind these mushrooms. We could wash it out a dozen times, and she'd still complain it wasn't clean enough."

"I agree. Brisa will be a problem, and the simplest solution is to conduct our test without her knowing about it. Which means we can't borrow her kitchen tools."

"We need a mortar from somewhere, my lady. I doubt a mouse will want to gnaw on a chunk of dried mushroom."

True, but Livia didn't want to purchase a new mortar and pestle to grind a single mushroom. "We need an alternative. Any ideas?"

"If we soak a mushroom in water to soften it first, we could grind it to a paste in a bowl," Grim said.

Roxana nodded. "That should work. And a stick could replace the pestle."

"Excellent suggestions."

How blessed Livia was to have slaves she could count on to work together and come up with creative solutions to their problems. "Now then, what will we use to hold the mouse? Do we have an old basket at home that can be sacrificed?"

"The basket you've been using to store hand linens in the dining room is about the right size," Roxana said. "It's old and lopsided, and it clashes with your new dining couch cushions."

She raised her eyebrows hopefully. Livia grinned at her. "I think it's high time I replaced that ugly old basket with something nicer, don't you?"

Problem solved.

Livia found a basket with a decorative rim to replace the ugly old basket in the dining room. Roxana talked a potter into giving them a cracked bowl for free, and Grim found a leg from a broken stool that would work as a pestle. Wouldn't Avitus be impressed when he heard how she'd anticipated the problems and solved them before arriving home and sending Brisa into a tizzy?

"Good work, everyone. Now remember, we don't want Brisa to discover what we're up to, so we'll work in the dining room."

"Yes, my lady."

They were greeted at the door by their ferocious watch dog, who threatened to lick them to death. As Livia gave the dog a friendly ear scratch, she caught a whiff of something nasty.

Ugh! Had Fumo been rolling in rotten cabbage? She pushed him away and sniffed her hands.

Not the dog.

"Momus, what do I smell?"

The doorkeeper rolled his eyes. "Brisa had another mishap in the kitchen."

How lovely. "What happened this time? Nothing was on fire, I hope?"

Momus shrugged. "Fumo and I stayed clear of things. Nobody came running for water."

Sigh.

In his years as a bachelor, Avitus had been satisfied with eating meals purchased from hot food stalls like the multitudes of poor residents who didn't have the luxury of a kitchen in their cramped apartments.

When they'd married, Livia had insisted that a man of Avitus's wealth and status needed a suitable cook. He'd agreed but asked Livia to train Brisa rather than add another slave to the household.

So far, the results had been disappointing (to put it kindly).

"I'd better see what the damage is."

Livia passed into the peristyle that served as the central hub of the house. The burnt odor was stronger here. Nissa, the household's other slave, was pulling weeds in the flowerbeds. She was a girl of fourteen with the disposition of a mule—hardworking but sullen and stubborn to a fault.

She rose at Livia's approach. "Good afternoon, Mistress."

"Momus tells me Brisa ruined another meal. What happened this time?"

Nissa made a sound of disgust in the back of her throat. "Brisa was supposed to be making stew while I weeded the flowers. I was finishing the bed in front of the dining room when the master's dog appeared, nosing at me to play, so I stood up and tossed the toy. He started barking, begging me for more, which brought Brisa running. Naturally, she yelled at me rather than the dog."

The shouting matches had become a daily occurrence. The petite Brisa, hands on hips, shrill voice quavering with indignation, facing off against the tall, silent bulk of Nissa. It never seemed to occur to Brisa that Nissa could knock her off her feet if she chose. Fortunately, Nissa was too smart to strike back. She let the older woman rant, then placidly returned to what she was doing (ignoring any advice Brisa had dispensed).

"While she was scolding me over the dog, I told her I smelled something burning. But did she listen to me?" Nissa made a sour face. "She kept right on with her rant. I had to drag her to the kitchen. By then, the whole pot was smoldering, and the kitchen was filled with smoke." Nissa clenched her hands and looked up at Livia. "Why do you let her ruin your food day after day? She's hopeless, anyone can see that."

"That will be enough, Nissa! Return to your work."

Livia crossed the peristyle and entered the passage that led to the home's tiny kitchen. The acrid odor of singed cabbage caught in the back of her throat, making her cough. Brisa was strenuously scrubbing the bottom of a pot, lips clenched and narrow face splattered with flecks of soot. The woman looked exhausted and miserable, but she brought it on herself. If she'd focus on mastering the kitchen instead of correcting the other servants and redoing half their work, everyone would be happier.

"I hear you had another accident."

Brisa threw her scrub brush to the floor. "It's all Nissa's fault."

"How is it her fault?"

"She was teasing the dog. I had to make her stop."

"Fumo isn't your responsibility. That's Momus's job."

"Well, he wasn't doing it." Brisa gave a disapproving sniff. "The dog was making a racket, and I've told that girl a hundred times that the master likes a quiet house."

"Avitus wasn't home this afternoon, so the dog wasn't bothering him."

"Nissa shouldn't have been tormenting the creature."

Oh, for heaven's sake!

"You had one task to do, and you failed to do it. As a result, you have a mess to clean up and a second meal to prepare. I'll leave you to get on with it."

CHAPTER FOURTEEN

Livia was sick of Brisa's incompetence in the kitchen. It was time to reopen the issue with Avitus and push him to purchase a cook. On a positive note, the fiasco would keep Brisa too busy to interfere with the mushroom test.

In the dining room, Roxana had spread an old towel over the table and set their test equipment on top. "I thought I'd get everything ready while we wait for Grim to catch a mouse, my lady."

"Good thinking."

Nissa entered, carrying a pile of rags. "Here you go, Roxana."

The girl turned to Livia, wide-eyed and eager. "Roxana says you're testing deadly mushrooms. Can I help?"

Triple fish pickle! Roxana's indecent curiosity about murder was bad enough. Livia didn't need Nissa poking her nose into things as well, but it was obviously too late to hide what they were doing. If Livia sent Nissa from the room, she'd almost certainly eavesdrop at the door. Then Brisa would notice Nissa and barge in on them.

Exactly what they wanted to avoid. Therefore, the best option was to let Nissa stay.

"You may help," Livia told her young slave. "But you must not breathe a word of what we're doing to Brisa. We don't need her fussing over things."

Nissa rolled her eyes before meekly saying, "I promise, my lady."

"Also, you must follow my instructions exactly because poison is not a game. We've been told that deadly mushrooms can kill you just by touching them, so we must be extremely careful."

That caused a wrinkle of concern in Nissa's eager face. Good. She must take this as seriously as the rest of them.

"You can help by taking the bowl on the table and filling it half full of water."

"It's got a crack in it."

"I'm aware of that. Off you go."

Nissa was back in a flash. "What next?"

"Set the bowl on the table and stand out of the way. You may watch but please don't interfere."

Nissa obeyed.

So far, so good. Livia handed the sack of mushrooms to Roxana, who carefully shook one mushroom into the bowl. While it soaked, Livia gave Nissa an abbreviated summary of what they'd been doing all day. The girl's eyes got bigger and bigger as the story progressed.

When Livia finished, Nissa cautiously approached the bowl. "These might be the same mushrooms that killed the lady?"

"Very possibly. That's what we hope this test will tell us."

By this time, the mushroom looked soft enough to grind. Hmm, they'd have to drain the excess liquid first, though. Livia presumed the liquid was poisonous, therefore they mustn't dump it out where some animal could lap it up. That meant they ought to pour it down the sewer, which was connected (somehow) all the way to the Cloaca Maxima, the ancient sewer which drained the city's wastewater into the Tiber River.

"Nissa, take the bowl outside and pour the liquid into the nearest sewer drain. And mind you don't spill any!"

Once the bowl was drained, Roxana worked the mushroom into a pulp. When she finished, Nissa peered into the bowl and crinkled her nose.

"Yuck! That slimy goo doesn't look appetizing. You should add a drizzle of honey."

"Why?" Roxana asked.

"Because mice love honey," Nissa said.

Roxana crossed her arms. "I've never heard that."

"That's because people who live in nice houses don't know what it's like to have mice scuttling about every night."

"For your information, I grew up in a crumbling Subura tenement. Our alleys were filled with vermin, and nobody ever said anything about honey."

"Tsk, Roxana," Livia said. "It can't hurt to add some honey."

The honey didn't make the mushroom pulp look any more appealing, but hopefully the sweet scent would entice a mouse to eat some.

Assuming Grim ever brought them a mouse.

"What took you so long?" Roxana demanded when he finally arrived with their test subject.

"I can't simply snap my fingers and catch a mouse," he replied. "It takes patience and stealth. Two things you know nothing about."

"Humph! Give me that basket before the filthy little beast escapes."

Roxana set the bowl with the mushroom paste in the bottom of the basket. Whiskers twitching, the mouse clambered over the rim of the bowl. After a tentative sniff, the creature started nibbling.

"I told you mice like honey," Nissa said.

Roxana gave her a glare.

"Thank you for your help," Livia said to Nissa. "Nothing will happen for a while, so you can return to your chores."

"Yes, my lady." Nissa hesitated. "I was wondering … Couldn't you let me cook instead of Brisa?"

Livia blinked twice as her thoughts switched to this unanticipated subject. "I wasn't aware you knew how to cook."

"I don't, but I can learn." Nissa darted a dark glance toward the kitchen. "I promise you I won't burn everything like *she* does."

The girl could hardly do worse than Brisa. If the solution was as simple as arranging lessons for Nissa, life would be better for everyone.

"I'll think about it."

The more Livia considered it, the more she liked the idea. Her Aunt Livilla had an excellent cook who would enjoy the challenge of training a novice. While they waited for the poison to take effect, Livia dispatched a brief letter to her aunt, asking if Nissa could come to her house for a cooking lesson.

Avitus arrived home to find his wife with her slaves in the dining room, peering into a basket. Livia looked up and smiled. "You're just in time. The mouse is beginning to show symptoms of poison."

Her enthusiasm for testing poison—in the dining room of all places—sent a fresh wave of anger surging through his limbs.

"We need to talk."

"Right now?"

"Yes."

Livia followed him to his study and dropped onto a stool. "You have news? Will Rutilia help us? How is it you know her, anyway?"

Avitus clenched his jaw. How could she act as if nothing was wrong? He settled into a chair facing her and took two deep breaths to quell the bile rising in his throat. He willed his hands to remain unclenched, his face calm, and his voice neutral.

"Can you begin to imagine the terrible things that could have happened to you today?"

Livia lifted her chin. "I was aware of the danger as was Calida. We took precautions."

As if her paltry precautions could protect her!

"What you should have done was refuse. I warned you not to get caught in Hortensia's schemes."

"This wasn't a scheme. It was murder. And for your information, I refused to go until Calida convinced me Gracchus was ill in bed."

"Don't be naive. In a large household, there are always slaves willing to win favor by tattling on the secrets of others."

Livia crossed her arms. "Let them talk. They think I was Calida's cousin Valeria, and since I wore a disguise, they won't even describe me correctly."

Avitus slammed his hand on the desk. "A disguise doesn't protect you from an angry assailant with a weapon."

"Really, Avitus! I wasn't walking down unsavory back alleys after dark. I was in the house of a senator, having quiet conversations with a handful of frightened and cooperative slaves. And nothing happened. I'm home, I'm safe, and Gracchus never saw me."

"He doesn't need to. He'll hear a woman matching your height and age was asking perceptive questions, and he'll begin to wonder. He hasn't forgotten you're the woman who poked her nose into his illegal water installations."

Livia made an exasperated noise in the back of her throat. "Please stop fretting. Gracchus won't suspect it was me because he knows you'd *never* let me near his house. Secondly, Calida told the servants I was a nosy but harmless busybody, and when I met Gracchus's body slave, I pretended I wasn't very bright."

Jupiter, Best and Greatest! Could this story get any worse?

"Melancton *saw* you?"

"He barged into the kitchen while I was talking with the cook, but all he *saw* was a frumpy woman with a provincial accent who meekly allowed him to boss her around."

"What if Melancton wasn't fooled by your disguise?"

"Oh, Avitus." Livia laid her hand on his and gave a gentle squeeze. "I know you don't like me taking risks, but I assure you the decision was sensible. You've been so worried by Gracchus's threats, and I thought this might be my best chance to help you. I did everything I possibly could to protect myself, including sending you a message so you'd know where I'd gone."

"No, you did not."

Her head snapped up. "Yes, I did. Hortensia sent you a note explaining—oh fish pickle!" A look of dismay crossed her face. "I never saw what she wrote to you."

Livia squeezed her eyes shut and huffed in frustration. When she opened them, they were filled with remorse. "She didn't tell you where I was going, did she? No wonder you're upset. You think I intentionally kept my actions a secret, don't you?"

That's exactly what Avitus had thought, but if it wasn't true...

The knot in his stomach began to loosen.

"What did Hortensia's note say?" Livia asked.

He plucked the message from the table and read it. "My dear Avitus, Livia and I are discussing a matter of some delicacy with a friend. The situation is complex, and we may not be finished until the ninth or tenth hour. Your wife did not want you to worry at her long absence."

Livia scowled fiercely. "She must have thought herself so clever, sending you that misleading message. I let her dupe me!" She slammed her clenched fists on her thighs. "That's the last time I trust Hortensia with anything."

His wife's fury loosened the remaining tension in Avitus's chest. Livia hadn't intentionally kept her actions hidden from him, after all. The blame lay squarely at the feet of his meddling, manipulative sister-in-law, who had no qualms about using Livia as her pawn. He would deal with his troublesome relative later.

Avitus looked at his wife and had to fight off a tear. How close he'd come to losing her today! Standing, he placed his hands on her shoulders. "Thank the gods you're safe. Promise me you will never, ever go near Gracchus or his house again."

Livia tilted her head to meet his eyes. "I promise. And I'm sorry for frightening you. That wasn't my intention." She kissed his cheek. The one scarred in his youth when Gracchus pushed him into a fire. "I hope my apology has made it up to you."

"Yes." Avitus pulled her tight against his chest. She nestled her head into his shoulder. He held her—this courageous, unpredictable, vibrant, exasperating woman who loved him enough to risk her own safety on his behalf.

Who would have thought that he would find a wife like Livia? Or that he would feel the glorious and terrible stirrings Livia caused deep in his being? He kissed the top of her head. She lifted her face to his. He leaned close. Their lips touched.

Then Brisa's shrill voice sounded from outside the room. "She's trying to murder us!"

CHAPTER FIFTEEN

Livia was through the study door in a heartbeat, her husband a step behind her. Grim stood in the peristyle, holding a flailing Brisa by the waist, while Roxana and Nissa glared at her from the dining room doorway.

Drat the woman for ruining a lovely moment.

"Master," Brisa shrieked. "Nissa is trying to poison us!"

"That's a lie," Nissa shouted.

"Quiet, both of you," Livia said.

Brisa ignored her.

"Master," she screeched, "we're all going to die a horrible death, and—"

"Silence!" Avitus roared.

His powerful bass voice, trained to project across the wide forum, reverberated in the small courtyard. The slaves immediately stilled, faces frozen in shock at this unaccustomed outburst from their master.

"Nobody is going to die," he said into the silence. "Your mistress has taken precautions to avoid any danger of accidental poisoning. Is that not so, my dear?"

"I have, indeed." Livia proudly told him the careful planning they'd done to keep the poison from contaminating the house.

"That won't protect us from her." Brisa pointed an accusing finger at Nissa. "Get rid of the poison, or you'll wake in the morning to a household of corpses."

"Don't be ridiculous!" Livia quelled an urge to grab Brisa by the shoulders and shake some sense into her. "Nobody is in danger. Please return to the kitchen and finish preparing dinner."

"I'm not serving dinner anywhere near that ..." Brisa waggled an accusatory finger at the dining room.

"No need," Avitus said calmly. "It's a pleasant evening. You can serve us dinner out here in the peristyle."

Brisa stomped off to the kitchen, shooting Livia dark looks.

"Sometimes I think she's going senile," Nissa muttered. "If anyone dies in this house, it'll be her cooking that's to blame."

"None of your lip." Livia gave Nissa a stern look. "How did Brisa find out about the poison when I gave all three of you explicit instructions not to tell her?"

"It wasn't me," Roxana said. "Grim and I were in the dining room the whole time. We didn't want Nemesis or Fumo to get at the mouse."

As expected, Nissa was the one who'd disobeyed. Livia turned to the girl. "Why did you tell Brisa?"

"It wasn't my fault. The old busybody came into the peristyle looking for somebody to boss around. She asked me where Roxana was. I told her Roxana was busy and she shouldn't interfere, but did she listen to me? She was heading for the dining room, so I had to say something to keep her out."

"And a right mess you made of it," Roxana said. "Thanks to you, she charged in waving her broom and shouting about deadly mushrooms that turn your face green and your intestines to mush. If Grim hadn't stopped her, she would have grabbed the basket and splattered the contents all over the house in her rush to toss it out."

Nissa jutted her chin. "I didn't say anything about her face turning green!"

"Don't try to get out of this," Livia snapped. "If you want to earn more responsibility in this household, you'll have to learn to follow orders and stop needling Brisa on purpose. Go sweep the floor in the atrium and try not to cause any more trouble."

Heaving an exasperated sigh, Livia turned to Avitus. "I'm sorry. I did my best to keep our experiment away from Brisa so she wouldn't have a fit over mice in the house."

"I hope the test was worth all the fuss."

"It was sir," Roxana said. "Would you like to know what happened?"

"Yes."

They followed Roxana into the dining room, where she gave them a detailed account of the mouse's symptoms.

When she finished, Livia held up the pouch of mushrooms. "Now we have proof! These evil mushrooms must be what Melancton used to kill Salvia."

Avitus clicked his tongue. "You're once again confusing probability with proof."

Sometimes being married to a lawyer was a sore trial! "Forgive my confusion, but why else would poisonous mushrooms be hidden in Gracchus's kitchen?"

"A more pertinent question is how the sack ended up in the pantry without Fortis and Zoe noticing."

Livia shrugged. "Maybe Melancton came back to the kitchen and hid it later to implicate the cook. I could see those two hated each other."

Her husband didn't look convinced.

"Do you at least agree the mushrooms were worth testing?"

He nodded. "It's prudent to consider all potential evidence. However, you had better clean this up so Brisa will stop worrying."

"Agreed." Livia sent Roxana to dispose of the basket and its deadly contents. Then she picked up the pouch of mushrooms. "I'll put this in our bedroom tonight so Brisa won't see it. In the morning, I'll show the mushrooms to Brother Titus to see if he can identify them."

Avitus made his I-don't-approve-of-that face.

"What's the matter?"

"We can't risk Gracchus hearing about our interest in the murder. I'd rather not involve anyone else in this crime."

"How is talking to Brother Titus any different than talking to Rutilia?" Livia asked. "I would think Gracchus's ex-wife is far less trustworthy than Brother Titus."

"An incorrect assumption. Rutilia has *personal reasons* to oppose Gracchus. The doctor does not."

"Brother Titus is my friend, and he has *personal reasons* to protect me because I'm a member of his church. If you knew him as I did, you'd know you can trust him with any secret."

"I had an interesting conversation with him earlier, so I understand why you trust him so readily."

Oh really? When was her secretive husband going to mention this fact?

"However, in this matter the risk is too high." Avitus crossed his arms.

"We don't need to tell Brother Titus the details. He'll answer our questions about the mushrooms without asking why we need to know."

"How will identifying the mushrooms benefit us?" Avitus asked. "We've already proved they're deadly."

"Gracchus must have purchased them from somebody. There can't be that many merchants who sell poisonous mushrooms. If we figure out who sold them, that person could verify who purchased them."

"Another incorrect assumption. Why would a merchant crooked enough to deal in poison willingly reveal his customers?"

"They wouldn't," Livia said. "However, I'm assuming my husband is clever enough to figure out the correct incentive to persuade the seller to admit the truth."

Her husband's frown slowly transformed to a grin. "I believe your idea has merit. We'll both go to see Brother Titus tomorrow. And I will do the talking."

"Fine."

Since he'd patched things up with his wife, Avitus slept well and woke eager to face the day. He dressed and headed for his atrium, where his clientes awaited him. As his loyal followers, these men were honor-bound to support him in public.

He told them about Salvia's suspicious death. "When this case comes to trial, I will count on all of you to attend and lend your support."

These men had witnessed trials where Gracchus had bribed his way to victory. They despised him as thoroughly as Avitus did and eagerly pledged their support. Avitus didn't have nearly as many clientes as Gracchus, but every voice helped.

After thanking his clientes and wishing them a good day, Avitus headed for his study, humming as he mentally sifted through his collection of legal scrolls for any mention of cases involving poison.

He was halfway across the peristyle before his wife's voice penetrated his thoughts. "Where is the pouch of mushrooms that your master and I were keeping in our bedroom?"

Uh oh! Livia only used that icily stern tone when she was furious. He looked up to find Livia glaring at Brisa, who stood with fists clenched at her sides, staring holes in a paving stone.

"Answer me," Livia snapped.

"It was left unattended. Nissa could have taken some. We'll have to dispose of all the food in the kitchen and scrub the entire house from floor to ceiling, and—"

"Stop right there," Livia broke in. She gave Avitus an exasperated look. "Are you hearing this?"

He nodded.

"Tell us what you've done with the pouch of mushrooms."

"I tossed it in the rubbish heap," Brisa said.

"What were you thinking?" Livia demanded. "You can't toss deadly mushrooms in the rubbish like a moldy piece of bread. Consider what would happen if a stray dog found them. Or a beggar child."

"But—"

"Quiet! You disobeyed my direct instructions, and as a result you've put others in danger. Until further notice, I forbid you from setting foot in the kitchen. Go scrub the dining room."

Brisa stomped away, narrow face twisted in fury and arms crossed tightly across her chest. Livia beckoned Roxana. "Find the pouch and make sure no mushrooms spilled out. Hurry."

"Yes, mistress."

Roxana trotted away. Livia turned to Avitus and glared at him as if this was his fault.

It wasn't! In all the years Brisa had served him, he'd never had a problem. He'd purchased her when he'd moved out of his father's house. She'd been malnourished when he bought her, but a few weeks of good food had given her a new lease on life. She'd been devotedly loyal to Avitus ever since.

Therefore, the problem must lie with Livia. She was too overbearing and impatient.

"Haven't you gone a bit far, banning Brisa from the kitchen?"

"Didn't you hear what she was saying? If I allow her in the kitchen, she'll empty it completely, for fear Nissa has poisoned something."

"But what about meals?"

"For the time being, I'll assign Nissa to the kitchen. She can't do any worse than Brisa has this past month."

That had yet to be proved, although his wife was probably correct. Brisa didn't show aptitude in the kitchen.

Roxana returned with the pouch. "I found it, and it's still tied shut."

"Give it to me." Avitus took the pouch. Blessedly, it was dry rather than oozing with slime from rotten turnips or putrid chicken entrails. This ugly little sack and its contents had caused enough turmoil in his house. Time to get to the bottom of this thing.

"We take this to Brother Titus immediately."

And once the doctor answered their questions, Avitus would lock the pouch in his strong box so nobody could touch it.

CHAPTER SIXTEEN

Livia and her husband headed for Brother Titus's apartment. The doctor's wife, Tirzah, greeted them when they arrived. She was a petite woman with black hair, a ready smile, and a heart of gold.

"Good morning, friends." Tirzah said in her melodious voice. She and Brother Titus had met in Syria, and her Latin still bore slight traces of her homeland.

"Is your husband at home?" Livia queried, returning Tirzah's smile. "We have a question for him."

"He's in the back room. He's not with a patient, so you can go in."

"Thank you."

Avitus and Livia passed through a curtained doorway into the larger room where Brother Titus treated patients and mixed his remedies. He was hunched on a stool, slowly grinding something in a mortar.

He stood with a groan and rubbed at the stubble on his chin. "Sorry. Not as young as I used to be. I was up all night day before last tending a patient, and I've not fully recovered."

"I hope your patient is on the mend," Livia said.

His face darkened. "She poisoned herself. I was too late to save her, and now I'm worried about the family. She left behind three small children."

"I'm so sorry. Anything I can do to help?"

"Not at the moment." Brother Titus glanced at Avitus. "But I assume you haven't come to commiserate with me. What can I do for you?"

"We need your expertise," Avitus said in a solemn voice. "My brother and I are dealing with a potential murder. Livia tells me we can trust you to keep this discussion confidential?"

"You have my word," Brother Titus said, matching Avitus's solemn tone.

The lines on Avitus's forehead softened. He handed Brother Titus the pouch of mushrooms. "This was found at the site of the death. We suspect the contents is what killed the victim. Can you identify it?"

Brother Titus shook one of the mushrooms into his hand. The cap was whitish and wrinkly with a skinny stem.

"I'm not an expert on mushrooms, and I couldn't say for sure what this is. It would help if you told me the symptoms. How long after ingestion did the victim begin to grow ill?"

"An hour or two."

"Many mushrooms don't show symptoms of illness so rapidly, so my best guess is that these are sweating mushrooms. Do you know if the victim was flushed and sweaty or drooling?"

"We don't," Avitus replied. "Are sweating mushrooms used for medicinal purposes?"

"Not that I know of."

"Therefore, they would not be sold by a reputable merchant. Do you know who might sell such deadly things?"

Brother Titus blew out his cheeks. "Not for certain. I can only guess. One possibility is Brassicus. He specializes in plants and resins from the provinces of Cyrene and Egypt, especially *sylphium*. Why a seller of an herb as rare and expensive as sylphium keeps a shop in the Subura, I'll never know. I could imagine a few unsavory explanations, but I don't know the facts, so I refrain from casting judgment. He'd be worth looking into, anyway."

He gave them directions to Brassicus's shop. It was in a poor and crowded section of the city not far from where they were. Maybe Livia could convince Avitus to look into the merchant before returning home.

"Any other sellers you can think of?" Avitus asked.

"You could check into Drash the Snake Charmer."

"A preposterous name," Avitus said with a frown. "Does he actually charm snakes?"

"Yes. He keeps a tame snake as a trick to astonish the credulous," Brother Titus said. "In addition to peddling medicinal herbs, Drash is a practitioner of magic arts who sells curses and amulets. He thrives on being as outlandish as possible, but he's not a total charlatan. He's knowledgeable about a wide variety of substances from poppy tears that ease pain to cardamom pods for counteracting venom to ground rhinoceros horn, which is said to be a powerful aphrodisiac. I occasionally purchase ingredients from him that are difficult to come by elsewhere. We disagree regarding the potency of magic, but I respect his knowledge nonetheless."

Brother Titus dropped the dried mushroom back in the pouch and handed it to Avitus. Then he washed his hands in a basin of water. "When handling plants that may be poisonous, it's always wise to wash your hands. Some can be harmful even on contact."

"I'll keep that in mind." Avitus frowned at the pouch in his palm. "Our discussion has made me aware how little prepared I am to deal with poison. How do I protect my household? What should we watch for? How do we detect poison, and what should we do if we suspect someone has ingested it?"

Leave it to her cautious husband to think of such things.

But Brother Titus seemed happy to provide answers. "Some poisons may be identified by a bitter, unpleasant taste. Some tingle on the lips, tongue, or throat. Unfortunately, there are others that are not so easy to detect by taste, smell, or sensation. With poisonings, I've found the sooner a patient vomits everything that has been ingested, the better their chance for survival. Once the stomach has been cleared, you can administer an antidote such as a decoction made from the roots of sliver thistle or viper's weed. Honeyed wine mixed with pine pitch is also helpful. I've read a decoction of acorns taken as a drink with cow's milk is sometimes effective, but I haven't tried it myself."

"You don't mention *theriac*," Avitus said. "Is the famous antidote used by King Mithradates only a myth?"

"I suspect it may be. Theriac is supposed to be the universal antidote to all poisons, but I have my doubts. The powerful elixir was said to contain over forty ingredients, including poppy, myrrh, saffron, cinnamon, and ginger. Unfortunately, the recipe was a closely guarded secret, and I've never heard a physician who could name the entire list of ingredients. In my opinion, it's better to trust simple but effective antidotes rather than rely on a magical mixture full of rare ingredients that were more likely chosen to impress the king rather than cure him."

Avitus nodded. "I am of your mind when it comes to simplicity over the exotic and expensive."

The men exchanged nods. Livia sent a silent prayer of thanks to God for the trust growing between her husband and Brother Titus. Then she rewarded Brother Titus with a grateful smile. "We both thank you."

"You're welcome. Please don't hesitate to send for me if you suspect poison. Or if you have more questions regarding our faith."

They thanked the doctor and took their leave.

"Brassicus's shop isn't far from here," Livia said. "We could go take a look."

Avitus harumphed. "Absolutely not."

"Why not? It won't take long to swing by his shop and ask a few questions." Livia narrowed her eyes. "Or have you decided the mushrooms aren't worth investigating after all?"

"I don't want my wife making the acquaintance of shady merchants who sell illegal poisons. Sorex and I will deal with them."

Before Livia could protest, Avitus turned to Sorex. "Once you escort us home, I want you to go to Turpio. Ask him who he suspects might sell poison on the sly. Then you may begin looking into the most promising merchants."

Turpio was the wily leader of an acting troupe who had many contacts among the lower echelons of Roman society. Avitus consulted Turpio when he needed information not available to an honorable, law-abiding senator's son. But Turpio's contacts weren't the only ones who could help them.

"I know a few honest, law-abiding herb merchants," Livia said. "I could ask them who might sell poison."

"No. I don't want you wandering the city asking about poison. I have a different task for you. Will you take a mushroom to Dioges and ask him whether it was what killed Salvia?"

Livia hid her annoyance with a thoughtful frown. "It would be better if you spoke with Dioges. He's made it clear he doesn't think women should be asking questions about Salvia's death."

Avitus shook his head. "You're forgetting that Dioges is Gracchus's loyal physician. If he told Gracchus that I was asking questions about the case, that would be a problem. Therefore, it's better if you return to him in the guise of Calida's cousin."

Fish pickle! Faced with her husband's logic, Livia could only acquiesce. Oh joy. Another delightful conversation with the city's grouchiest doctor.

Mistress Livia returned home with unpleasant news. "We need to visit Dioges again," she told Roxana. "But I'm not going to see anyone until I've been to the baths."

"Yes, my lady."

While Mistress Livia checked on Nissa and Brisa, Roxana gathered the bathing things, including scented oils, an ivory-handled *strigil* for scraping away dirt, and a pair of wooden-soled sandals to protect bare feet from heated floors.

Then Roxana wandered to the front door, nodding to Grim and Momus before stepping out to the street. Odd. The food dish she'd left for Nemesis this morning was untouched. Normally, the greedy cat gobbled the food immediately.

Not today. Where was that cat? Roxana gave a warbling whistle and waited, searching the street for the lithe black form.

Nothing.

She poked her head inside. "Have either of you seen Nemesis this morning?"

The men shook their heads.

"I hope that nasty dog didn't chase her away."

"Don't start looking for trouble where there isn't any," Grim said.

"I'm not looking for trouble. It's already happened, and I want to know why."

"Your cat's probably off causing mischief," Grim said. "You have no business blaming Fumo. He's a well-behaved dog."

"Even well-behaved dogs can be ordered to chase cats. Do you both swear that didn't happen?"

Momus filled his chest in indignation and shook a finger at her. "For shame, girlie. Are you accusing us of abuse?"

"Nobody in this house would intentionally harm Nemesis," the mistress said, joining them. "Maybe she's searching for a place to have her kittens. You can look for her on the way to the baths. Keep an eye out for Dap while you're at it. I want him to go to Auntie Livilla and ask her if today will work to bring Nissa for a cooking lesson."

Dap was a young scamp who hung around the neighborhood doing odd jobs. When the boy wasn't running errands for someone, he amused himself (and Roxana) by teaching Nemesis to do tricks.

But today they saw no sign of the cat or the boy. After several blocks, Grim spotted some of Dap's friends. He hailed them. "Any of you know where Dap is?"

"Nope," said one.

"Haven't seen him today. Or yesterday neither," said another.

"In that case," Mistress Livia said to the boys, "which of you will take a message to the Caelian Hill for two *quadrans*?"

After sending the messenger on his way, they continued to the bathing complex. While the mistress soaked in the warm pool, Roxana questioned the other servants who lived near them. No one had seen Dap or Nemesis this morning.

"Why would I notice a stray cat or scrawny boy?" one maid scoffed.

"You should warn your mistress to stay away from street urchins like him," another maid said. "They're nothing but trouble."

Dap wasn't a troublemaker, but it was pointless to argue. What did these ninnies know about Dap? Nothing! All they saw was a poor boy with tattered clothes. They didn't bother to look past his attire to the resourceful, courageous young man underneath. Rich lady's maids had no idea about the realities of life on the Roman streets. They'd never appreciate a boy like Dap.

But Mistress Livia did, and it made Roxana proud to be her maid.

After the mistress finished bathing, she asked Roxana to create a lopsided hairdo so she could once again pretend she was Calida's cousin from Marruvium. Appropriately costumed, they headed for the odious doctor's apartment.

While they walked, the mistress told Roxana and Grim what Brother Titus had told them about the nasty mushrooms and who might sell them.

"I hope you're not planning to visit these merchants," Grim said.

"No," the mistress said tartly. "Avitus asked me to question Dioges instead."

"I'm glad," Grim muttered, scowling to show how happy he was.

What a hopeless grouch. He was almost as bad as the prickly doctor.

When they arrived at the building, Dioges was on his way out. He had a large leather bag slung over his shoulder, and he held a walking stick with a coiled serpent carved into the top—the symbol of his profession.

"You again!" he said by way of greeting. "I thought I told you it isn't seemly for women to ask questions about death."

He gripped his staff as if he might use it to strike them. Grim shifted to the mistress's side, ready to protect her.

The mistress didn't flinch. "I've come on behalf of my cousin Calida," she said calmly. "We may have found what killed Salvia." She handed him a parcel wrapped in a scrap of cloth.

The doctor's eyes bulged out of his head when he opened it and saw what was inside. He muttered a rude phrase that made Roxana's toes curl. Beside her, Grim sucked in his breath, as shocked as she was at the doctor's lack of manners.

The mistress was too much a lady to react. She merely pointed at the shriveled mushroom in his hand. "Do you recognize this? Could it be what killed Salvia?"

"Where did you get this?"

"It was given me so I could ask you whether you thought it could be what poisoned Salvia."

Dioges scowled at the mushroom. "I'm not an expert on mushrooms. They may be poisonous. I can't say for certain."

"We know they're poisonous. We tested one on a mouse."

"*Aesculapius* preserve us!" The doctor waved the mushroom in Livia's face. "Women shouldn't meddle in things beyond their understanding. You're lucky you didn't kill yourself, dabbling in poison. Who else have you told about these mushrooms and your foolish experiments? Does Senator Gracchus know you and your cousin are poking into his wife's death?"

"No."

"Then you're lucky. The noble senator would consider it a grave insult if he knew you were nosing into his private tragedy. You'd better drop the matter before he finds out what you're doing." He slammed his staff into the ground for emphasis. Then he re-wrapped the mushroom and dropped it into his bag. "Leave this dangerous thing with me and ask no more questions."

"But I wanted to—"

"No more. Begone. I don't want to be late for Salvia's funeral rites." Dioges pushed past them, slamming his door behind him, and stomped away, his stick thwacking the ground with each step.

Roxana watched him go, stunned by his incivility. "That may be the rudest, most obnoxious man I've ever met!"

The mistress clicked her tongue. "Don't judge him too harshly. He's grieving over Salvia's death. I bet he's also worried that Gracchus will blame him for not being able to save her."

"That doesn't excuse his behavior. Grim and I thought he was going to hit you."

Mistress Livia grimaced. "So did I for a moment. But we must forgive his prickly behavior as Brother Titus urges us to do."

Roxana wasn't sure she could ever learn to forgive a man who had insulted her mistress like Dioges had. (Nor, to be honest, did she want to.) She followed her mistress home, pondering how it was humanly possible to love your enemies or extend mercy to those who didn't deserve it.

CHAPTER SEVENTEEN

What would compel Gracchus to murder his wife? Avitus kept returning to that question as he searched his legal scrolls for precedents. He would never understand the cold-hearted thinking behind premeditated murder. A murder of passion made more sense. Avitus kept firm control of his emotions, but he could imagine how a man who lacked self-control might lose his head in the heat of the moment. Is that what had happened with Gracchus? Had he discovered Salvia had a lover and assumed she'd been to see him that night?

Probably not. Gracchus was too devious to act rashly. More likely, he'd been planning the death for days. But why?

Avitus pushed his musings from his head and went back to work. So far, he and his secretary Timon had read through dozens of documents without discovering any clear precedents they could utilize. Poison had been used in too many ways by too many people. Avitus finished scanning one scroll and started another. This one included a reference to a criminal who'd been convicted of several poisonings.

AN ODE to POISON

An alarming thought! If Gracchus was willing to use poison on his wife, might he use it again? Against Avitus? Did Gracchus have plans to bribe one of Avitus's slaves to add a deadly elixir to a cup of wine?

Which of his slaves might do such a thing? Sorex and Timon were utterly loyal and could never be bribed at any price. So were Momus and Brisa, but what about the newer staff? How far could Avitus trust them?

Roxana was deeply loyal to her mistress, who had once saved her life. Roxana would never allow anyone to harm Livia. Grim had proved himself loyal in several tense situations, including a courageous rescue when Livia was kidnapped by Gracchus's henchmen. There was no love lost between either Grim or Roxana and Gracchus.

Which left the sullen Nissa. If someone wanted to infiltrate the household, the disgruntled Nissa would be a prime target. Hades! Why hadn't he thought of this earlier before he'd given permission for the girl to be their household cook?

He'd have to bring the matter up with Livia. Not a pleasant thought. No use worrying about it now, though. Avitus stood and stretched the tension from his neck.

Timon looked up from the scroll he'd been studying. "Anything new, sir?"

"No. I need a break." Avitus returned the scroll to its pigeonhole. Opening the door, he found Fumo waiting just outside. The dog scrambled to his feet and nudged Avitus's hand with his nose.

"Hello boy." Avitus fondled the dog's ears. "Shouldn't you be in the atrium where Momus can keep an eye on you?"

"You're his master," Momus said from the arched entryway to the atrium. "He's been waiting patiently for you to play with him."

"Is that so?"

"Yes, sir." Momus retrieved a length of braided rag and held it up. Fumo stared at it, eyes bright and ears perked. Momus commanded the dog to sit, then tossed the toy. Fumo quivered with tension, but he remained obediently seated.

Impressive.

"You release him like this." Momus pointed to the toy and whistled a staccato signal. Fumo raced to the toy and brought it back to the old slave.

"Drop."

The well-trained dog did so.

Momus picked up the toy and held it out to Avitus. "Your turn."

Avitus accepted the length of rag, now damp with dog slobber. In his head, he heard Brisa's sniff of disgust. The soggy piece of rag would earn at least a how-can-you-abide-the-filth sniff from the fussy old woman.

Avitus grinned down at the dog. "Some things are more important than clean hands, isn't that right, boy?" He held up the toy. "Fumo, sit."

The dog obeyed, eyes glued to the toy. Avitus tossed the rag across the peristyle toward the door to his bedroom, counted to ten, then gave the signal. Fumo made a beeline for the toy. Unfortunately, the dog's trajectory went directly through a clump of flowers, sending petals flying and snapping several stalks.

Uh oh!

More stems were trampled as Fumo returned, proudly holding the toy. "Good boy." Avitus exchanged a sheepish look with Momus.

"Better ask Brisa to tidy up the mess before Livia comes home."

"Yes, sir."

Avitus looked down at the dog. Fumo gazed back, happily ignorant of the damage he'd done. "I guess even Jonas can't train a dog to respect the sanctity of flower beds. We'd better shift our game to the colonnade where there aren't any plants to trample."

He led the dog to a corner of the peristyle and tossed the toy down the length of one colonnaded side. After ten tosses (and no further floral casualties), he handed the toy to Momus. "Thank you. I needed the break."

"Do you think we can win the case this time, sir?" Timon asked when Avitus returned to the study.

It was a valid question. Avitus and Publius had an impressive record of legal successes—except against Gracchus, who always cheated justice by one underhand method or another.

But this time was different. Because this time the crime was murder.

"Salvia comes from a prestigious family. They'll demand that someone is punished for her death, and they're powerful enough they won't let Gracchus intimidate them. In addition, Calida's husband Merenda is Urban Praetor. Between them, they have enough clout to prevent Gracchus from buying off the judges."

"Even so, we can't win the case without testimony and proof," Timon said.

Avitus nodded. "Which is why we must find men willing to testify regarding Gracchus's true character so we can convince the judge he's dishonorable and capable of killing his wife."

If they could build a strong enough case against Gracchus, he'd be forced to commit suicide rather than face the shame of a public execution. Then the city would be rid of him forever.

Once Gracchus was dead, Avitus could breathe easily at night. But they wouldn't succeed without help. Fortunately, help arrived a short time later—the list of men wronged by Gracchus that Rutilia had promised.

Breaking the seal, Avitus read quickly through the list of names. Men whom Gracchus had cheated or abused and who might have the courage to publicly proclaim the truth.

He handed the list to Timon. "What do you know about these men?"

Of the twenty-seven names, Avitus only recognized four. Timon filled in details on another six, but that still left over half the list they knew nothing about. Presumably, the men were newly wealthy members of the equestrian class whom Gracchus had conned into agreements of one sort or another.

To defeat Gracchus, Avitus needed to know which of these men he could trust as allies and who would provide the most convincing testimonies. Unfortunately, they didn't have the luxury of months to delve into the men's backgrounds.

"Salvia's family will want a trial as soon as possible, and we must be prepared. No time to waste."

"I understand, sir." Timon was already mouthing the names, memorizing the list.

"You can check with your informants," Avitus told him. "Then I want you to go to Publius. See what he knows about the men. Also, search his scrolls for information on poison cases we've not yet studied. I know he has some scrolls that mention Gaius Aculeo's cases."

"Yes, sir."

Meanwhile, Avitus would go to Livia's brother Curio. He'd lived a rascally youth before settling down to take over his late father's business running apartment buildings. Curio had a knack for befriending people who engaged in a wide variety of occupations—both legitimate and questionable—and was therefore another of Avitus's trusted sources for finding useful information.

A babble of voices in the peristyle announced the return of Livia, home from questioning Dioges (and bristling over it).

"Talking to Dioges was a waste of time," she informed Avitus. "He refused to answer my questions and insulted me in the process. Now I'm off to visit Aunt Livilla."

A visit with her aunt would keep Livia out of trouble for the rest of the day, but it would leave Nissa unmonitored.

"Before you leave, I've been rethinking our discussion earlier. In retrospect, I wonder if assigning Nissa to the kitchen was a bit hasty. She is untried."

Livia crossed her arms. "I'm aware of her inexperience. That's why I'm taking her to get a lesson with Auntie's cook."

"Ah." Avitus could see by the set of her jaw that Livia wouldn't be easily dissuaded. A lengthy argument would waste time and energy better spent seeking allies. And Nissa would be under the watchful eye of Aunt Livilla's cook. That would have to suffice, for today at least.

CHAPTER EIGHTEEN

After telling her husband about Dioges's rudeness, Livia went to inform Nissa she was getting a cooking lesson. Then she headed for the atrium, where she found Roxana pacing.

"My lady! Nemesis still hasn't eaten her food. I'm worried she's gone off to have her kittens in some nasty hole where rats and stray dogs can get to them. May I go look for her?"

Livia checked the angle of the sun. They needed to leave for Auntie's soon to allow Nissa sufficient time for a cooking lesson. "Sorry, no. We're off to Aunt Livilla's."

"Couldn't I stay behind to search while you go to your aunt's?"

Livia's first instinct was to refuse. After all, cats had been successfully raising kittens in the city of Rome for centuries. But sometimes kindness was more important than pragmatism.

"Yes, you may."

"Thank you, thank you, thank you!"

"You're welcome."

Smiling to herself, Livia collected Grim and her cook-in-training and headed for her aunt's house.

AN ODE to POISON

While women like Hortensia took pains to hide every imperfection beneath cosmetics and expensive jewelry, Aunt Livilla made no attempt to disguise her graying hair or wrinkled skin. Although she was past fifty and widowed, she moved with energy in her steps and a sparkle in her eyes.

"Livia dear, so good to see you." Auntie gave Livia a quick kiss then turned to Nissa. "And this must be Nissa."

"Yes, ma'am." Nissa gave Auntie a bow (surprisingly graceful despite her large, stocky frame).

"I understand you want to learn to cook," Auntie said. "Why?"

"Anybody can scrub a floor. Cooking is more interesting. I know there's lots to learn, but I'm young, and I promise I'll work hard."

"I like your attitude, my dear." Auntie turned to Livia. "I've decided on a pork stew with raisins and broccoli simmered with olives for the first lesson. Cook will teach Nissa the entire process, and I'll send her home with the finished meal when it's ready."

"Thank you, Auntie, but I don't mind waiting. You know I love spending time with you."

Auntie beamed at Livia. "I know, dear, but I have plans this evening."

Livia grinned back, delighted her aunt still enjoyed a social life. "In that case, I accept your offer."

"Splendid. I'll take Nissa to the kitchen and get her settled. Meanwhile, why don't you check on the painters?"

She meant the fresco painters who had redone Livia's dining room. Auntie had liked their work and hired them to "freshen up a few rooms" as she put it. Livia went to find them.

The head painter saw her and set his brush aside with a smile. "Good afternoon, my lady. What do you think?"

Two-thirds of the room was complete, and the art was stunning. "Beautiful. How do you create flowers that are so lifelike? I feel I could pluck one and put it in a vase."

Livia crossed the room to inspect a finished panel up close. She wished she could create something this lovely. As a child, she'd been scolded for doodling little pictures instead of attending to lessons. Her fascination with drawing had reawakened when the painters were working on her dining room. She'd been so enthralled at their ability to capture an object in a few brief lines that she'd asked them to teach her how to draw. The head painter had happily obliged.

Since then, Livia had been sketching whenever she had the chance. "I've been practicing, but I can't draw a flower blossom that looks real."

"Then let me show you another of our secrets."

"Yes, please."

When Livia returned to the peristyle after the impromptu art lesson, her aunt was nibbling from a tray of food. Grapes, toasted chickpeas, and figs.

"Sorry I took so long," Livia said. "The painter was showing me a new drawing technique."

"I assumed that's what was keeping you. I remember when you were a little tot, you used to 'paint' pictures with water on the pavement by dipping a stick in the fountain. You'd get so angry when they dried up and disappeared."

Auntie chuckled fondly, then patted the bench beside her. "Join me and tell me what exciting things you've been up to."

"I'm involved in solving another murder." Livia told her aunt everything from Hortensia's summons to questioning Gracchus's servants to the experiment with poisonous mushrooms.

"My, you have been busy," Auntie said when Livia's account came to a close. "How can I help?"

"Can you think of a reason Gracchus killed Salvia? The kitchen maid overheard Gracchus accusing her of infidelity. Could that be a possibility?"

"I suppose so, but why wouldn't he simply divorce her rather than kill her? Although, he wouldn't want to risk humiliating her publicly just now, would he? Not when her brother-in-law Merenda is serving as Urban Praetor."

Hmm. Livia hadn't thought about it from that angle. The Urban Praetor was the magistrate who presided over civil lawsuits in the city. Among other things, he assigned which judges heard which cases. Gracchus wouldn't want to alienate him. On the other hand …

"Wouldn't killing Salvia damage his relationship with Merenda far more than a divorce?"

"Only if Gracchus looks guilty. He's far too clever for that, isn't he? He must plan to shift blame to someone else. Then he'd divert Merenda's animosity toward that person."

How diabolical! Livia's neck prickled as she imagined Gracchus poisoning Salvia to make some enemy look guilty.

"Poor Salvia," Auntie said. "I felt sorry for her when she married Gracchus. I have it on good authority Salvia agreed to the marriage to win Gracchus's help in getting her brother elected praetor two years ago. And Gracchus helped Merenda win his post as Urban Praetor too. Honestly, I can't see why Gracchus would risk disrupting his relationship with Salvia's family when everything is working to his advantage."

Livia munched a handful of chickpeas while she considered her aunt's words. The more they probed, the less this murder made sense. Perhaps Auntie could shed light onto a different issue instead.

"What can you tell me about Rutilia?" Livia explained how Avitus had asked Rutilia to help him oppose Gracchus.

Aunt Livilla wrinkled her lips. "I can see why Avitus might form an alliance with Rutilia, but don't make the mistake of thinking this means you can trust her. Avitus is a good man, respectful of the law and temperate in his character. Rutilia is more like Gracchus. Ambitious, manipulative, devious, and bitter. She'll only help Avitus for as long as it benefits her."

Livia had feared as much. "Do you think we should break off our alliance?"

"Not necessarily. Rutilia may prove useful. I'm sure she has several of Gracchus's servants feeding her information. But don't let down your guard. The moment her goals stray from yours, she'll leave Avitus in the dust. If you work with her, watch your back."

"I see."

Livia had better get home and make sure Avitus realized how dangerous Rutilia was.

CHAPTER NINETEEN

Unfortunately, Avitus was still out when Livia returned home. That turned out to be fortunate because she found Nemesis curled up on her bed. Roxana sat beside the cat, mending a tunic hem, blithely ignoring the fact cats were banned from the house.

"Tsk, Roxana. I said you could search for Nemesis. I never said you could bring her inside and coddle her. I hope Brisa didn't see you."

"We were careful, weren't we?" Roxana stroked the cat's cheek. "You'll never believe where I found Nemesis, my lady. I walked the streets, whistling for Nemesis and asking people if they'd seen her, but no one had. Eventually I came across some of the young scamps that Dap plays with. One of them said he'd seen Nemesis way down at the base of the hill, sitting outside a basket maker's shop on Long Street.

"I said it must be another black cat because why would Nemesis be all the way down there. But the boy swore he'd seen 'the cat Dap likes,' as he called her. *What does he know*, I thought to myself. He's only a boy, and one black cat looks like another. But then I thought, *what if he's right?* Since I'd searched everywhere else, I decided it couldn't hurt to look, so down the hill I went."

Roxana pantomimed walking down the hill with two fingers. "And there was Nemesis, sitting outside a basket shop just like the boy said. She came running to me when I called and demanded to be stroked. But she refused to tell me what she'd been doing there. Didn't you?"

Nemesis purred smugly as Roxana stroked her cheek.

"The basket maker claimed Nemesis had been sitting there off and on for the last two days, always staring across the street. That sounded odd, so I asked him if he'd seen Nemesis before. He said yes, he'd seen her now and then over the last few months, usually in company with a young lad. Right away, I suspected he meant Dap. When I described him, the basket maker nodded. So I asked around and learned Dap lived nearby. I also learned Dap was attacked two nights ago, and he's hurt. I'm certain that's why Nemesis was down there. She's worried about Dap, and so am I."

Roxana gave Livia a pleading look. "Now that you're back, may I go visit Dap and see how he is?"

Livia stroked the cat's head as she considered the question. The boy wasn't her responsibility, but they owed him a debt of honor. "You and Nemesis may go check on him."

Roxana broke into a wide smile. "Thank you, my lady."

"Take a basket of food with you. I'm sure his family can use it."

"Yes, mistress. Thank you." Roxana scooped the cat off the bed. "Oof, you're getting heavy. I bet those kittens are coming any day now."

"Speaking of kittens," Livia said, halting the maid in the doorway, "I'll remind you of your master's rule. There will be no kittens in the house, no matter the circumstances."

"I know, my lady." Roxana settled the cat with its chin and front paws draped over her shoulder, the back legs held in the crook of her arm. "While we're at Dap's apartment building, we'll look for a good hiding spot for a mother cat with kittens."

Once Roxana was gone, Livia straightened the bed cover where Nemesis had formed a nest. Then she checked on Brisa, who was scrubbing the walls in the dining room with the intensity of a gladiator in combat.

Livia left Brisa to her scrubbing and retrieved the smooth slab of pale wood she used as a sketchpad. She sat down in the peristyle and settled the board on her lap to practice the new technique she'd learned from the fresco artists.

What to draw? Livia let her eyes drift around the flowerbeds. Not much was blooming this late in the season, but the marigolds bravely flowered on. She chose a bloom that looked almost iridescent in the sunlight. She wished she had color so she could capture the vivid orange, but she didn't. Instead, she brought to mind the advice the fresco painter had given her.

"Sometimes you need to forget about colors and visualize something only in shades of white, gray, and black."

Easier said than done. Livia squinted at the sunlit flower, trying to see the pattern of light versus dark. She started with the darkest parts, focusing on the shadows rather than the shape of the flower as a whole. At first the drawing looked like a mess, but eventually a recognizable image emerged. How fascinating.

As she sketched, she mulled over Aunt Livilla's warning about Rutilia. How was she going to convince Avitus of the danger without sounding pushy?

Roxana headed off with a basket of food in one hand and Nemesis draped over her shoulder.

Grim stopped her. "Where are you going?"

"To visit Dap. Not that it's any of your business."

He narrowed his eyes. "What's the matter with Dap?"

"Who said anything's the matter?"

"Why else would the mistress send you to visit the boy with a basket of food? I'm coming with you."

"No, you're not."

"Yes, I am."

Roxana glared at him. "I don't need your protection. I can take care of myself."

"It's not you needs protection, it's Dap. You'll talk the boy's ears off."

Very funny. Roxana gave him the stink eye.

Grim turned to Momus, who'd been watching with an amused smirk. "She thinks I'm joking."

Momus shook his head in mock dismay. "You don't need to explain it to me, boy. The girlie has been sassing me since the day she arrived. Can't shut her up."

He winked at Roxana. "But maybe her nonsense is exactly what a lonely boy needs to brighten his day."

"See that? At least Momus understands. I can't cheer someone up with Mister Gloomy tagging along." Spinning on her heel, Roxana marched out to the street.

"Wait." Grim followed her out. "What happened to Dap?"

"I heard he was in a fight and he's been hurt. We're going to check on him." She set Nemesis on the ground. "But I'm not carrying you. You'll have to follow."

Grim snorted. "You realize the cat doesn't understand what you're saying."

"Says who? Nemesis is highly intelligent. She saved my life."

"Sure, she did."

"It's true! She led the mistress to me when I was stuck under a collapsed building." Roxana bent to stroke the cat's head. "Ignore the nasty man. He thinks the worst of everyone, so don't take it personally."

Then she straightened. "I've apologized for you, but if Nemesis decides to bite you for the insult, I can't be blamed."

Grim rolled his eyes. "Do you plan to stand here all day babbling nonsense, woman? Or can we get started?"

The man was impossible. One minute he was ordering people to wait and the next he was impatient to go. Humph!

Dap's apartment building had seen better days. The stairs to the fourth floor reeked of garbage, and the hallway was dim, lit by one small window at the far end. At Roxana's knock, the door opened a crack. A thin-faced woman with scraggly brown hair peered out, a pouting child on her hip.

"What do you want?"

Roxana gave the woman her friendliest smile. "My name is Roxana, and this cheerful man is called Grim. We heard Dap was injured, and Nemesis wanted to come cheer him up."

She shifted so the woman could see the cat cradled in her arms. The woman's face softened. "Is it you, Cat?"

Nemesis meowed. The woman opened the door a little wider and reached out a hand to stroke Nemesis. The cat meowed again, and a young girl peeked out from behind her mother's skirts. "Hello, Cat."

"Is that Nemesis?" Dap's voice called from inside the apartment. "Please, mother, can she come in, just this once?"

The woman hesitated, staring at the cat. Then she sighed. "I guess you can come in."

Nemesis squirmed from Roxana's grasp and scampered through the door. Roxana followed the cat into the apartment. It was small and stuffy, but the walls and floor were clean, and a pile of clothes was neatly folded atop a wooden chest in one corner.

Dap sat on a sleeping mat in the opposite corner. He was bare-chested. Without his baggy tunic, he was skinnier than Roxana had realized. His chest, arms, and face were covered in bruises and scrapes, and he cradled one arm in his lap. Nemesis walked up to him, placed her front paws on his bare chest, and sniffed him over. He grinned and stroked her with his good arm.

Beside her, Grim stiffened.

"Don't embarrass the boy," he murmured. "Talk to the mother while I see to him."

Roxana complied, turning her back on Dap and giving the woman and her children another warm smile.

"How do you know my son?" the woman asked.

"Sometimes my mistress hires Dap to run errands," Roxana said. "He always does a good job, so the mistress wanted to thank him."

She held out the basket. Instead of taking it, the woman pulled back, face hard and wary. "What's all that for?"

"It's a gift."

The woman eyed the basket longingly (the contents would feed her family for two days), but she made no move to take it. Was she too proud to accept the charity of a stranger? Or afraid accepting the gift meant obligations?

Roxana set the basket on the floor and began to talk about her mistress. How kind and generous she was. How much she appreciated Dap's honesty. How she enjoyed watching the antics Dap and Nemesis performed.

It worked. By the time Grim finished his whispered conversation with Dap, Roxana had convinced the woman to unload the items from the basket.

Grim picked up the empty basket. "Good day, ma'am. We won't take up any more of your time. C'mon cat."

He headed out the door without bothering to see if Roxana was ready. She murmured goodbyes and followed. Grim didn't say a word on his way down the stairs, but the rigidity of his back and the set of his jaw spoke volumes. He reached the street and turned for home, his pace swift and angry.

Roxana hurried to catch up. "How bad is he?"

"Arm looks broken, and you saw the bruises. He was taking the family's rent to the landlord when he was attacked by thieves."

A series of juicy words ran through Roxana's head, but she clamped her mouth shut. Maids of wealthy ladies didn't use coarse language. Neither did followers of Jesus. She drew a breath and rephrased her thoughts in more polite language.

"Have they reported the crime? We must help them find the filthy thieves and force them to repay."

Grim shook his head "You'll never find them."

She glared at him. "There you go, always believing the worst."

"I'm simply being realistic. Dap didn't recognize who attacked him, so there's nothing anyone can do."

Fish pickle! There must be some way to help. "Has he seen a doctor?"

"Doubt it. The boy's father has a bad leg and doesn't earn much. With three children to care for, the family doesn't have money to spare for a doctor."

"The mistress will pay. We can ask Brother Titus." Roxana planted her fist on her hip. "Any objections?"

Grim shook his head, and some of the worry eased from his eyes. They found Brother Titus in his front room showing a customer how to apply a salve. After bidding the customer goodbye, the doctor gave Roxana a puzzled greeting.

"We've come about a boy named Dap," Roxana told him. "Grim thinks he has a broken arm."

"I know Dap," Brother Titus said. "A good lad. I hire him when I can. His family needs every quadrans he can earn."

"I'm sure the mistress will pay your fees."

"No need to pay. I came to Rome to serve the sick, not to make a profit on them." Brother Titus grabbed a sturdy leather bag and threw the strap over his shoulder. "I'll go at once."

"Thank you."

Back on the street, Roxana stopped and turned to Grim. "Before we go home, I have an idea. Since we're not far from the Subura, we could look for Brassicus's shop. He's one of the merchants Brother Titus said might sell poisonous mushrooms."

Grim crossed his arms and gave her a withering look. "This is why I insisted on coming with you, woman. You can't stay out of trouble for an hour."

"How is looking for an herb merchant trouble?"

He gave a cynical snort, but he didn't start home in a huff. Which meant he was at least a *little* curious.

"What I have in mind," Roxana said in her most reasonable voice, "is for us to locate Brassicus's shop. Then if you think it's safe, we could ask some local residents what they know about him."

"Bad idea. Remember what happened the last time you tried something like this? Almost got the mistress kidnapped."

"That's why I'm suggesting we go. If we find the shop now, then the mistress won't be tempted to look for it later."

That got him. Grim turned and stared toward the Subura. "I'll go on one condition," he said without looking at her. "You keep your mouth shut and let me ask the questions."

"Deal."

CHAPTER TWENTY

Livia's shading skills improved with each try. As she sketched, she wondered what had compelled her husband to talk with Brother Titus. She'd been praying Avitus would accept their faith. Was this an indication he was softening? If so, how could she encourage him? Should she invite him to join her for prayer meeting tomorrow morning?

It couldn't hurt to ask, surely?

That settled, she lost herself in her drawing until Roxana and Grim appeared looking pleased with themselves.

Livia set her drawing board aside. "How's Dap?"

Roxana's face fell. "He was beaten up, and we're pretty sure his arm is broken, so we went to Brother Titus. I promised him you'd pay his fee, but he said he won't charge them. I hope you don't mind?"

Livia's mother would be appalled at a maid daring to act without permission, but Livia was proud her slaves could think for themselves and make wise decisions.

"You did the right thing. What else can we do for the family? Should I send you back with more food?"

"They have a bigger problem than food, my lady. Dap was taking the family's rent payment to the landlord when he was attacked. With the money stolen, I don't know how they'll scrape together enough to pay the rent."

"Say no more," Livia said. "I'll offer to replace the amount that was stolen."

"I wouldn't recommend doing so," Grim said.

"Why not?"

"Dap and his family are hardworking and proud. Think how Dap's father would feel if a rich stranger handed him money he didn't ask for."

Fish pickle! Why did other people's feelings so often get in the way of practical action?

"We have some good news, too." Roxana's customary smile reappeared. "Since we were down in the valley, Grim and I went looking for Brassicus's shop."

"Is that so?"

Roxana nodded, eyes shining with pride. In contrast, Grim stood stiffly, jaw clenched, staring at the floor. He'd relaxed in the two months since joining the household, but he reverted to this grim expectation of punishment whenever something unexpected occurred. Unfortunately for Grim, unexpected things happened to Livia and Roxana all the time. It kept life interesting.

Livia rewarded her slaves' initiative with a delighted smile. "How clever of you."

Roxana beamed and nudged Grim in the ribs. His stance relaxed.

"Everyone gave us odd looks when we asked about Brassicus," Roxana said.

"No, they didn't," Grim broke in.

"Yes, they did. Maybe you didn't notice the looks, but I did. Anyway, we found the shop, but it's closed. The entire neighborhood is wondering why Brassicus up and disappeared. Very mysterious!"

"Quit embellishing the facts, woman," Grim growled.

Roxana crossed her arms. "If you don't approve of my version, you can tell her yourself."

He shot her a dark look.

"Go on." Roxana put a hand to hear ear. "Start talking."

"*One* shopkeeper—" Grim gave Roxana a pointed look. "—told us Brassicus left town four days ago and might be gone a month. He didn't know where the merchant has gone or why."

"We were told Brassicus almost never leaves Rome," Roxana said (forgetting it was Grim's turn to talk). "Doesn't that sound suspicious, him leaving the city one day before Salvia died? I bet Brassicus used his secret smuggling contacts to get those evil mushrooms for Gracchus, and soon as Gracchus paid him, he fled the city so he can't be blamed for Salvia's death. We should send someone down to the port and find out which ship he booked passage on."

"Stop it!" Grim spluttered. "There you are, making up stories again. Nobody said anything about Brassicus taking ship or smuggling."

"Thank you for locating the shop," Livia said before Roxana could argue. "I'll tell Avitus what you've learned."

AN ODE to POISON

Livia excused Grim and asked Roxana to sit down on a bench that caught the afternoon sunlight. "Turn a little more to the left. Now hold still."

Livia sketched her maid's narrow face with its pointy chin and full lips under large, expressive eyes. Her maid's straight brown hair was twisted into a simple but elegant bun with a few artful strands framing her face. Roxana was staring at a flower with fierce concentration. Was she trying to figure out where Brassicus had run off to, or did she find it taxing to sit still?

Whatever the reason, capturing Roxana's expression was a challenge. But the drawing turned out rather nicely. Livia showed her maid the result. "What do you think?"

"Oh, Mistress! It's wonderful. It looks just like me."

"Thank you. Return to the bench, and let me try a different angle."

By the time Livia had completed her next sketch, Avitus was home. He sank to a bench facing Livia and stretched his legs in front of him. Livia offered him a cup of water. "You look tired and thirsty. I hope your afternoon was productive?"

"Yes." Avitus drained the cup. "Thank you. How is your Aunt Livilla?"

"We had a lovely visit. I told her about our investigation, and she suggested Gracchus may have a more sinister motive. She thinks he might have murdered Salvia to frame someone else. Have you heard who Gracchus is blaming for the crime?"

Avitus shook his head, face taut with worry. "But I've been wondering who he might blame. He could claim you poisoned Salvia at the party."

"That's preposterous! We know the poison was in the cup Salvia drank after she returned home. Pansa and Placida are witnesses that we tested it."

"True." Avitus's worry eased. "Did your aunt suggest anyone Gracchus might want to frame for the murder?"

"No. She was more worried about Rutilia." Livia kept her voice carefully neutral. "Aunt Livilla says Rutilia is a lot like Gracchus. She manipulates people for her own ends and tosses them aside when they're no longer useful. You had best beware her selfish motives and her shifting allegiances."

"I'm not blind to the risks of working with her."

"Promise me you'll be on guard when you're with her."

Avitus quirked an eyebrow. "Do I detect a note of jealousy in your voice? If so, you needn't worry. I'm well aware of her nature and know to guard against it."

What did this scholarly man know about guarding himself from a seductress like Rutilia? Livia stepped close.

"If Rutilia chooses to work her seductions on you—" She ran a finger along his jaw, then touched it to his lips. "—I'm afraid you'd succumb faster than you think. Remember, it's those who believe they are invincible who topple first and hardest."

Avitus took her hand. "Rutilia has a beauty that is artful and breathtaking, but it's also cold and dangerous. I prefer the beauty that resides inside you."

He kissed her hand before continuing, "Others are drawn to Rutilia, but she sets my nerves on edge. She reminds me of all I'm not. Therefore, I loathe every minute I spend with her. Not so with you."

Avitus drew Livia into an embrace. "You help me see the best in myself, and I thank the gods you are my wife."

Livia melted into his embrace. This inscrutable man who rarely showed emotions could sometimes surprise her in the most delightful ways. In moments like this, Livia dared hope that one day she and Avitus might share the kind of marriage Brother Titus and his wife Tirzah enjoyed. Mutual love and admiration comfortably working together.

She smiled up at him.

He kissed her. She kissed him back.

The moment was shattered by Fumo barking a welcome. They pulled apart as Sorex strode into the peristyle.

"Report," Avitus said, once more the dispassionate, pragmatic lawyer.

"I talked with Turpio. Checked two of the herb merchants he suggested, then paid a visit to Drash the Snake Charmer. Loud, flashy, full of big claims. Insists his love potions are the best in Rome and senators flock to buy them. When I scoffed, he gave me a list of important customers."

Sorex rattled off ten names. The names meant nothing to Livia until he got to the last one—Gracchus.

Even her inscrutable husband couldn't hide his surprise.

"Do you believe him?"

"I checked. Drash described Gracchus's servant. Called Melancton. Big man, small eyes, prominent forehead."

"Your description fits him," Livia said with glee. "This confirms our theory that Melancton poisoned Salvia."

Avitus harrumphed and waved a finger. "Don't jump to conclusions. Just because Drash knows Melancton doesn't mean he sold him poison. Besides, I thought you told me Gracchus doesn't trust anyone besides Dioges to make him medicines."

"True, but consider this logic," Livia said. "If Gracchus planned to poison his wife, he wouldn't want Dioges to know about it, would he?"

Avitus's eyebrows rose, and a hint of a smile played on his lips. "Excellent point, my dear."

He turned to Sorex. "Go back tomorrow and see what else you can dig up about Drash and his customers. Then investigate Brassicus as well."

"Don't bother. Brassicus isn't home." Livia told them what Grim and Roxana had discovered, making it clear it was their idea.

Avitus took it well. "Since Brassicus is out of the city, we'll focus on Drash and hope we can pry the truth from him."

CHAPTER TWENTY-ONE

By the time Avitus finished recording notes on all he'd learned from Curio, Sorex, and Livia, Nissa had returned, and dinner was served.

Unfortunately, it was delicious.

Nissa had prepared a mixture of olives and broccoli that Avitus hoped might prove disgusting, but the combination was surprisingly tasty. Then there was pork stew. The pork was tender and moist, not scorched or tough as leather. The sauce was a piquant balance of sweet, spice, and tanginess, not so vinegary it made his mouth pucker.

Then he noticed there were little bits of leafy something sprinkled over the stew. He touched a few with the tip of his tongue.

Ugh! They tasted bitter!

He spat the noxious stuff into his napkin.

Livia frowned at him. "What's wrong?"

He pointed to the stew. "What are these green specks?"

"Minced coriander leaf from Auntie's garden." Livia licked a dab of the sauce from her finger. "*Sophisticated* cooks use herbs to enhance a dish. The sharpness of the coriander adds a brilliant contrast to the sweetness of the raisin sauce. Don't you agree?"

Coriander, eh? He tentatively put another morsel in his mouth. His wife was right, the balance of flavors was delicious. Hades! How would he ever convince Livia to ban Nissa from the kitchen after this meal? He took another bite. No point ruining the best dinner in weeks with an argument. They could discuss it tomorrow.

Avitus had eaten his fill (and then some) when Timon entered the dining room, sweaty and out of breath. "Your brother sent me to fetch you, sir. He requests you come at once. There's been a poisoning."

Jupiter, Best and Greatest!

Avitus got to his feet. Livia stood also. "I'm coming with you."

He drew breath to argue, then paused. What better opportunity to discuss his concerns regarding Nissa and the risk of poison?

"I've been afraid this would happen," Avitus told his wife as they headed across the valley. "Gracchus successfully killed his wife, and now he's discovered how easy it is to rid himself of enemies through poison. It's possible Gracchus is behind this poisoning. If he's attacking Publius, we may be next."

"I know you don't believe in coincidences," Livia said. "But blaming Gracchus seems a bit premature. We don't know what's happened or who's taken ill."

Avitus silently berated himself for sounding illogical. "Allow me to rephrase my concerns. Whether Gracchus is responsible or not, this tragedy highlights the danger of attack by poison. I've thought through the situation with some care. If Gracchus intends to poison us, Nissa is the slave he could most easily bribe.

Therefore, even though her cooking is far better than Brisa's, we cannot have her in the kitchen."

Livia made an angry noise in the back of her throat. "I agree that Nissa's loyalty hasn't been tested, but I hate to pull her away from the kitchen. Cooking has changed her from sullen to happy. Do you know, I found her humming earlier."

There Livia went, trying to counter logic with emotion. When would she learn emotions were never to be trusted?

"I'm sorry, but I insist. It's easy for someone of Gracchus's resources to bribe Nissa to slip deadly poison into our food or wine. We must protect ourselves. I admit Brisa is not adept in the kitchen, but she could never be bribed to harm us."

"She wouldn't intentionally poison you, but I'm not convinced her cooking won't kill us both someday."

"This is no time for levity. Do you trust Nissa with your life? Are you utterly sure she would resist a large bribe from Gracchus?"

Livia huffed an annoyed sigh. "No."

"Then we can't trust her in our kitchen."

His wife was quiet for several paces.

"Can Nissa return to the kitchen once Gracchus has been found guilty?"

He ran his tongue around his mouth, remembering the delicious dinner.

"Yes."

"Then I concede your point." Livia pointed a finger at his chest. "But only until this is over. Then, Nissa becomes our cook."

"Agreed."

A weight lifted from Avitus's chest.

Only to settle back again when they arrived at his brother's house. They found Publius pacing his peristyle.

"We came as soon as we could," Avitus said. "How many are ill?"

Publius gave them a ferocious scowl. "Just Fortis, curse that woman! I should never have allowed her into my house."

Avitus exchanged puzzled glances with Livia.

"What woman? Are Hortensia and the children safe? Have you forbidden the household from eating or drinking anything?"

"Calm down, Avitus. This wasn't an attack on my household," Publius said. "Fortis is the one who's been poisoned, and it's all Zoe's doing. The little viper has been playing us for weeks, letting Fortis think she was working for us when all along she's been feeding Gracchus information about me. I must go back and reexamine every fact Fortis reported to me."

"You're not making any sense. If Gracchus was using Zoe to draw information from Fortis, why kill him off?"

"To send me a warning, proving he can hurt me any time he wants."

Avitus gave Livia an I-told-you-so look before turning back to his brother. "Tell us what happened from the beginning."

"Right." Publius ran a hand through his thinning hair. "It started early this afternoon. Zoe appeared at the house. She'd come to warn Fortis not to visit her because Gracchus was in a rage over Salvia's death and the entire household was terrified of doing anything to anger him. Or so she claimed. After I'd questioned her about the state of Gracchus and his household, I allowed her a few moments with Fortis. How I rue that decision!"

Publius started pacing. "A while later, my steward informed me that Fortis was ill. By the time I saw him, he'd been sick for at least an hour. He was in a sorry state but was still lucid. He insisted the only thing he'd eaten since morning were some date cakes Zoe brought from Gracchus's kitchen. He swears it couldn't be Zoe's fault because she'd eaten one too. Humph. Blinded by love. Logic says Fortis was targeted on purpose. Why else is he the only one dying?"

Why else, indeed? Could this be the breakthrough they'd hoped for? Was killing Fortis Gracchus's fatal error that would lead them to proof of Gracchus's guilt in Salvia's murder?

They must not waste the opportunity.

"Have you tested the pastries Zoe brought him?" Avitus asked.

"Not yet. I was waiting for you to arrive. You're the criminal experts. Now you're here, let's see what you can learn. Follow me."

Publius led them to an unused storeroom and gestured for them to enter. Avitus remembered hiding in the room as a child to avoid his father's rages. He'd spent many hours sitting on the floor of this room, reading by the light of an oil lamp. The room was still mostly empty. Two oil lamps lay discarded in a corner along with a folded blanket. In another corner, he saw a plate with a few crumbs embedded in a puddle of sticky residue and a pottery cup containing a few dregs of wine.

"I ordered that nothing be touched until you had a chance to study it," Publius said.

Livia lifted the plate to her nose and sniffed. Then she touched the tip of her finger to the sticky residue. Before Avitus could stop her, she licked it.

"Jupiter, Best and Greatest!" Avitus lunged across the room and pulled her hand away from her mouth. "What do you think you're doing? Trying to kill yourself?"

She pulled free and gave him an annoyed look. "Calm down. If Dioges tested poisons by tasting a drop on his finger, so can I."

"Dioges is a trained physician who knows what to look for. Do you taste anything odd or bitter? Do your lips tingle? Does your throat feel numb?"

"No, no, and no." Livia raised an eyebrow. "Satisfied?"

Avitus nodded and stepped back, showing that he trusted her. "Carry on."

Next, she picked up the cup and sniffed. She wrinkled her nose then swirled the dregs and sniffed again. Then she stuck her finger in the cup and brought a drop of wine to her lips.

"Ugh!" Livia grimaced and spat several times. "That tastes even worse than it smells."

Served her right!

"And it's set my lips tingling like I've eaten nettles."

CHAPTER TWENTY-TWO

Livia didn't know which frightened her more, her tingling lips or her husband's look of terror. He was immediately at her side, gripping her shoulders so tightly it hurt.

"You must vomit immediately!"

"Why? I only tasted a drop."

"Don't argue!"

Someone handed her a feather to tickle the back of her throat. She reluctantly obliged. After vomiting, Avitus led her to a guest room and made her lie down while he gave a flurry of orders to the servants. Someone handed her a cup. She took a sip. Honeyed wine that had been mixed with water and some pine resin. It cleared the bitter taste of bile from her mouth.

Livia drained the cup and handed it to Avitus. He refilled it, sloshing some onto the floor in his haste. "Drink more."

When he started to fill it a third time, she held up her hand. "Avitus, stop! I'll be fine. Please take me back to Publius so we can continue our discussion."

He studied her, eyes filled with worry. "You're sure you're up to talking?"

"I'm sure." Livia stood. "My head is spinning with questions, not poison. The sooner we find some answers, the better I'll feel."

When they were seated in her brother-in-law's study, Publius gave her a wry smile. "You, my dear, are the most courageous woman I've ever met. I was planning to have the cake crumbs and wine dregs tested on mice, but it seems you've saved us the trouble."

Avitus drew an angry breath. Livia laid a hand on his arm. "Relax. He's only trying to lighten the mood."

Then she grew serious. "The poison was in the wine, not the cake. Where did Fortis get it?"

"We shall find out." Publius sent for his cook and asked if Fortis had obtained wine.

"Yes sir," the cook replied. "Fortis begged me for a cup of wine. He claimed he had a special powder that would enhance his, er..." He gave Livia a sidelong glance.

"Where did Fortis get the powder?" Publius asked.

"He didn't say, sir."

"Was his girlfriend with him?" Avitus asked. "Could she have touched anything in the kitchen while you were getting the wine?"

The cook shook his head firmly. "I don't let anyone in my kitchen who doesn't belong there, sir. The two of them stayed in the doorway until I handed Fortis the cup."

Publius sent the cook away, then shook his head in disgust. "A love potion. How ironic. I bet the little viper found it amusing to kill her lover that way."

Why was he so set on blaming Zoe? Livia glared at her brother-in-law. "Fortis could have purchased it himself, you know."

"She's right," Avitus said. "Is Fortis lucid enough to tell us where he got the powder?"

"Let's hope so." Publius stood and turned to Livia. "Will you join us?"

Her stomach churned, remembering the reek of vomit and acrid herbs in Salvia's bedchamber. Her troubled stomach couldn't face that particular stench right now.

"Thank you for asking, Publius, but I suspect Fortis doesn't want a woman seeing him in his present condition."

While the men were gone, Livia considered the facts. Publius assumed Zoe was responsible. Could she have brought the love powder and given it to Fortis? Had she added something to the cup when Fortis wasn't looking? Either was possible, but why?

If Zoe was secretly wheedling information from Fortis, why suddenly kill him? Unless... what if she was the one who'd added poison to Salvia's cup? Then Fortis would have seen her, which meant she needed to kill him to prevent him from talking. But if that was true, why hadn't Fortis told them about it yesterday?

Livia groaned and rubbed her forehead. Her poor brain was going in circles. Time to look at a different possibility. Where might Fortis have purchased love tonic powder laced with poison? Could some fiend (like Drash the Snake Charmer) be selling toxic aphrodisiac powders to unsuspecting victims all over Rome? How sick was that, killing men desperate to find love?

Whoa. This was starting to sound as far-fetched as one of Roxanna's stories.

And as unlikely. If some twisted merchant had been selling deadly powders, the forum would be abuzz with news of men dropping dead. That wasn't happening. So then, why was Fortis poisoned? And by whom?

Too many questions.

The men returned carrying a cracked clay jar containing a dark, brownish powder. Publius plunked it on the table. "You're not going to believe where Fortis got this powder."

"I'm all ears," Livia said.

"Gracchus's kitchen."

She blinked. "You're not serious."

"We are. Apparently, Zoe told Fortis about Gracchus's aphrodisiac, and they couldn't resist taking some to try."

That explained why Zoe had acted so guilty when Livia questioned her about who had a key to the medicine chest. Livia picked up the jar and took a whiff. Blech! It smelled like the nasty wine dregs she'd tasted. But wait...

"This can't be what killed Fortis. Dioges tested every one of those medicines. If one drop of this made my lips tingle, I'm sure Dioges would have noticed, so this can't be where the poison came from."

Publius frowned at the jar of powder. "That means Zoe must have brought poison with her and added it to the cup when Fortis wasn't looking."

"There may be a third option," Avitus said. "Dioges tested the medicines several hours after Fortis and Iris were in the kitchen. Therefore, I propose that between those two events the killer returned and switched the poisoned jar for an identical one that was not poisoned. We can test this powder to verify the theory, but for now let's assume it contains poison."

Livia followed his convoluted logic. "Then according to your theory, the poison was in the jar of tonic powder *before* Iris mixed the cup for Salvia?"

Avitus nodded. "It's the most logical explanation given our new information. Unfortunately, it means we can no longer limit our suspects to the few who were in the kitchen when Iris mixed the tonic. The poisoner could have acted days ahead of time."

Publius nodded his agreement. "However, according to your theory, the killer must have been in the house that night in order to switch the jars after Salvia sickened."

"Which means the killer obtained two jars of love tonic before acting."

While the brothers traded logic, Livia's mind traveled in a different direction. Who had access to a key to unlock the medicine chest during the night? And what about ... Oh! A thought struck Livia with a sickening jolt.

"When the poisoner placed the jar of deadly aphrodisiac powder in Gracchus's medicine chest and waited for his trap to take effect, he wouldn't be expecting to kill Salvia."

Livia watched as understanding dawned on both men's faces.

"Jupiter Best and Greatest!" Publius thumped his desk. "The murderer was trying to kill Gracchus."

AN ODE to POISON

Avitus grappled with Livia's shocking revelation that Gracchus might not be guilty of Salvia's death. Which meant Avitus and his brother were in trouble because without a murder charge they had no case against Gracchus. And if they had no case, how were they going to destroy their enemy before he destroyed them?

On top of that, if Gracchus was innocent, he'd be looking for somebody to blame and he'd beat his servants unmercifully until he found a culprit. What if Zoe confessed that Fortis had been at the house? What if Iris described Livia so well that Gracchus saw through her disguise? What if…?

"Oh!" Publius suddenly straightened, a wolfish grin on his face. "This may not be a disaster. I've been assuming the gods had answered our prayers by granting us the chance to bring Gracchus down through a murder charge. What if that wasn't their plan? What if the gods have decided that Gracchus should be punished a different way—death by poison?"

An intriguing thought. Avitus explored his brother's logic. If the gods had decided Gracchus should die, they would have wanted the poisoner to succeed.

"If you're right, the gods must be angry at Iris for ruining their plans and killing Salvia by mistake."

Publius raised a finger. "Ah, but the gods won't allow a mere maidservant to thwart their will. This isn't over. If the gods have decreed that Gracchus must die, the poisoner will try again."

And maybe the next time he would succeed. The hard knot of despair in Avitus's gut unclenched. He'd dreamed of playing a part in Gracchus's downfall, but what did it matter so long as Gracchus could no longer threaten them?

"We dare not interfere with divine justice," Publius said gravely. "Therefore, we must cease our investigation and allow the poisoner to succeed."

"I can't believe you said that." Livia glared at Publius, quivering with indignation. "You can't sit back and do nothing."

Publius clucked his tongue. "You must look at the matter in the correct light. If the gods have chosen to use the poisoner as their instrument of justice, who are we to question it?"

"It sounds to me like you're confusing justice with your private thirst for vengeance," Livia said, frowning. "The killer has already poisoned two innocent victims. It's your duty to prevent him from killing more. On top of that, Salvia deserves justice."

"Not so," Publius said. "Salvia wasn't murdered. She died of a tragic accident, unintentionally poisoned by her own maid. Ergo, there has been no crime."

"Wrong!' Livia pounded her fist on her knee. "Salvia was killed by whoever poisoned that jar. And we need to find who's responsible."

Uh oh! Avitus recognized the set of his wife's jaw. She was working herself up to become Salvia's champion of justice. He stood, making sure he had Livia's full attention. "*We* are not relatives of Salvia. Therefore, *we* have no responsibility to find her killer. None. At all."

He held her gaze, watching until her indignation softened to acquiescence.

"Fine. I'll tell Calida the sad truth and let her deal with it."

"You will do nothing of the sort!" Publius cried.

Livia gaped at him. "Excuse me?"

"Were you not listening? We must allow the gods to enact their justice, which means Calida must know nothing of our suspicions."

"Why not?"

Publius raised his eyebrows. "Who was in Gracchus's home that night with sufficient wealth to purchase two jars of expensive love tonic?"

Livia refused to answer, so Publius said it for her. "Calida arrived at the house before Dioges did. She could have gone to the kitchen and switched the jars. Therefore, we must consider her a suspect. And that means you must tell her nothing."

Livia crossed her arms. "Calida asked me to investigate Salvia's death, and I promised to bring her a report tomorrow. If I suddenly refuse, she'll wonder why. Therefore, if you don't want Calida to become suspicious, I *must* talk with her."

It was Publius's turn to glower.

"Livia has a point," Avitus said to his brother. "We should proceed as if we are still seeking Salvia's killer. To do otherwise would make the killer—whoever it is—become suspicious."

"I stand corrected," Publius said with ill grace. "But we can't tell anyone what we've discovered tonight. Including Calida."

CHAPTER TWENTY-THREE

That night Avitus's sleep was disturbed by uneasy dreams. He woke at dawn, body weary and mind churning, to find his wife missing. Icy panic raced through his veins until he remembered she and Roxana had gone to their early morning prayer gathering. He lay back and closed his eyes, but he was too jittery to return to sleep.

Throwing on a tunic, Avitus went to the peristyle. As the dawn light grew, he paced, trying to identify what had troubled his slumber. A battle had waged through one confusing dream to the next. Was it a message from the gods? If so, what did the battle symbolize?

He examined his marriage, household, and pending cases. Nothing fit. When he'd exhausted other options, he considered Gracchus and their unexpected discovery. That must be it. The battle symbolized his long struggle against his enemy.

But his gut disagreed. Why?

Avitus stopped pacing and closed his eyes, attempting to recall his dreams. A scene came to vivid life, two great gods at war with each other. One was Mars Ultor, god of vengeance, the other Justitia, goddess of justice. At first, it was not apparent what they fought over, and then he noticed a lone figure between them.

Who was it? What did it mean?

"I don't understand," he whispered. "Help me."

Surprisingly, he heard an answer. *They battle for your heart. Your thirst for retribution wars against your love of justice. You must decide who wins.*

Chest tightening, Avitus felt compelled to choose. But weren't the two compatible? In the strengthening light of morning, he considered the matter objectively. Gracchus deserved to die. That truth was incontrovertible. However, neither Avitus nor his brother had the authority, either under the law or under the rule of the gods, to mete out death.

Was that the crux of the matter? The decision to stand back and allow the poisoner to murder Gracchus? How many times had Avitus stood up to his peers, insisting that justice belonged to all men regardless of their status, popularity, or birth? Would he now recant his position to fulfill his wish for vengeance?

Could he live with himself if he did nothing to prevent an unjust murder?

No.

He would hold fast to the virtue of justice and not allow the baser instinct of hatred to prevail. Avitus forced himself to state his decision out loud. "Gracchus deserves justice as much as any other citizen of this empire."

There. He'd admitted it.

Immediately, the tension eased, and he could breathe again. He sat down, weary but filled with a peace he hadn't felt in weeks.

Fumo padded over and nosed Avitus's leg. Absently, he scratched the dog's ears as he considered what to do next. To honor justice, Avitus must continue to pursue the killer, whether Publius liked it or not. But a man who killed once might kill again to prevent his crimes from being exposed. Which meant they couldn't allow the poisoner to realize they knew the truth. They must work covertly.

By the time Livia returned, Avitus had formed a plan to seek the murderer as safely as possible. Now to convince his wife.

"Good morning, my dear. How was your prayer gathering?"

"Hopeful." She searched his face, an odd eagerness in her eyes. "How are you?"

"The gods sent me a dream." Avitus told her his vision of the battle between Vengeance and Justice. "Therefore, I no longer agree with Publius. We can't turn a blind eye to murder without dishonoring justice no matter how much Gracchus deserves death."

Livia rewarded him with a beaming smile. "I've been praying fervently that you'd come to that conclusion. Praise God!"

Avitus opened his mouth to deny her God had anything to do with it.

And closed it.

Because his heart confirmed the truth of her words. Somehow, her God had shown him the meaning of the dream and guided him to the right decision.

And it had brought peace to his troubled soul.

"I prayed you would come to see that taking the law into your own hands would plague your conscience."

"That's the conclusion I've come to as well, but we must proceed with caution." Avitus paused to capture his wife's gaze. "As you've discovered, a murderer who fears exposure is liable to kill again to hide his deeds."

Fear flickered across her face. Good. He rammed home his point.

"You know how dangerous Gracchus is. Any man who would dare to kill him is equally dangerous. It must appear to everyone that we still believe Salvia was the intended victim. Please promise me you won't tell anyone about Fortis's death or what we learned from it. Not Calida. Not even your aunt."

"What about Roxana and Grim?"

Avitus was instantly wary. His clever wife had used her slaves to get around her promises before. "You may tell Roxana and Grim, but none of you may mention Fortis or the love potion or speak with anyone belonging to Gracchus's household."

That ought to suffice to keep her safe.

"We will keep that promise," Livia said solemnly. "Thank you for thinking of my safety. I appreciate it even if sometimes I don't show it."

His gaze softening, Avitus stroked his wife's cheek with a finger. "I'm glad we understand each other."

And glad his strong-willed wife had complied without a lengthy fight. "When you return from Calida's, we can discuss the best plan to proceed."

"I was planning to stop in on Curio after I spoke with Calida."

"Oh? What business do you have with Curio?"

"Do I need a reason to visit my own brother?"

Avitus crossed his arms and waited.

After a few heartbeats, Livia sighed loudly. "I'm worried about Dap and his family."

She told how the boy had been attacked and his money stolen. "I thought we could help them by paying their rent anonymously. I'm going to ask Curio to handle it for me."

"Did you plan to inform me of this decision before or after the arrangements had been made?" Avitus asked dryly.

"I'm informing you now," she said, matching his tone. "Dap was indispensable the night Grim rescued me. We owe him a debt of gratitude, so this is a matter of honor."

Avitus didn't understand his wife's interest in helping poor nobodies, but he understood the debt of gratitude they owed the boy for his part in rescuing Livia. Her suggestion was honorable, and acquiescing would please her.

"Very well, I approve."

"You're a good man, Aulus Avitus. I'm fortunate to be your wife." Livia kissed his cheek. The warmth of her lips spread from his cheek through his entire body.

She stepped back and smiled up at him. "I have one more question. Now that we know Gracchus didn't poison his wife, can we assume he isn't planning to poison us either?"

Uh oh! That sounded like a loaded question.

"Maybe. Why do you ask?"

"Because I want to keep Nissa in the kitchen."

Ah. He should have seen that coming. And he couldn't fault her logic.

"Nissa may remain our cook so long as you continue sending her to your aunt for lessons."

"Thank you. I'll send her off at once."

AN ODE to POISON

Livia's heart was bursting with gratitude. She sat down on her bed and murmured a prayer. "Thank you, Lord Jesus, for answering my prayers and changing Avitus's mind. Please continue to draw his heart and soul to you and your truth."

Then she called Grim and Roxana into the room and told them about Fortis's death and the shattering realization that Gracchus might be the intended victim rather than the killer.

Roxana's hands flew to her cheeks. "But that means Salvia's death was an accident. How tragic! Poor Calida must be heartbroken."

"She doesn't know, and we aren't allowed to tell her."

"Why not?" Roxana gaped at Livia.

"We need to treat Calida as a suspect. She was in the house that night and could have switched the jars."

"Calida wouldn't kill her sister!"

"Do you *ever* think before you speak, woman?" Grim said. "The killer *wasn't* trying to kill Salvia."

Roxana stared daggers at him. Then her face crumpled. "How horribly tragic if Salvia's death is Calida's fault. How would she ever forgive herself? And …Oh! I just thought of something even more horrible. What if Salvia herself is to blame?"

The maid clutched her hands to her chest and intoned in a voice worthy of a tragic actor, "A wife killed by the poison she intended for her husband."

Grim rolled his eyes. "Sounds like the plot of a bad play."

"Let's hope the truth isn't so melodramatic," Livia said with a chuckle. "I don't think either Salvia or Calida is guilty. Why would they have gone to the effort to meet me at the party and work out a plan to spy on Gracchus if they were planning to kill him?"

"I hope you're right, my lady."

Livia did, too. Her gut told her Calida was innocent, but her gut had been wrong before. She would proceed as if Calida might be guilty.

"Before we head out, I want to rethink everything that happened the night of the murder in case there are details we've overlooked."

She held up two dainty glass perfume bottles. "This green bottle represents the jar of love tonic that contains poison, and this clear bottle is the jar that isn't poisoned. We'll use this bench to represent the chest in Gracchus's kitchen where the jars are kept."

She set the clear bottle on the bench and held up the green one. "At some time—possibly days before Salvia's death—the murderer added poison to this jar and put it in the chest in place of the unpoisoned one." She reached for the clear bottle then stopped.

"Hmm. The killer would need to unlock the chest. Salvia, Gracchus, and the steward are the only ones with a key. However, Zoe told me she knew where Salvia kept hers. We can presume other slaves knew as well."

Livia pantomimed unlocking the chest. She switched the perfume bottles and held up the clear one. "I guess the killer kept the unpoisoned jar so he could put it back later."

She set the clear bottle aside and touched the green one. "The poison is in the chest. Since Gracchus is the only one who's supposed to use the love potion, we assume the killer must have been after Gracchus."

"Only that's not what happened," Roxana said.

"Correct. Let's see if we can recreate what transpired. We know Zoe and Fortis stole some of the tonic before Iris appeared, so the poisoned jar was in place before Fortis arrived at the house. When Iris comes to the kitchen, she adds poisoned love tonic to Salvia's cup by mistake. Then she leaves the cup in the kitchen while she takes food to the back door."

"What if Iris was only pretending to leave food?" Roxana asked. "Maybe she was really letting in the killer. Didn't the cook say something about the back door being left unbolted?"

Grim shook the green perfume bottle at Roxana. "Wrong. The poison was already in the chest."

"But it's possible the door was unbolted earlier," Livia said. "We don't know who else might have taken advantage of it. I'll ask Calida."

Next, Livia talked through the actions of Iris, Melancton, Zoe, and Fortis. "After all four of them leave the kitchen, the room is empty until the steward sends the cook to heat water. So whoever the poisoner was, it appears he or she used that window of time to sneak into the kitchen, remove the poisoned jar, and replace it with the original one."

Livia reached for the green bottle.

"Wait," Grim said. "At this point, Salvia is in her room. How could a slave sneak in and borrow her key?"

"Excellent point. With Salvia's key unobtainable, we must limit the possibilities, which makes the steward a prime suspect."

Grim nodded. "He was told about Salvia's illness before anyone else. He could have switched the jars before waking the cook."

"Good thinking." Livia pantomimed unlocking the chest. She swapped bottles, then stared at the green bottle in her hand.

"Ooh!" Roxana sucked in a breath. "Once he swapped the jars, the killer would need to hide the poisoned jar."

"Maybe that's why the door was unbolted," Grim said. "The killer hid the poisoned jar outside the house so nobody would find it. And then he hid the mushrooms in the kitchen to make the cook look guilty."

It all made sense to Livia.

"Excellent work, everyone. Let's see if we can confirm our suspicions. While I talk with Calida, you two can question her staff. Just remember, Calida could be the poisoner, so be very careful what you say."

CHAPTER TWENTY-FOUR

When she arrived at Calida's house, Livia was shown to a tasteful sitting room. Calida was seated on a backless couch featuring red cushions embroidered with a pomegranate motif in silver and black. Very elegant. She gave Livia a sad smile. "Thank you for coming. Please join me."

Livia sat down beside her host and laid a hand on her arm. "How are you holding up?"

"As well as could be expected. I think Salvia would have been pleased with the ceremony." Calida paused, fighting tears. "Gracchus may not have loved her, but he knows how to put on a good performance. He played the role of mourning husband well enough to fool most people."

Her bitter tone implied she still held Gracchus responsible.

"Who is Gracchus blaming for your sister's death? Not Iris, I hope?"

Calida shook her head. "He claims his wife's murder was intended to threaten him, but he didn't say who he's pretending was behind it."

"Was Gracchus upset with you because your 'cousin' was asking nosy questions?"

"No, you don't need to worry. No one saw through your disguise. Now tell me what you've learned." Calida took Livia's hands in hers, her voice fierce. "Were we correct about the poison in the wine?"

Livia saw the grief etched on Calida's face. She was not the killer. Of that, Livia was sure. But promises were promises, so she kept to her pretense.

"Salvia's wine contained poison, and Dioges assured me none of his medicines would have caused death even at the wrong dosage." Livia summarized the pertinent facts, including the sack of poisonous mushrooms.

"Then we have him!" Calida said. "Gracchus and Melancton must be guilty."

"The facts point to that conclusion, but to convince a judge, we must eliminate all other possibilities. Can you ask your spies in Gracchus's household to find out who else might have been in the kitchen that night, either before or after Iris?"

"I can do better than that." Calida's face brightened. "Gracchus is quite fond of his sons. They're his one soft spot, so yesterday I asked if he would allow me to visit them. I said they needed a woman to help them with their grief since they were close to their stepmother. He agreed. That means I can go and ask whatever is needed. Wasn't that clever of me?"

"Brilliant!" Livia said.

"Thank you. What do you want me to find out?"

"To begin with, who Gracchus intends to blame. Verify who has a key to the medicine chest. Find out if the house was searched for poison. And one last question. The cook told me he'd found the back door unbarred. Can you ask Iris if the door was barred when she left the sack of food for the midwife? What was her name?"

"Nerilla."

"She's a loose end we ought to clear up. Tell me more about her."

"I don't know much." Calida wrinkled her nose. "She was once a respectable midwife, years ago. There was some controversy that tainted her reputation, and she was reduced to working for the lower classes. Salvia claimed Nerilla was as knowledgeable as any physician, but I wouldn't want anything to do with her."

"Where can I find her?

"No idea. Why are you so interested in Nerilla?"

"I thought if Salvia confided in her, she may know something."

"Salvia wasn't in the habit of confiding in mere acquaintances."

So much for that line of inquiry. "Have you thought of any other reason Gracchus might have had for murdering Salvia? She mentioned something about him dishonoring your family. What did she mean?"

"I don't know. There was never any love lost between our brother and Gracchus, but they were allies. As far as I know, Gracchus has fulfilled all his promises."

They chatted for a few minutes longer, but Calida had nothing else of note to add. Livia took her leave, promising to return soon.

On the way to their next visit, Livia told Roxana and Grim all she'd discovered. "What have you two learned?"

"That Calida's husband Merenda has been friends with Gracchus for years," Roxana said. "They sometimes dine at each other's houses. But when Gracchus comes to Calida's, he's never satisfied with the menu and always asks for something else. Gracchus pretends it's because of his weak stomach, but the cook says it's really an excuse to demand special service."

It would stroke Gracchus's ego to demand special treatment. The cur!

"Guess what else I found out!" Roxana continued, eyes shining in her enthusiasm. "The last time they dined together, Salvia had a whispered discussion with her brother-in-law Merenda. They were overheard arranging to meet the next day at the house of someone named Lucius."

Livia's stomach lurched. Please, let it not be true that Salvia was having an affair with her brother-in-law. That could get ugly in so many ways.

"What have you learned, Grim?"

"Merenda was dining with friends the night Salvia died," Grim replied. "He didn't return home until after Calida had been called away to nurse her ailing sister. Also, I got several people talking about Gracchus's steward. Everyone says he's bitter at Gracchus and has enough backbone to take action. I think there's a high chance he's the poisoner."

Livia's neck prickled. If the steward were the killer, nothing prevented him from trying again. Would more innocent victims die in his next attempt? Were Gracchus's sons at risk?

Very possibly.

What could she do to protect them?

Avitus opened a blank tablet and considered the facts one by one. Someone had attempted to kill Gracchus by poisoning his aphrodisiac, which meant the killer knew Gracchus used it. Avitus wrote: *Killer knew about love tonic.*

Livia had informed him that all the jars of medicine powder looked the same, therefore Avitus assumed they came from the same source—Dioges. Could the doctor be the killer? He had opportunity but not motive. As Gracchus's personal physician, Dioges's best interest was served by keeping Gracchus happy and healthy so the senator would continue recommending Dioges to all his friends and clientes. Thus, Dioges's ambitions and success were tied to Gracchus. Furthermore, Dioges was too intelligent to use his own medicine to poison someone.

Did that mean the poisoner was hoping to make Dioges look guilty? Highly plausible given how carefully the poisoner had planned his crime. So then, would a killer as clever as this purchase his means of death from his victim's loyal physician? Not likely. Which meant the poisoner must have obtained the love tonic from an alternative source.

Drash the Snake Charmer, perhaps? Was his touted love tonic similar enough that Gracchus wouldn't have noticed the difference?

One way to find out.

Avitus called Sorex and explained his suspicions. "It's time for you to go back to Drash. While you're there, obtain a sample of his love tonic. Also, try to find out what Melancton purchases from the charlatan."

Sorex departed, and Avitus returned to his cogitations of the murder. The poisoned love tonic had been removed sometime during the night before Dioges tested the medicines. Therefore, either the killer was a member of Gracchus's household or the killer employed one of Gracchus's slaves as an accomplice.

Killer has access to household or possible accomplice.

Was there a slave in Gracchus's household angry enough to hasten the master's voyage to the underworld if the bribe was high enough? The cook, for example? He had access to the kitchen whenever he wanted. Also, by using the love tonic instead of food, he would shift the blame elsewhere.

Check into cook.

However, the poisoner had been smart enough to remove the poisoned jar when his plans went awry, and Salvia had succumbed instead of Gracchus. Which meant the man was able to think independently.

Killer or accomplice capable of adjusting plans as needed.

Was the cook clever enough to do that, or should they be considering someone like Gracchus's steward instead? Avitus had no way to find out.

So then, a different line of inquiry. Who wanted Gracchus dead? More men than Avitus could count, so the question must be more specific. Who wanted Gracchus dead *at this moment?* Something must have occurred to precipitate the crime.

Killer needs compelling reason to act now.

That should be a more promising line of inquiry. Avitus considered how best to approach the puzzle. He was interrupted by a tap on his door.

Timon poked his head into the study. "Sorry to interrupt, but your brother requests you come at once. There's been another emergency."

Avitus's stomach clenched. "Jupiter Best and Greatest! Another poisoning?"

Timon shrugged. "He didn't say."

They found Publius's household in a frenzy of activity. Carpets were being rolled, silver goblets were being packed, and Hortensia could be heard scolding maids from a bedroom. Publius was in his study, pulling scrolls from his strongbox and tossing them into the arms of his harried secretary. He spun around when Avitus entered.

"You're here, thank the gods."

"What's going on?" Avitus asked. "It looks like you're fleeing town."

"Gracchus is accusing me of sending Fortis to poison Salvia. He's threatened to go to the praetor to lodge official accusations. I've ordered Hortensia and the children out of the city. I'm sending them to our uncle's villa in Herculaneum."

No, no, no! This couldn't be happening.

"How did Gracchus find out about Fortis?"

"He beat the truth out of his cook, who admitted Fortis was Zoe's lover and that he'd been in the house the night Salvia died. Gracchus claims I sent Fortis to poison Salvia and then I sent him to coax Zoe here—not the other way around—so he could kill her too. Apparently, she succumbed to poison last night. More proof that infernal love tonic is the cause of all this. Anyway, Gracchus is saying Fortis is responsible for killing both Zoe and Salvia, and I am guilty of ordering Fortis to act."

This was worse than Avitus could have imagined. His mind whirred, considering the legal implications.

Publius closed his eyes, grimacing in pain. "After I get Hortensia and the children to safety, I'll begin preparing my defense. I'll need your help."

"You won't beat Gracchus by focusing on defense. No amount of clever rhetoric can negate the fact that Fortis was in his kitchen. Therefore, we must go on the offensive, uncover the killer, and prove who actually killed Salvia."

"We agreed not to interfere with the gods."

Avitus's neck prickled as his dream flooded into memory. "Either you fight for justice as a Memmius should or play the coward and allow Gracchus to blame you for the crime. The choice is yours."

Publius's face darkened at the implied insult. Then he slumped into a chair. "I concede your point. How do you propose we find the killer?"

"The same way we solve any problem. We start with what we know." Avitus held up a finger. "First of all, we know the killer added poison to the jar of love tonic, which means the killer knew Gracchus used the stuff. Secondly, the killer is either part of the household or bribed a slave who is. Thirdly, the killer was desperate enough to attempt the murder of one of the city's most dangerous senators. We must look for someone with a compelling reason to get rid of Gracchus. Find him, and we may have our killer."

Publius ran a hand through his hair. "What a time to lose my spy. We need someone with access to Gracchus's house. You'll have to go back to Rutilia and ask for her help."

Avitus had considered it already. And rejected it.

"We can't trust her. She's a potential suspect. As his ex-wife she'd be familiar with the love tonic, she has ample reason to hate him, and she knows which household slaves are capable of being bribed."

Publius waved the argument away. "If Rutilia had wanted her ex-husband dead, she'd have killed him before now. I think we can trust her."

Avitus shook his head. "It's too great a risk. Consider this. No one benefits financially from both Salvia and Gracchus dying as much as Rutilia's sons."

"We need her help, risk or no."

"What if you're wrong and she's the killer?"

Publius gave him an exasperated look. "You're an experienced lawyer. You'll have to determine that when you talk to her."

Beard of Jupiter, what a mess!

CHAPTER TWENTY-FIVE

Livia found Curio in his study shuffling through a pile of wax tablets and semi-unrolled scrolls. His face brightened when she appeared. "Livia! How delightful. Have you come to rescue me from the evils of contracts and rents-past-due?"

"Yes, for a few minutes."

"Wonderful." He shoved the tablets into a teetering pile and offered Livia a seat. Then his features hardened into a mock scowl. "Avitus told me about your investigation. Reckless of you to set foot in Gracchus's house. That's like walking into the den of a hungry lion."

"The hungry lion was sick in bed, so I was perfectly safe." Livia scowled back at him. "And I didn't come here to get scolded by you."

Curio gave her his lopsided grin "Sorry. Couldn't resist a little teasing. Honestly, I'm proud of you and all you've managed to learn in so short a time."

"Thank you." Her big brother's grin warmed Livia's heart. She'd had precious few smiles from her parents over the years, so Curio's praise meant a lot. He was one of the few people who loved her without trying to change her. He was also one of the few people who knew about her faith in Jesus, so she was eager to share her story of answered prayer.

"Guess what happened this morning. Roxana and I were praying with Brother Titus that Avitus would change his mind on an important decision. By the time I got home, he had! And when I told him I'd been praying for him, he didn't argue. I think he's softening toward our faith."

"I think so too. He asked me about my beliefs yesterday when he was here. He knew me before when I was a bitter degenerate. I explained how I'd pretended I was enjoying life as a wastrel but in truth I was miserable. I was furious at the gods who had allowed my reputation to be destroyed, I hated Father for disowning me, and I loathed myself. I told Avitus how I'd felt trapped in that life until Pansa explained that God loved me despite my lifestyle and all the mistakes I'd made. God offered me forgiveness and a second chance. I took it."

"Thank God you did," Livia said, remembering the joy of being reunited with the brother she'd thought had abandoned her. "I'm glad the angry Curio is gone for good."

"So am I," Curio said. "Avitus watched my transformation, so he can't deny it. And I made it clear it was the power of our Lord Jesus that made it possible."

It was wonderful news, yet Livia felt a pang of disappointment. "I wish he'd told me about your conversation. That's twice he's had a conversation about Jesus without telling me."

"Don't let his reticence upset you. He'll talk about it when he's ready." Curio gave her another crooked smile. "Once Avitus is curious about something, he won't leave it until he's satisfied. Be patient and keep praying. 'Trust God to do what you cannot' as Pansa so often reminds us."

Easier said than done. Sigh.

Maybe she couldn't control her husband's faith, but she could make a difference in Dap's life.

"I have a favor to ask." Livia told her brother the situation with Dap and the stolen rent money. "I can't stand the thought of Dap and his family being thrown out on the street. Will you help me pay the landlord anonymously? I was thinking two month's rent."

"I applaud the idea. You've taken our Lord's teaching on serving others to heart. But I must ask, does Avitus agree with your decision?"

She met his concerned gaze with steady eyes, thankful she and Avitus had talked the matter through. Curio knew her tendency to act first and ask permission later.

"He knows and agrees."

"Good. Where does the boy live?"

Livia described Dap's apartment building.

"I think I know who owns that building. I'll take care of it."

"Thank you."

She hugged Curio goodbye and headed around the corner to Pansa's bakery. Placida was in the workroom, deftly shaping balls of sweetened dough that would rise into her pillowy must cakes. She welcomed Livia and Roxana with her usual motherly embrace. "How are you, my dears? I hope you're not still playing with poison?"

"No," Livia said. "There's a related issue that's bothering me, but I can't tell you much because I promised Avitus I wouldn't."

"Tell me what you can. The Lord knows the truth, and he can guide us."

"Other people in Gracchus's house could be in danger, but Avitus has forbidden me from speaking with any of the household. What should I do?"

"You've always been resourceful when it comes to accomplishing what you think is right, my daughter. Why are you hesitating now?"

"Because I want to honor my promise to Avitus," Livia answered immediately.

But was that the whole truth? She searched her heart and realized that part of her *wanted* Gracchus dead. He deserved it, and it would make everyone's life easier. *Sorry, Lord. I'm struggling here. Loving my enemies isn't easy.*

As if she could read Livia's thoughts, Placida said, "If it were Curio's household that was in danger, what would you do?"

"Warn them at once."

"Should you act any differently in this case even though the household belongs to your enemy rather than your brother?"

Livia shook her head. "But how can I warn them without disobeying my promise to my husband?"

"By finding someone who can tell Gracchus for you."

That made sense. Unfortunately, the only person Livia knew who fit the description was Dioges.

A whole barrel of rancid fish pickle!

"I have another question. Calida told me about a healer woman named Nerilla. Do you know where to find her?"

"Why are you interested in Nerilla?"

"We think she visited the house the night Salvia died. She might have seen or heard something that could help us find the killer. Do you know her?"

"No, but I've heard of her. Some say Nerilla is the best midwife in Rome. Others say she has no training and relies on magic more than skill. Yet others say she's an unholy sorceress who curses those who cross her so they sicken and die."

Placida scrunched her face. "I don't believe the cruelest rumors, but there's too much about her that worries me. She's never married, yet she lives on her own rather than under the protection of a male relative. I fear she carries dark secrets in her heart, and I don't trust her."

Nerilla sounded fascinating, but Placida didn't understand why independent and eccentric women inspired Livia. She patted her concerned mentor's hand. "Please don't worry. I'm not planning to become Nerilla's patient. I only want to question her about Salvia. How do I find her?"

"I don't know."

"Any idea who would?"

"Let me think."

Livia waited while Placida methodically shaped her dough and murmured a prayer. Would Livia ever develop her mentor's habit of asking God to solve her problems instead of charging ahead to solve them on her own?

Placida finished a tray of must cakes and wiped the flour from her hands. "I know a woman who's just given birth. We've been short-handed, and I haven't had a chance to visit her since the baby arrived. You can deliver a gift for me. I don't know if she used Nerilla as her midwife, but it's possible."

"That sounds like a good plan. Thank you."

It turned out Placida kept a stock of supplies for new mothers. Livia left the bakery a few minutes later, followed by Roxana lugging a basket piled with bread and a bundle of infant cloths.

The woman who answered Roxana's knock peered out at them, holding the door half-closed as if she feared Livia would invade her tiny apartment. From behind her came the mewling of a newborn followed by the shout of an older child.

"What do you want?"

Livia gave the hostile woman her friendliest smile. "I bring a gift from Placida, the baker's wife. She sends her greetings and wishes you well with your little one."

The woman softened at the sight of the parcel Roxana held out. "Tell Placida I'm grateful."

"Perhaps you can help me in return?" Livia said before the woman turned away. "I'm looking for Nerilla. Placida thought you might know where I can find her."

The woman looked at Livia's midriff and frowned. "What do you want with Nerilla?"

"I have some questions for her. It's a private matter. I've heard I can trust her."

"It's true," the woman said. "Nerilla is the wisest, most patient midwife in Rome. Some say she's short-tempered and bossy, but she has a heart of gold. My labor lasted all night, but Nerilla never left my side. I wouldn't have managed without her."

"Praise God for his mercy," Roxana said. "When was your little one born?"

"Three nights ago."

That meant Nerilla was with this woman the night Salvia was poisoned. So much for considering her a suspect. But it wouldn't hurt to question her just in case.

"How can I get in touch with Nerilla?"

The woman gave Livia's slender form another searching look, then shrugged. "The usual way."

"Which is?"

"Leave a message with her landlord, One-Legged Lurco. His building is on the Viminal Hill not far from the baths and a few blocks up from Marius's Tavern."

"Thank you. May God bless you and your child."

Logic said Nerilla couldn't be involved in Salvia's murder if she'd been attending a birthing that night, yet something in Livia's gut urged her to talk with the woman. Perhaps it was simple curiosity.

Was that so wrong?

She turned to Grim. "I want to speak with Nerilla."

Roxana gave an excited gasp. "Is it true, my lady? I've been wondering if you were with child."

Fish pickle! Roxana must have noticed Livia's monthly cycle was late.

"It's too soon to be sure," she said briskly.

But Roxana squealed in delight and clapped her hands. "I knew it. A baby! How excited you must be."

How wrong she was. Excitement wasn't the emotion filling Livia's chest.

"Hush, woman," Grim muttered. "You're making a scene."

"Grim's right. No more talk of babies. We have a murder to solve."

They found the building owned by One-Legged Lurco. As the name suggested, Lurco was missing the lower half of one leg. The scars on his face and arms indicated he'd served in the legions before his injury. He was still a large and commanding figure despite the missing leg.

"How may I help you?" he asked in a gruff voice.

"I'm told Nerilla the midwife lives in this building. I'd like to speak with her."

Lurco gave Livia a once-over, gaze lingering on her midriff so long she felt her face grow warm.

"Nerilla isn't home," he said finally. "Leave your message with me, and I'll see she gets it. If she's interested in speaking with you, she'll find you."

Uh oh! Livia had hoped to speak to Nerilla privately. If the midwife appeared at their home, Avitus would immediately assume Livia was pregnant and begin fretting over her health. Worse, if either Momus or Brisa got wind of it, the entire neighborhood would be told that Avitus's wife was expecting.

Rancid fish pickle! Livia couldn't risk that happening.

She needed an alternate location to meet with Nerilla. Somewhere they could talk without people jumping to conclusions about Livia expecting a baby. Hmm, her friend Elpis's perfume shop would work. Elpis was good at keeping secrets.

Yes, excellent solution.

They could stop by on the way home and let Elpis know about the plan. She'd be thrilled.

CHAPTER TWENTY-SIX

Roxana walked beside her mistress, humming happily. The mistress was with child! In a few months, there'd be a baby in the house. By then, Nemesis's kittens would be mostly grown. Roxana and Dap could pick the nicest one and train it to be the child's special pet.

Her daydream was shattered when Mistress Livia stopped suddenly. "Change of plans. We have one more errand to see to." The mistress spun on her heels and headed back the way they'd come.

"Why can't a woman ever make up her mind?" Grim muttered under his breath.

Roxana jabbed him in the ribs. "I heard that."

Grim gave her a dirty look, then turned to follow the mistress. "Where are we going, my lady?"

"To see Dioges," Mistress Livia answered. "My conscience can't ignore the fact that Gracchus and his household may be in danger. I can't warn them through Calida, so that leaves Dioges."

Roxana made a face. "Why bother. He won't listen to you."

The mistress glared at her, eyes smoldering. "I don't like him any more than you do, but our Lord commands us to love our enemies, so I expect you both to cooperate. Let's get it over with as quickly as possible."

"Yes, mistress. But what about your disguise?"

"Fish pickle! You'll have to help me."

Roxana loosened a few plaits of hair, loaned the mistress her worn arm bangles and traded shawls. It would have to suffice.

"Waste of time," Grim muttered as they continued on.

"No, it's not!" Roxana said hotly.

"What's with you, woman? A moment ago, you hated the idea. You're as fickle as she is."

"Am not. Dioges is an arrogant misogynist, but the mistress is following her conscience, and God will honor it."

"Don't try to distract me with fancy words. I bet you don't know what misogynist means."

"I do too. I heard the master using it with Timon. A misogynist is someone who hates women."

Grim rolled his eyes to show how impressed he was. "I bet you five quadrans the doctor won't listen and this trip will be a waste of time."

"You're on! Just you wait and see what happens, oh you of little faith."

The scowl Grim gave her made Roxana giggle. But Grim's scowl was nothing compared with the scowl the doctor gave them when he opened his door. His face was ferocious enough to send small children running for their mothers.

"You again," he growled. "I'm not answering any more of your questions."

"Good morning to you too, Doctor," Mistress Livia said with frosty politeness. "I haven't come to ask questions. I'm here to warn you."

Somehow, Dioges managed to scowl even more fiercely. "About what?"

"My cousin Calida and I suspect Salvia was poisoned by accident, and we're worried the poisoner might try again."

That startled the old grouch. He stared at the mistress, pop-eyed. Then his brows lowered, and his ferocious scowl returned. "I warned you to stay out of this."

Mistress Livia continued as if he hadn't spoken. "Calida is afraid to warn Gracchus about our suspicions because of his temper. I suggested we tell you because you're Gracchus's physician. I'm sure you know what precautions the household ought to take to protect themselves from harm."

"Of course I do," Dioges said haughtily. "I don't need foolish women telling me my business. You can take your suspicions right back to Calida and inform her she's wrong."

"She isn't wrong. We have proof the poison was in one of your medicines."

"Impossible!" Spittle flew from his mouth, and his nostrils quivered in rage. "I tested each medicine myself. There was no poison."

"We think the killer switched the poisoned jar with another one before you arrived. That means the killer was using *your* medicine to do his dirty deeds, which means *your* reputation is at stake."

Oh, good work, Mistress! Clever to appeal to the doctor's reputation.

Dioges gaped at Mistress Livia. "It's not possible ... Who would dare ... Oh!"

His face darkened to purplish red. "The cook. I've been suspecting he's the cause of Gracchus's stomach ailments. The wicked slave must have been slowly poisoning his master for months, and when that didn't work, he tried something more potent."

"How terrible," Mistress Livia said. "Isn't it your duty to warn Gracchus of the possibility?"

The doctor's eyes narrowed. "Go back to your cousin and tell her I'll handle it. If she tries to interfere, she's liable to regret it." He gave her a final dark look and shut the door.

They all stared at the door for three heartbeats. Then the mistress shook herself and said, "That's over with. Let's go home."

Roxana followed her mistress, a slow grin spreading over her face. Because the doctor had agreed to cooperate.

She turned to Grim with a smirk. "You owe me five quadrans."

The slit-eyed look of disgust he gave her was worth as much as the coins. How men hated to be wrong! Ha!

Rutilia agreed to meet with Avitus two hours after midday. He was led to the formal study, where Rutilia was waiting for him. Today, she was dressed in a tunic of deep green with ornate embroidery on the cuffs and neckline. She took her chair with the grace of a lioness and waved Avitus to a seat. He took his time, studying her out of the corner of his eye. He would need all his skill in reading emotions to determine whether he could trust her.

"I thought you might show up today," Rutilia said. "I've heard the rumors. Everyone is saying Publius killed Salvia. Is it true?"

"No." Avitus took a deep breath and let it out slowly, his inscrutable mask firmly in place. "How would killing Salvia benefit Publius?"

Rutilia gave a little nod of satisfaction. "As I thought. Publius isn't that stupid. Was his slave in Gracchus's house that night?"

"Yes."

"That is unfortunate." She clicked her tongue. "Poor Publius is looking mighty guilty. You must be worried."

An interesting comment. If Rutilia were guilty, she'd not be so willing to discredit a rumor that focused blame elsewhere.

Unless she was being intentionally deceptive? He must stay alert.

"I hear Gracchus will make official accusations," she said.

"You're exceedingly well informed."

"I pay good money to keep myself informed. That's how I survive." Rutilia leaned forward and dropped her voice to a menacing purr. "And when it comes to Gracchus, I take pains to stay *very* well informed. Fortunately, Gracchus has made an enemy of his steward. He promised to free the man years ago but has yet to keep that promise. The steward resents it bitterly. His highest ambition is to gain his freedom. With the money I pay him, he'll soon have enough to purchase it."

If Rutilia wanted to conceal a crime, she wouldn't have volunteered the identity of her spy. That was twice she'd failed to respond like a guilty murderess.

However, by revealing information she'd put Avitus on the spot. To continue the game, he must reciprocate.

"Publius and I believe the poisoner was not trying to kill Salvia. If her death was an accident, the killer may try again." He let the sentence dangle, watching Rutilia's face for telltale signs.

She gripped the arms of her chair, alarm in her eyes. "Are my boys in danger?"

Her first thought was for her sons' safety. What did that tell him? If she was behind the poison, she'd have known they were safe. And the woman's fear wasn't feigned.

"We don't believe your boys are being targeted," he said. "We think the killer is after Gracchus."

Rutilia sat back, nodding to herself. "I've been wondering. After all, who would benefit from Salvia's death? But Gracchus is another story."

Would a murderer admit that fact so readily? He was almost convinced. Except … "It seems to me no one benefits from Gracchus's death more than your sons."

Rutilia's striking face turned hard and sharp as flint. "Are you threatening me? Then let me tell you something. Much as I despise Gracchus, until my sons come of age, they're better off with their father alive."

She leaned forward, jaws tight with rage. "Furthermore, if I were going to kill Gracchus, I'd want him to suffer longer than an hour or two. And I'd want him to know it was me who was making him suffer."

The icy hatred in her voice sent chills up Avitus's spine. Had he been too hasty in disregarding her as a suspect?

Sitting back, Rutilia gave Avitus a sheepish smile. "Foolish of me to admit my true feelings to a lawyer searching for a murderer."

His chest relaxed. The woman was not as invulnerable as she pretended. Nor was she the killer.

Avitus explained about the stolen aphrodisiac and Fortis's subsequent death. "Thus, we now believe Gracchus was the intended victim rather than Salvia. Tell me about this love potion. Did he use it when you were his wife?"

"Ugh!" Rutilia grimaced. "That noxious brew. I blame Calida's husband Merenda for it. He was bragging at dinner one night, claiming he had a potion that made him—" She cleared her throat. "You can imagine what men with big egos might say. Gracchus craves anything that makes him feel powerful, so he ordered Dioges to make him a similar concoction."

She made a face. "I think Dioges intentionally made it taste as disgusting as possible so Gracchus would be impressed by its potency."

"You've tried it?"

"Gracchus insisted."

"Did it work?"

Rutilia gave a sardonic laugh. "All I ever noticed was the horrible taste. It made one's breath foul for the rest of the night."

Interesting. Where better to disguise the bitter taste of poison than in a foul-tasting love potion?

"Who else does Dioges sell this potion to?"

"Gracchus doesn't like to share. He made Dioges promise not to offer his precious aphrodisiac to anyone else." Rutilia gave a disdainful sniff. "Although I suspect Dioges has been selling it on the sly and charging a premium."

"Who else knows Gracchus uses the love tonic?"

AN ODE to POISON

"How should I know?" Rutilia dismissed the question with a wave. "It's the kind of thing men discuss when women aren't present."

Apparently, he'd gotten all he could on that topic. Moving on...

"The crime appears to have been carefully planned. In your opinion, who has a strong enough motive to kill Gracchus at this particular time?"

"That is the question, isn't it?" Rutilia tapped one perfectly manicured finger on the polished wood of a table. "My dear ex-husband has cheated and swindled his way to power, so his list of enemies is long. It's possible the killer is someone Gracchus has been blackmailing. Someone faced with an imminent threat of exposure because he can no longer pay Gracchus's exorbitant demands. Also, I'd look closely at Senator Merenda."

"Why?"

"First of all, Merenda resents Gracchus. It's common knowledge Gracchus was instrumental in helping Merenda gain the praetorship. You can be sure Gracchus will expect repayment. With interest. Secondly, Merenda knows about the love tonic since he's the one who introduced the idea. Thirdly, I happen to know that Merenda pays Gracchus's cook to spy for him. And you mentioned it was the cook who suggested Fortis was to blame."

Amazing how a few facts could bring a baffling puzzle into focus.

Avitus thanked Rutilia and hurried back to Publius's house. He needed to catch Hortensia before she left the city and ask her what she knew about Calida's husband Merenda.

CHAPTER TWENTY-SEVEN

On her way home, Livia pondered Dioges's suggestion that Gracchus's cook was the killer. The cook had easy access to the medicine chest, but how did he unlock it? Also, if he were the poisoner, would he have given Livia the sack of deadly mushrooms? Unlikely.

So then, what if the killer was trying to make the cook look guilty? That seemed more likely. He'd hidden the mushrooms in the kitchen on purpose so when they were found, it would point blame to the cook. The cook was fortunate he'd discovered the sack of mushrooms and given them to Livia before anyone else knew about it.

Unless the cook was guilty and only pretended to find the mushrooms?

Ugh. She was thinking in circles. Time to turn her attention elsewhere for a while. They crossed Long Street, passing a beggar with a bandaged arm. It reminded her of Dap. She ought to tell Brother Titus about the rent money.

Livia turned toward the doctor's apartment. His wife Tirzah welcomed them into the waiting room with a maternal smile. "Good afternoon. Look who I get to hold while my husband is tending a patient." Tirzah beamed at a baby in her arms. "This little dear is four months old. It's been a long time since mine were this tiny."

"How adorable," Roxana cooed, bending to take a closer look.

Livia forced a smile as she watched the two women fuss over the baby. She'd never been drawn to infants the way Tirzah was. Livia's mother had been cold and distant, forever scolding Livia for her many failings. Livia felt ill-prepared to face motherhood and didn't want to consider it yet.

"Is something the matter?" Tirzah asked.

Oops. Livia gave her friend a confident smile. "Nothing. I dropped by to give your husband a message about Dap, the boy with the broken arm. I've arranged to pay the family's rent for two months. Anonymously. I wanted Brother Titus to know about it in case there's a problem. I don't want a dishonest landlord taking my money and still demanding rent from Dap's family."

"That's generous of you."

"Dap's been a good help to us, so we're happy to help him in return."

The baby squawked, and Tirzah shifted him, absently giving him a finger to suck on. Which gave Livia an idea.

"Do you know a midwife known as Nerilla?"

Tirzah ran a concerned eye down Livia's form. "If you're in need of a midwife, I can give you more suitable names."

"What's wrong with Nerilla?"

"Nothing. I think you'd like her, actually. She's a strong, independent woman with firm opinions and boundless energy. But I'm not sure your husband would approve of her. Or she of him. She often criticizes the ruling classes. She's fiercely protective of the women she serves and shares their mistrust of the wealthy and powerful.

"Then too, there are cruel rumors about her. Total poppycock. Nerilla is a worthy healer. She's as devoted as Titus, and her patients are fortunate to have a healer as capable as she is. She's clearly been given medical training, although I don't know where or how. She doesn't talk about her past, and we don't pry."

"I see." Nerilla sounded more and more like someone Livia would admire. Livia couldn't wait to meet her.

A woman emerged from the back room. The baby cooed and waved her arms. Tirzah returned the infant as Brother Titus came into view. He handed his patient a cloth-wrapped parcel and bid her goodbye. Then he approached Livia with his compassionate smile.

"Good morning. What brings you here?"

"She's been asking about Nerilla," Tirzah said.

"Oh?" His eyebrows rose.

"I don't need a midwife," Livia added before he started asking awkward questions. "As my husband told you, we're trying to find who poisoned a friend of my sister-in-law. The victim had contact with Nerilla. From what Tirzah told me, Nerilla sounds like an intelligent woman. I'm hoping she might have insights others have missed."

"I wouldn't doubt it." Brother Titus tilted his head and regarded Livia, brow wrinkled in thought. "I would say you are equally observant. May I have a private word with you?"

He beckoned Livia to follow him into the examination room. Once out of sight of Tirzah, his face turned grave. "I may be involved with a murder myself. A patient died recently of poison. I was told she killed herself, but I don't believe it. Fausta was an intelligent woman with a good husband and happy children. She had no reason to take her life. My spirit is troubled over this. It prods me to dig deeper. Would you be willing to talk with Fausta's servant and see what you can find out about the death? I think the servant will be more willing to confide in a woman than with me."

"Wouldn't Tirzah be a better person than a total stranger?"

Brother Titus shook his head. "I love my wife dearly, but she isn't the best choice in this matter. Tirzah would be too worried for the children and too focused on comforting everyone. I doubt she could bring herself to ask uncomfortable questions. Whereas God has given you a heart for fighting injustice and the ability to ask questions others wouldn't think to ask. It's a rare gift. Just as I serve others with my medical knowledge, would you serve me with your talent for solving mysteries?"

Warmth flooded Livia's heart. She'd never been praised for her passion for justice before. The idea that she could serve God by probing into crimes and seeking justice—amazing!

"I'll be happy to help you."

"Thank you. I'll contact the family. If they agree, I'll let you know."

Livia arrived home shortly after midday expecting Avitus to bombard her with questions about why it had taken her so long to return. Instead, she found him gone. Called to his brother's house. Nissa was busy in the kitchen, and Brisa was in the peristyle mending one of Avitus's long-sleeved tunics.

Hallelujah. Everyone was doing their job without fighting. And since Brisa wasn't spending half the day on kitchen duties, she had time to work on mending off-season clothing. Livia approached her with a smile. "I'm glad to see you taking initiative to get Avitus's wardrobe ready for cooler weather."

Brisa didn't reply, her eyes on her work.

"Roxana and I are having a reading lesson soon. I don't believe I ever asked if you would like to learn to read?"

The housekeeper gave a what-kind-of-stupid-question-is-that sniff. "Waste of time, learning to read." She stabbed her needle through the cloth with more force than was necessary.

So much for winning the old woman with kind words. Settling on the opposite side of the peristyle, Livia sent Roxana to fetch the scroll they were working on, the first volume of Homer's Odyssey. At Roxana's stumbling pace, it might take them months to get through the entire story, but the maid was improving with each session. Livia listened patiently, encouraging Roxana to sound out unfamiliar words.

Despite her earlier grumbles, Brisa was clearly following the story, her needle pausing whenever Roxana got stuck on a difficult word.

AN ODE to POISON

Suddenly—thump! An object landed next to Brisa, who lurched sideways with a shriek.

What on earth?

Oh. The disgusting length of braided rag the men used as a toy for Fumo. Livia drew a breath to scold them when a gray form hurtled through the atrium doorway, heading straight for Brisa, who shrieked again and jerked her feet off the floor. Fumo grabbed the toy and raced back to the atrium, oblivious to the damage he'd wrought.

Livia shot to her feet. "Grim. Momus. Come here!"

The two men sheepishly approached. The dog followed, tail drooping.

She pointed to Brisa, who was nursing a pricked finger. "I will not have Fumo rampaging through my house and scaring my servants. Which of you threw that toy?"

The men exchanged guilty glances.

"I did, mistress," Momus said. "I didn't mean to throw it so far, but it slipped from my hands—"

"I don't want excuses. Apologize."

Momus hung his head. "I'm sorry, my lady—"

"Not to me. Apologize to Brisa."

The old woman's brow crinkled in astonishment.

Momus obediently turned to Brisa. "Sorry, I didn't mean to throw the toy at you. I hope you aren't hurt."

"Just a pricked finger."

The men slunk away. Brisa darted a sideways look at Livia, then returned to her mending, but her frown wasn't as stiff as before.

Progress!

CHAPTER TWENTY-EIGHT

Brother Titus sent for Livia later that afternoon to interview the dead woman's nursemaid. She was a short, stocky woman of thirty or so with a kind face, sad brown eyes, and skin a few shades darker than Livia's. Her name was Abru, and she'd been tending Fausta's children for eight years.

"I'm glad someone's asking questions about the mistress," Abru said to Livia. "It's not right, what happened. Mistress Fausta didn't up and kill herself no matter what anyone says. I don't believe it for a moment, and I don't think the master does either even though that's what he's been telling people."

Livia felt the familiar pull in her gut, a resolve to help those who needed help. But she mustn't allow this family's plight to distract her. This suspicious death was not her battle. She was only assisting Brother Titus with a few questions.

"Please tell me about your mistress. What was she like?"

"She loved life, did Mistress Fausta. She adored her children, and they adored her. She often told me she didn't want to miss a single day of their growing up. That's why I know she wouldn't have done away with herself no matter how upset she was." Abru planted her fists on her hips. "My mistress was murdered, and that's the only story I'll believe."

"You mentioned your mistress was upset. Why?"

"Her sister's been poorly the last few months," Abru said. "One more thing weighing on her heart."

Livia made sympathetic murmurs. "What else weighed on your mistress' heart?"

"The children, naturally. And the money."

Aha. Where crimes were concerned, it was often a good idea to follow the money.

"There are financial problems?"

"Didn't used to be, but early last year the master lost a big shipment, and that started the troubles. He had to ask his patronus for a loan." Abru clicked her tongue. "The mistress wasn't happy about it, but what else was he to do? Things were fine for a while until his patronus demanded the loan be paid back in full. The master begged for an extension, but the patronus refused, and he's not a man you defy." Abru shook her head for emphasis.

So the family faced a desperate financial plight. Was that what had led to murder?

"Poor Mistress Fausta was worried sick," Abru continued. "She started going to temples to beg the gods for help. One of them must have listened to her because the master got word the loan was extended."

"What a pleasant surprise. I'm sure it was a big relief."

The nursemaid pursed her lips. "You'd think so, but the mistress didn't act like it. She smiled and pretended she was happy, but something was wrong inside her. I could see it. Like someone had died, only she was afraid to tell us."

Hmm. A loan unexpectedly extended *and* a secret Fausta was afraid to talk about. Now they were getting somewhere. Fausta must have done something besides visiting temples in her desperate attempt to alleviate the money problem.

"Think carefully about the day your mistress died," Livia said to the nurse. "Did she go anywhere unusual or talk to anyone significant?"

"No, my lady. She was at home all day and then went to visit her ailing sister in the evening like she often does. She'd been spending more time with her sister of late. The master doesn't like her out alone after dark, but she always insisted she'd be fine. It's only two blocks."

Aha! Fausta was going out alone at night. That had potential.

"When your mistress returned that night, did she act oddly? Was she upset or afraid?"

"Not that I noticed. She felt a bit sick to her stomach so she went straight to bed. Some while later, the master woke me. He said the mistress was ill and I should run and fetch the doctor, which I did. By the time I returned home, the mistress was moaning and thrashing—" Abru clamped her lips together and stifled a sob.

Livia looked away and waited for the nurse to compose herself. It was sounding more and more like Fausta had worked a deal over the money and something had gone wrong.

"You've been very brave," Livia murmured. "Just a few more questions. Who is your master's patronus?"

"Senator Gracchus."

The name sent a jolt of energy coursing through Livia. But she kept her voice calm and steady. "Tell me again, what night did your mistress die?"

"Three nights ago, it was."

The night of Salvia's death! Could the two deaths be related? Was that possible?

After bidding Abru goodbye, Livia told Brother Titus all she'd learned. "Abru's story has me wondering if Fausta's death could be related to the one Avitus and I are investigating. They both died on the same night."

"I don't think so," Brother Titus said. "The death your husband is investigating was caused by sweating mushrooms while I suspect Fausta died of wolfsbane. Her skin was cool and clammy rather than sweaty. Also, she suffered from painful tingling in the tongue and throat and labored breathing."

Fish pickle! Two different poisons.

But wait.

The drop of love tonic Livia had tasted had made her lips tingle, and Iris had mentioned Salvia complaining of a burning throat.

"Do sweating mushrooms give the victim a burning throat or stinging lips?"

"I don't think so. I was taught a burning throat was a telltale sign of wolfsbane."

There was nothing like being met at the door by an ecstatic dog. Avitus grinned like an idiot as he knelt and ruffled Fumo's ears. "I'm glad to see you, too. How would you like to go for a walk?"

Momus beamed at them. "Exactly what he needs, sir. The mistress has stepped out, and no one is waiting to see you. It's a perfect time for you to take a stroll. Shall I fetch his rope?"

"Yes."

Man and dog wandered the street, stopping to sniff and piddle at whatever caught their interest. Or rather, the dog sniffed and piddled while Avitus thought through what he'd learned. The more he considered Merenda's potential guilt, the more likely it seemed. Gracchus's cook, who was in the perfect position to have switched the poisoned tonic, was in Merenda's pay. Moreover, by using medicine instead of food, the cook was shifting blame away from himself.

As for motive, Gracchus had aided Merenda in winning the role of Urban Praetor. Which meant Gracchus was surely putting pressure on Merenda to use that position for his benefit. What if Gracchus was pushing Merenda further than he was prepared to go? A power struggle of that proportion was worthy of murder.

Altogether, a likely scenario. Too bad Fumo's busy nose couldn't sniff out the evidence they needed to prove Merenda's guilt.

They returned to the house to find Nemesis lounging like a malevolent black lump on a bench outside Avitus's door. The beast's distended abdomen made it look twice as large as usual. It was glaring at them like a gorgon with a toothache.

Fumo barked, tail wagging in anticipation of a playful chase. But the cat didn't run. It flattened its ears and hissed. Fumo scrambled backwards when the cat swiped at him with a dagger-tipped paw.

Avitus whistled Fumo to heel and hustled him inside. "Don't let that cat worry you," he said as he untied the rope. "You are part of my family. That cat will never be."

He gave his loyal friend a final pat and headed to the peristyle, where he found Livia waiting for him.

"Good afternoon, husband. I hope your day has been successful?"

Uh oh! She had that fiery-eyed look that meant she couldn't wait to divulge some great discovery. To her credit, instead of blurting whatever it was, she waited for him to speak. So Avitus told her Gracchus was accusing Publius of murder.

That got her attention.

"As you can imagine, my brother's house was in an uproar," Avitus said. "Publius has ordered Hortensia and the children out of the city. He was so shaken he suggested you ought to join Hortensia at the villa."

Avitus raised a sardonic eyebrow. "You'll be relieved to know I took the liberty of declining for you."

Livia shuddered in mock horror.

"You'll also be glad to hear that once I calmed my brother enough to listen to reason, I convinced him our best defense against Gracchus's accusations was to locate and expose the poisoner."

"Good for you. Publius is lucky he has you to talk sense into him."

"Thank you." Her compliment warmed his heart almost as much as Fumo's adoration. "Once Publius agreed, we got to work identifying potential suspects. We think we've found our killer. Senator Merenda, Calida's husband."

Livia's smile vanished. Avitus held up a hand. "Please hear me out. I'm not suggesting Calida is guilty. It's unlikely she knows anything about it. She and her husband are not close. According to Hortensia, they act the dutiful couple in public, but in private they avoid each other."

"Merenda can't be guilty," Livia said. "While I was talking with Calida, Grim learned that Merenda was at a friend's house the evening Salvia was killed. Therefore, he couldn't have done it."

Avitus hid a smile as his wife's naiveté.

"You aren't thinking like a criminal. If Merenda were guilty, he'd make sure he had an alibi. Also, he'd hire someone else to do the dirty work. Someone like Gracchus's cook, whom I learned Merenda has been paying to bring him information."

Livia pursed her lips. "Calida confirmed the cook brings the information, but he doesn't have access to the medicine chest key. Gracchus's steward seems a more likely accomplice."

Avitus brushed her argument aside. "Acquiring a key is a minor issue easily overcome."

"Maybe so, but I have another reason to doubt the cook's guilt. I had a thought-provoking conversation with Brother Titus about those mushrooms."

Aha. Was this the momentous discovery she'd been waiting to tell him?

"Brother Titus told me that tingling lips and throat are symptoms of wolfsbane rather than sweating mushrooms. I don't remember either Salvia or Fortis suffering from excessive sweating or drooling, so I'm beginning to doubt the mushrooms were what killed them. And if so, why was a sack of poisonous mushrooms hidden in the kitchen?"

"To mislead anyone seeking the killer," Avitus answered.

"That's the only conclusion that makes sense to me. Therefore, if the cook is the culprit, why would he tell me he'd found poison in his kitchen rather than claiming they'd been found elsewhere?"

A well-reasoned argument. Avitus gave her a grin. "I concede your point, my dear. The steward may be Merenda's accomplice rather than the cook."

Livia grinned back, her eyes shining. "Thank you."

He hated to disturb their moment of accord. But he must.

"I'm curious, though. Why were you talking to Brother Titus about poisons?"

"It was an odd coincidence. I stopped by to let him know we were anonymously paying Dap's rent. He'd been brooding over a patient who'd died of poison. He suspected foul play and asked me to help him dig up the truth."

Livia plunged into a story of a woman named Fausta who had died under suspicious circumstances. "And wait until you hear the part that really caught my attention. Guess who the husband owed money to."

Avitus raised his eyebrows.

"Gracchus." Livia crossed her arms and gave him a self-satisfied smile. "What do you make of that? Same night. Both poisoned. Both had symptoms of burning lips and throat. And both had connections to Gracchus. I don't see how the two are related, but it's too many coincidences to ignore."

A *cliens* of Gracchus whose loan was suddenly extended. Suspicious, yes, but that didn't mean the two deaths were related.

Unfortunately, Livia had already convinced herself they were because she said, "I'm sure Brother Titus would introduce you to Fausta's husband. You ought to question him."

Wrong! Avitus mustn't allow her to sidetrack their investigation chasing random coincidences.

"I'll keep the offer in mind in case we decide Merenda isn't the killer."

Livia's jaw stiffened into stubborn lines. "Is that a polite way of saying my discovery isn't worthy of your attention?"

Hades! How had they gone from cooperation to arguing so quickly?

"I haven't discounted your information. I merely choose to focus on the most likely suspect first."

Before he could explain further, Momus interrupted them. "My lord? A visitor."

"Send him in."

Their visitor was none other than Brother Titus. He strode across the peristyle, face crinkled in concern. "Sorry to bother you, but I've discovered alarming news."

He turned to Avitus. "Permit me to explain. Your wife kindly assisted me in looking into the mysterious death of one of my patients."

"We were just talking about it." Livia gave Avitus a pointed look.

"Then I will get right to the point. After Livia left, I decided to talk with Fausta's ailing sister. I'd hoped she might know something. The sister claims Fausta didn't visit the night of her death.

It isn't like Fausta to lie." Brother Titus's expression grew grave. "I'm more convinced than ever that she was murdered."

"I knew it!" Livia said. "That's why I suggested you and Avitus should question Fausta's husband Equitius."

"And I declined," Avitus said, his tone making it clear he would brook no argument. "This matter is not my responsibility. I have more pressing duties."

Instead of taking the hint, the doctor looked Avitus in the eyes. "Your wife told me plainly that she was not at liberty to disclose the details of the suspicious death you've been looking into. But I've heard the news about Gracchus accusing your brother of his wife's death."

The doctor paused before adding, "By poison."

"What are you implying?"

"That we can help each other. You wish to prove your brother innocent of murder. I want to find who killed my patient. I suspect Equitius knows more about his wife's death than he's told me. Will you help me talk to him? Together, we might learn something that would lead to justice in both our cases."

Avitus ground his teeth. He hated being pressured into action, but there was an outside chance the doctor was correct. A prudent man checked into every snippet of evidence no matter how unlikely. Also, it would give Avitus a chance to see what else this perceptive doctor guessed about the nature of their investigation.

"I will come."

CHAPTER TWENTY-NINE

As they walked together, Brother Titus filled Avitus in on Equitius and his situation. "He's a wine importer. Prosperous, well-liked, and generally good-natured, although his wife's death has sent him spiraling into brooding anger."

The doctor went on, describing the man and his family. By the time they arrived at the wine merchant's apartment, Avitus had constructed a reasonable image of the man—helpful when questioning a witness.

Before they entered the house, the doctor said, "Equitius's servant warned me he'd been drinking heavily. I suggest you allow me to speak to him first to assess what kind of shape he's in before I introduce a stranger."

Avitus nodded his agreement.

They were let in by a nervous maid. As agreed, Avitus hung back while the doctor greeted their quarry. Equitius was slumped on a stool in the corner of a stuffy room lit by two guttering oil lamps. The man's hair hadn't seen a comb in days, and his cheeks were darkened by stubble. The room was as unkempt as he was, empty plates and cups lying on the floor and a half-eaten loaf of bread on the table beside him.

Equitius didn't bother to rise at their arrival. He lifted his head, glanced at Brother Titus, then turned away.

"Why are you here, doctor?" he demanded in a voice slurred by wine. "Afraid I'll poison myself next?"

"I don't believe Fausta poisoned herself. And neither do you."

The wine merchant's head snapped up. "Are you calling me a liar?"

"No," the doctor continued in his slow, calm cadence. "I think Fausta was the victim of a crime, and I'd like to help you find justice for her."

"Justice?" The man barked a cynical laugh. "I know you mean well, but there's nothing you can do. Leave me and go home to your family."

"I've brought an acquaintance to help us. He is seeking justice in a similar case."

The doctor moved aside, and Avitus stepped into the light.

Equitius blinked. Sat up straight. "I recognize you! You and your brother have opposed Gracchus in court. Your brother should have won that lawsuit a few months back, only Gracchus bribed the judge."

Bile flooded Avitus's throat at the memory.

"You hate him as I do," Equitius said. "I see it in your face."

"I hate him," Avitus said, voice taut with anger. "He and I have been enemies for many years."

Equitius leaned forward, eyes smoldering. "Do you hate him enough to accuse him of murder?"

"Yes, if it's true."

"It is! He killed my wife."

Avitus locked eyes with Equitius, goosebumps running up his spine. "Tell me."

The man's gaze shifted to the opposite wall. He rubbed a hand across his stubbled cheek as if marshaling his thoughts.

"When my wife realized she was dying, she confessed everything. She told me she'd gone to Gracchus and begged him to give us an extension on repaying the money I owed. The jackal pretended to sympathize. He arranged a private meeting with her, and he warned Fausta not to tell me lest she injure my pride."

"She did as he asked. He gave her an ultimatum. If she slept with him, he would give me an extension on the loan. If she didn't, he would demand every last sestertius and sell our children into slavery to make up the difference." Equitius's voice grew hoarse with impotent rage. "What choice did she have?"

White hot fury shot through Avitus. Gracchus was the worst kind of man! No, he was too degenerate to be called a man. He was an utterly evil fiend! Muttering a curse, Avitus asked the grieving man to continue.

"The night she died, Gracchus insisted they both drink a cup of vile tonic. He wanted her to be more *enthusiastic*." Equitius's lips twisted in disgust. "Fausta said the tonic made her lips tingle. She was so frightened she dropped her cup, and it shattered on the floor. That infuriated Gracchus, so he forced her to drink the rest of his cup. Every last drop. That's how he killed her. He had his fun, and then he discarded her."

Avitus's fury turned to ice.

If not for the accident of a clumsy woman, Gracchus would have drunk the poisoned tonic. He should have died that night!

How the gods must be laughing.

Stomach roiling with the awful truth, Avitus dragged his attention back to Equitius. "Gracchus wasn't trying to kill your wife."

Both men turned to stare at him.

"Don't you see? Gracchus was drinking from his cup before he gave it to your wife. He didn't know the wine was poisoned."

He watched sickening realization dawn on their faces.

Equitius swore. "You're telling me Gracchus didn't murder my wife and you won't help me drag him into court?"

"We can't accuse him of murder, but there are other options." Avitus held the man's gaze, looking into the depths of his anguished soul. Was he angry enough to fight? Did he have the courage?

"There will come a day when my brother and I have sufficient evidence to bring Gracchus to trial. When that day comes, can I count on you to tell your story? A damning testimony from one of Gracchus's clientes should help us expose our enemy's true character."

"I will do it," Equitius replied without hesitation.

"Excellent. Now, do you also want to find who poisoned your wife?"

"Yes!"

"Then help me figure out who is desperate enough to attempt poisoning Gracchus."

The man frowned. "It must be a man who has nothing to lose."

"I agree."

"I know a wine importer who recently lost a lawsuit because the Urban Praetor assigned him a biased judge, one who had a personal grievance against him and a well-known preference for Gracchus. My friend lost the case, and his business is now in ruins.

If you want a man furious enough to murder, look at that man or others like him who have been cheated of justice for Gracchus's benefit."

Although his face didn't reveal it, Avitus exulted at the man's news. Here was proof that Gracchus had been coercing Merenda to twist justice to his own ends—giving Merenda motive for murder.

Avitus left Brother Titus consoling Equitius over his tragedy and headed home. In his role as lawyer, Avitus was often exposed to the sordid deeds of men, but Equitius's story sent horror icing through his veins. What might Gracchus do to Livia if she fell into his hands?

That. Must. Never. Happen.

The moment he arrived home, he sat Livia down to explain the facts. "You were correct. The two cases were connected, and it has me worried."

Avitus relayed the tragic story. As he spoke, Livia's expressive face registered shock, horror, and then grief.

"The poor abused woman. Her husband must be devastated."

"He is." Avitus held Livia's gaze. "Let this be a warning. The tragedy happened because Fausta usurped her husband's authority and acted behind his back instead of trusting him to handle things. By approaching Gracchus, the unfortunate woman set herself up to be preyed upon—and suffered the consequences. Please take Fausta's mistake to heart."

Livia swallowed. Took his hands in hers. "I promise."

After a delicious meal and a pleasant sleep, Livia should have awakened feeling happy and content. But her cycle was late. This morning made it six days past due.

She ought to be elated. After all, producing an heir was her highest duty. But was she ready? She wasn't the nurturing type like Placida or Tirzah. Was she capable of loving a squalling, stinking infant? She'd faced kidnappers and knife-wielding madmen and kept her nerve. But having a baby set fear curdling her stomach.

And she hated being afraid.

Nothing she could do about her late cycle, however, so she got up to prepare for the day.

"Good morning, Mistress," Roxana said as she helped Livia dress. "What's the matter? Are you unwell?"

"I'm fine."

"No, you're not. Something's eating at you."

No point trying to hide the truth from Roxana. Her loyal maid knew her moods too well.

"I'm not ready to face being pregnant."

"You're young and strong, my lady. God will protect you when it comes time to give birth."

"It's not the birth I'm worried about. The moment Avitus finds out I'm carrying his child, he'll treat me like I'm an invalid. He'll smother me and I'll go crazy."

Not to mention all her other fears.

Roxana bit her lip, studying Livia with concern. "Well then, my lady. Brother Titus says we should take all our worries to our Lord."

Right. Why did Livia so often forget to bring her anxious thoughts to Jesus? With Roxana at her side murmuring encouragement, Livia poured out her fears and frustrations to God. When she finished, her heart felt lighter.

She pulled Roxana into an embrace. "Thank you for taking good care of me and being my sister in the faith."

"You're welcome," Roxana said, blushing.

"And thank you, Lord Jesus, for hearing our prayers. We ask that you guide us today. Help us find the poisoner so we can stop him from killing again. Amen."

"Amen," Roxana echoed.

"Before we get on with our day, let me remind you we aren't yet certain I'm expecting. You may not tell anyone else about it yet. Not even Grim."

"Why would I tell Grim of all people?"

Livia didn't bother to answer. She finished dressing and went to check her household. She assigned chores to Brisa. Reminded Momus to water the flowers. Went to the kitchen to discuss the day's meals with Nissa.

Her young cook had ambitious plans for the evening meal, a roasted fish with an herb and olive sauce.

"Are you sure you're ready to cook a fish?"

"Yes, my lady." Nissa confidently recited the recipe. "Your aunt's cook explained how to do it, and I'd like to try it on my own. May I go to the market and purchase a fish?"

Could this eager young woman be the same girl who only days ago had frowned and grumbled at every order? Moving Nissa to the kitchen had done wonders for her attitude. Livia gladly handed over sufficient coins and sent the girl off to the fish market.

Next, she wrote a quick note to her aunt, explaining that Nissa would not be coming for a lesson today. Tablet in hand, Livia headed for the atrium. "Momus, I need a boy to carry a message to my Aunt Livilla. Can you find me one?"

Momus grinned. "I think you'll find a suitable lad outside."

Dap was sitting on the bench outside their door, petting Nemesis. His left arm was held snug against his chest with a length of knotted fabric.

"What are you doing here? Shouldn't you be in bed?"

Dap shook his head, grimacing. "I couldn't bear it any longer, my lady. The doctor said I could get up if I kept my arm in a sling. Then my mother said if I was well enough to get out of bed, I was well enough to get out of the apartment and do something useful."

He looked up at Livia, eyes hopeful. "Do you have a job for me?"

She studied him critically. It was a long walk to her aunt's house, but if she didn't hire him, he'd find other work. "Are you up to delivering a message to my Aunt Livilla?"

"Yes."

She gave him a curt nod. "Wait here."

"Yes, ma'am." Dap gave her a gallant bow, grinning from ear to ear. Then he sat down and rubbed Nemesis behind her ears. "Hear that, my friend? I've got a job. Mama will be happy."

Livia opened the tablet and added a few lines about Dap and his injury, concluding with: *Please stall him as long as possible while you write a reply. I know you can come up with a clever excuse so he doesn't realize you're making him rest.*

That ought to keep Dap from overexerting himself. She bid the happy boy goodbye and reentered the house. What next?

She'd hoped to talk through the latest developments on Salvia's murder with Avitus, but he'd gone to an early morning appointment, leaving Livia with nothing to keep her mind off the impending pregnancy.

Fish pickle!

Perhaps Livia could return to Calida and wheedle information about Merenda. Avitus couldn't complain about her visiting a female acquaintance. And while she and Calida chatted, Grim and Roxana could find out where Merenda had gone the night of Salvia's death.

Wouldn't Avitus be surprised if she brought him that information!

CHAPTER THIRTY

A maid led Livia across Calida's peristyle to a room that faced east toward the morning sun. As they passed the study, Livia peeked through the open doorway, catching a glimpse of a large, fleshy man with a thick neck and jutting jaw. This must be Merenda. He was frowning at something he was reading. He looked haughty and unpleasant. Not a man you'd want to cross.

Fortunately, he didn't glance up as Livia walked past.

In contrast, Calida's smiling countenance made Livia feel welcome. "Good morning. I wasn't expecting you back so soon, but after yesterday's news about Gracchus accusing Publius of murder, I'm not surprised. Is that why you've returned?"

"Partly," Livia said. "You don't believe Publius killed Salvia, do you?"

"Not for a moment," Calida said. "Merenda doesn't either, although he'll support Gracchus's accusations in public because they're allies. My husband knows how upset I am over Salvia's death, but he won't jeopardize his reputation by getting in the middle of it."

That comment could be interpreted more than one way. Was Merenda's reluctance to get involved merely political, or did he suffer from a guilty conscience? How to find out more without arousing Calida's suspicions?

Livia helped herself to a honey-soaked sesame cake while she considered the best way to pursue the truth. Perhaps an oblique approach?

She adopted a conversational tone. "Gracchus's accusations caught us all off guard. It's sent Avitus and his brother chasing at shadows. Avitus has a new theory about who is to blame, and he insisted I ask you some questions. I didn't see how I could refuse him."

The women shared a look of long-suffering. Roman ladies were expected to obey their husbands without question. Naturally, women found ways to exert their own wills when possible, but they had to keep up appearances.

"If your husband insists, then by all means ask away," Calida said with mock solemnity. "What does he wish to know?"

"Avitus says we must consider Gracchus's cook as a possible suspect."

"Unthinkable! The cook was trained in our father's household and remains completely loyal to our family. He would never do anything to harm Salvia."

"What about the steward?"

"Why would Avitus consider either of them?" Calida asked. "I thought we'd proved it was Melancton who poisoned Salvia's cup."

Livia heaved a sigh. "You have to understand my husband. He's meticulous. He considers each suspect, however unlikely.

He's also considering the possibility that somebody else paid Melancton to poison Salvia. If that were so, it would mean somebody was violently angry with Gracchus. Might your husband know of any recent conflicts between Gracchus and other men? I believe the two men are close friends?"

"I wouldn't call them close friends, but we socialize in the same circles. Gracchus was vital in helping Merenda become elected praetor. A fact he frequently reminds us," Calida added sourly.

Livia nibbled another cake, giving Calida time to say more.

"Merenda has been under a lot of strain. Being appointed Urban Praetor was a big honor, but there have been days he's regretted the title. He's earned as many enemies as friends fulfilling his new role. I don't think he was prepared for the pressure from all sides. For example, the other week my brother was here. Normally, Merenda and Lucius get on well, but this time I heard raised voices."

"What were they discussing?"

"I don't know," Calida said with a frustrated sigh. "It wouldn't cross either of their minds that I might be interested in what was bothering them. I learn more about my husband's actions by listening to gossip in the forum than I do at home. But enough of my complaining. Merenda's political worries won't help my sister, will they?"

Livia shook her head.

"I do have some useful information for you," Calida said, brightening. "I was able to speak with some of Gracchus's servants when I went to visit the boys yesterday. The steward told me they searched the house for poison and found nothing."

Interesting. Was the poison truly gone, or had the steward conveniently "overlooked" it during his search?

"Also, Iris doesn't remember if the back door was unbarred that night. She does remember checking later that day, and the sack she'd left for Nerilla had been taken."

"I don't suppose there's any way to know when Nerilla came to fetch it?"

Calida shook her head.

Livia asked a few more trivial questions and received equally trivial answers. Time to bid the woman goodbye.

"Before you go, I have another tidbit you may find interesting. Guess who was at the door yesterday afternoon annoying the doorkeeper with questions about my 'cousin' Valeria.'"

Uh oh! A chill went down Livia's spine. "Who?"

"That arrogant physician, Dioges. He was so rude and demanding our doorkeeper was all in a huff when he told me about it."

Not Gracchus, just nosy old Dioges. Phew.

"What a pest!" Livia said. "I bet he wanted to make sure I'd passed on his warning that you shouldn't be looking into the murder. He told me that if we don't leave it to the men, one of us is going to get hurt."

Calida gasped. "The horrid man said that to your face?"

Livia nodded. "Like your husband, Dioges is convinced women aren't capable of intelligent thought. He believes women who stick their noses into men's business are likely to do something stupid and get in trouble. In his opinion, it would serve us right."

The women shared a look. Men! Humph!

On the way home, Livia asked her servants what they'd learned.

"As you requested, I found out where Merenda dined," Grim said. "He was at the home of his brother-in-law. He wasn't looking forward to the meal, apparently, and he returned home late that night in a foul temper."

"I learned he's been in a foul temper for days," Roxana said. "Ever since he had that whispered discussion with Salvia. Remember, I told you about it?"

"I do."

Livia had been purposely ignoring it because she didn't want to discover that Merenda's motive for killing Gracchus was a love affair with Salvia. Hopefully, Avitus would be able to uncover an alternate motive.

"Thank you both for your efforts. Let's go home and see what Avitus has to say about our information."

Livia found her husband in his study. Timon stood at Avitus's side, a note tablet and stylus in his hand. Sorex leaned against the wall beside the door, arms crossed and eyes alert as always.

"Livia, please join us," Avitus said, beckoning her to a seat. "We've been discussing the story Equitius told me last evening. When I asked him who he thought had reason to want Gracchus dead, he mentioned an associate who feels cheated of justice. Timon has uncovered three more instances of men who lost lawsuits because Merenda assigned biased judges who favored Gracchus unfairly. I propose this issue underlies Merenda's motive to kill Gracchus. What if Gracchus is demanding Merenda sway too many cases, and Merenda is unwilling to cooperate?"

It was a better motive than a love affair.

"That makes sense to me," Livia said. "I've just come from talking with Calida. She doesn't know anything about her husband's legal dealings, but she says he's been tense lately and feeling the pressure of his role as Urban Praetor."

"Which confirms my suspicions," Avitus said.

"While I was chatting with Calida, Grim and Roxana did a little snooping too. They found out where Merenda was the night Salvia died. He'd been invited to dine at his brother-in-law's house. Apparently, he wasn't looking forward to it. And one more thing that may be important. Not long ago, Salvia and Merenda were overheard arranging a rendezvous to meet at the home of someone named Lucius. The slave who overheard the conversation thought the two were having an affair, although I hope that isn't the case."

Avitus shook his head. "Allow me to set your mind at ease regarding Salvia's intentions. Her brother's name is Lucius, so we can assume that's who she meant."

"Why would Salvia arrange to meet Merenda at her brother's house?"

"I don't know, but I find it curious. Salvia urges Merenda to talk with Lucius, and then a few days later she's killed while Merenda and Lucius dine together. I believe it's time I had a chat with Lucius and find out what he and Merenda have been discussing. Thank you for bringing it to my attention."

"You're welcome." Livia's cheeks warmed as she shared a smile with her husband.

"And now I need your help on another matter."

"Oh?"

"Yesterday, I sent Sorex to Drash the Snake Charmer to obtain a sample of his love tonic. I suspect Drash may have supplied the tonic Merenda used to poison Salvia, since—according to Drash, at least—Merenda is a regular customer. Can you tell me if Drash's love tonic tastes like the tonic you sampled in Fortis's cup?"

At some signal Livia didn't see, Sorex stepped forward and placed a small leather sack on the desk. Avitus pushed it toward her. Livia grimaced at the thought of the disgusting stuff, but Avitus had asked for her assistance.

She sent for a cup of wine, stirred a spoonful of powder into it, and lifted the cup to her nose. Same strong, acrid scent that made her grit her teeth. From the corner of her eye, she saw all three men watching her intently.

Fish pickle! She'd actually have to sip the nasty stuff. She tipped the cup and let the liquid touch her tongue. Bitter and earthy with undertones that reminded her of rotten cabbage. Blech! Drat Avitus for making her taste it.

Hmm. That gave her an idea. She hid her disgust, adopting the thoughtful expression of a connoisseur tasting wine. She swirled the cup and pretended to take another sip. "I think I detect a hint of myrrh, but I'm not sure. Would you taste it and see what you think?"

Avitus stared at the wine as if it were poisoned. His gaze flicked to her face, then back to the cup. He lifted it to his lips.

Ha! Her ploy had worked.

With a strangled cry, Avitus slammed the cup down so hard liquid sloshed over the side. "That is the most disgusting thing I've ever tasted."

Livia gave him a playful smile. "I'm glad you agree."

"You did that on purpose!"

"I did," she said with a straight face. "The love tonic is important evidence. I thought you should have your own opinion of the taste. For the trial."

Avitus glowered at her.

"To answer your original question, this tonic tastes like the stuff that killed Fortis. But would Gracchus notice it tasted different than his usual tonic? To find out, you'll have to obtain a sample of Dioges's version and compare the two side by side."

There. Let him argue his way out of that logic.

Avitus gave the cup a baleful glare. Then he huffed a sigh. "You're right. Sorex and I will obtain a sample."

It was hard not to gloat, but Livia did her best.

CHAPTER THIRTY-ONE

Avitus could have sent Sorex or Timon to purchase a sample of Dioges's love potion, but the physician's testimony would be important when Salvia's case came to trial. Purchasing the love tonic in person would give Avitus an opportunity to assess the man.

They found the doctor's abode, but no one answered the first knock. They could hear someone moving inside the apartment, so Sorex knocked again and shouted in his rumbling voice, "Is Dioges there?"

"Coming! I heard you the first time."

The door was yanked open to reveal a short man with a jutting chin, humped shoulders, and a face creased by a permanent frown. Behind him, his shop was a cluttered mess, baskets and bundles of herbs lying helter-skelter and two wooden chests sitting open as if they'd just disgorged their contents all over the floor.

"May I help you?" the man asked in a voice that made it clear he would rather not.

Avitus raised his chin and gave the man an imperious sniff of high-born disdain. "You are Dioges, the physician who serves Senator Gracchus?"

At the name, Dioges underwent an instantaneous transformation, his frown of annoyance melting into an obsequious smile. "I am he. How may I be of service, sir?"

"I was told you can supply me with a potent aphrodisiac."

Dioges's eyes narrowed. "Who told you that?"

"A friend. He promised me you weren't a charlatan like the others. He promised me your powders work wonders. Is he correct, or am I wasting my time?"

Dioges drew himself up. "Few men who call themselves physicians are as knowledgeable as I am."

Which didn't answer Avitus's question. This doctor was a slippery one. Good to know.

"Was my friend correct regarding the efficacy of your powders to enhance one's virility?"

"He was."

Avitus feigned a relieved smile. "Excellent. I'll take a jar at once."

The doctor looked away. "I'm terribly sorry, sir, but I can't help you. My powders are in such demand that I've run out of a crucial ingredient. I'm forced to wait for next year's spice caravans to arrive before I can replenish my stock."

The man's eyes said he was lying.

Why?

Had Gracchus forbidden the doctor from selling his special aphrodisiac to anyone as Rutilia claimed? If so, a bribe ought to work.

"I'm willing to pay double what it's worth if you give me a jar." Avitus gestured to Timon, who pulled a handful of coins from his belt pouch.

Dioges's eyes locked onto the coins. He licked his lips with the tip of his tongue as fear and desire battled on his face. Desire won out.

He gave them an oily smile. "I may be able to find a small quantity of the ingredients I need, good sir. If I may have your name, I will deliver a jar of the tonic this evening."

"Excellent." Avitus gave Dioges his name and the directions to his house.

"Memmius Avitus?" The doctor's eyes sparked in recognition. "Am I correct that you are the gentleman who recently married Denter's daughter?"

"Why do you ask?"

"I trust she is strong and healthy?"

"Yes, she is." The conversation had taken a decidedly odd turn. Why had the doctor asked after Livia's health?

Oh! A surge of bile rose in Avitus's throat. This boorish man was implying Avitus was unable to father children. He clamped his jaws tight, hiding the surge of embarrassment.

"Don't let me keep you any longer." Avitus gave the doctor a haughty sniff. "You will send the medicine without delay?"

"I will, sir. I promise."

Avitus strode away, embarrassment turning to anger. What if the vile doctor started a rumor about Avitus asking for love powders? Olympus! Why had he given Dioges his name?

AN ODE to POISON

Livia hurried to the kitchen to find something to rid her mouth of the disgusting tonic. She helped herself to a handful of olives. Nissa had purchased a nice-looking fish, which she was busy scaling. After admiring the fish, Livia left Nissa to her work.

Since Avitus was out and the household was running smoothly, Livia decided it was a good time to assess the aging walls of her husband's study. The frescoes were old and faded. Besides, scenes of Bacchus gamboling with satyrs and the birth of Venus weren't the most suitable subjects for a scholarly jurist.

When she'd first met Avitus, she'd thought him overly tidy. Now she knew it was Brisa who kept the house spotless while Avitus tended to set things aside and forget them. Timon kept his scrolls and tablets in order, and Brisa picked up his discarded olive pits and abandoned sandals. It fell to Livia to bring the home's neglected decor up to date.

She spent several minutes standing in the middle of the room, visualizing the possibilities. Then she got her drawing board and sat down to sketch out ideas. When she tired of that project, Livia sent Roxana for the scroll of Homer and doodled while Roxana read. Livia was putting the finishing touches on a drawing of Penelope, Odysseus's long-suffering wife, when a flicker of movement caught her eye.

Fumo was trotting along the colonnade, nose to the ground. Where was Momus? Probably so engrossed in a game of knucklebones with Grim he hadn't noticed Fumo wander off.

The dog turned to cross the peristyle. Livia drew breath to scold him, but he circled the flower beds without trampling a single leaf. He meandered along, nose working busily. What on earth was he doing?

Suddenly, he veered sharply and entered her bedroom. Roxana stopped reading and clicked her tongue. "That naughty dog! I'll get him, my lady."

As Roxana stood, Fumo began barking furiously. A moment later, an angry feline yowl erupted. Nemesis raced out of the bedroom with Fumo in pursuit, baying like a hound of Hades. The cat zigzagged between two clumps of flowers. Fumo plowed through them.

Drat that animal!

The pair raced across the peristyle, veered around a startled Brisa, and headed for the kitchen hallway. Brisa grabbed a broom and added her screeches to the cacophony as she chased after the animals.

A whole barrel of fish pickle!

Livia followed them into the kitchen. Nissa was shouting at Brisa. The dog was barking his fool head off while the cat hunched on the worktable, back arched and ears flat, growling at the dog. Behind Livia, Roxana added her voice to the confusion, vainly commanding the dog to stop barking.

Livia bellowed for everyone to stop.

No one listened.

"Scat, you filthy beast!" Brisa jabbed her broom at the cat. Nemesis sprang out of the way, and the broom struck a clay pitcher of oil, which fell to the floor with a crash.

AN ODE to POISON

Livia grabbed for Brisa's broom, missed, and was forced to duck as the broom swept past her head before crashing onto a corner of the worktable. The blow jolted the platter with the fish onto the floor.

Fumo's barks instantly ceased as he sank his teeth into the fish.

"Oh no, you don't!" Nissa lunged at Fumo and tried to wrest the fish from his jaws. Roxana grabbed Fumo's backside and tugged. "Fumo. Bad dog! Drop it!"

Brisa raised the broom for another swing. Livia grabbed it. "Stop, Brisa! Get out. Back to the peristyle. Now!"

Glowering, Brisa stomped off. One problem dealt with.

Nissa and Roxana got control of the dog and pried the mangled fish from his jaws. Two problems down.

"Roxana, take the dog to Momus and tell him to keep Fumo in the atrium."

"Yes, mistress."

Roxana manhandled the squirming dog out of the kitchen while Livia surveyed the damage. The floor was covered in shards of broken crockery and a spreading puddle of olive oil. Nissa held the remains of the fish. Fumo had all but bitten it in half. "Look at this! A whole morning's work, ruined!"

She tossed the pulpy mess on the worktable and kicked at a chunk of broken pottery. "What a mess. And it's Brisa's fault."

"That's not entirely true. Nemesis is also at fault." Livia shook a finger at the cat. "You shouldn't have been in the house. I hope you learned your lesson."

The cat hissed in reply, ears laid back like an angry owl and tail fluffed to three times its normal size.

Livia sighed. "Put the cat out, and then we'll deal with the mess."

Nissa scooped up the cat. "Ew, her backside is all wet."

She pulled a hand away and gasped. "Olympus, my lady. Nemesis is bleeding. Oh, you poor baby. Did that horrible dog hurt you?"

Lovely. A wounded cat. Could anything else possibly go wrong?

Just then, Roxana ran into the kitchen. "I saw blood on the tiles. Did Fumo bite Nemesis?"

"Must have. She's bleeding. Look!" Nissa shifted the cat in her arms.

All three women saw the problem at the same instant.

The cat was giving birth.

That was more than Livia cared to face. "You two deal with the cat."

Turning her back on the mess, she emerged into the peristyle to find Momus and Fumo crouched outside her bedroom. "Why is that dog not in the atrium like I ordered?"

Momus laid a hand on the dog's back. "He's acting like there's something in your room, my lady. It could be a rat. If you hold the dog, I'll take a quick look."

Livia took hold of Fumo's collar while Momus slowly pushed the door all the way open and peered into the bedroom. The dog whined and tried to pull away.

Brisa charged past them, wielding her broom. "We'll not have rats in this house!"

Livia lost hold of Fumo, who raced into the bedroom after Brisa, barking with glee.

Rancid fish pickle! Had Brisa gone completely mad?

"Fumo, come!" Momus yelled. The dog ignored him, pawing at a tunic Avitus had left in a crumpled heap on the floor.

"I see the rat," Brisa shrilled. "Out of my way, dog."

Instead of moving, Fumo turned and growled at Brisa, who jumped backward with a frightened gasp. She raised her broom. "Don't growl at me, you mangy dog."

"Stop, woman!" Momus grabbed Brisa around the waist and hauled her from the room.

The dog stayed put, so Livia grabbed his collar. "Steady, Fumo. What have you found?"

Two tiny black forms lay atop Avitus's tunic. Too small for rats. And their tails weren't naked. Livia finally realized what she was seeing—newborn kittens.

She went to the door and shouted for Roxana. "Bring the cat. I've found two kittens in the bedroom, and they need their mother."

After leaving the odious doctor, Avitus considered his next task. He wasn't acquainted with either Merenda or Lucius, so stopping them in the forum wasn't likely to get the answers he needed. Fortunately, Rutilia had promised him she could broker an alliance with Lucius. Avitus would hold her to that promise.

He was admitted to Rutilia's house and led to a room off a corner of the peristyle. This was further into the house than he'd been allowed before. A good sign.

But then he was left to wait.

And wait.

The message was clear. Avitus was still nothing more than a supplicant. When Rutilia finally deigned to join him, her hair was twisted into an intricate sculpture of braids that looked like it had taken hours to create. Had she purposely taken time to have her hair arranged just to annoy him?

Anger stiffened his resolve. He stood tall and raised his chin. Rutilia respected strength, therefore he would exude confidence no matter how she toyed with him.

"Good afternoon, Avitus. Sorry I took so long, but I had other important business to attend to."

Rutilia settled gracefully onto a chair and arranged her skirts with a practiced twitch of her wrist. She regarded Avitus silently for a moment, then arched her perfectly shaped eyebrows suggestively. "If I didn't know better, I'd suspect you of inventing reasons to visit me."

"My wife wouldn't be pleased to hear you say so," he replied, imitating her gently teasing tone.

"I keep forgetting you're married. I'd like to meet Livia. Quite a feisty young lady, by all accounts. Not the type of wife I would have expected you to marry. But then, you're not the timid sparrow I thought you were. You're a determined hawk, willing to wait silently and patiently for the right moment to swoop in for the kill."

Was that a compliment?

Avitus acknowledged her words with a nod and a polite smile. Then he hardened his features. "I've come because our opportunity to swoop might be at hand."

Rutilia leaned forward, all amusement gone from her eyes. "Oh?"

"At your suggestion, I've been looking into Merenda. I think he's been using his praetorship to cheat men of justice for Gracchus's benefit."

"Of course he has. Why else would Gracchus have helped Merenda win the position?"

"But I think he's angered his brother-in-law Lucius Calidius in the process. Salvia arranged a meeting between Merenda and Lucius a few days before she was murdered. I suspect whatever was discussed at that meeting pushed Merenda into murder. Therefore, I'd like to question Lucius Calidius. Can you arrange it?"

"I know something about that meeting," Rutilia said. "Lucius's wife told me that the last time she'd seen her sister-in-law alive, Salvia had been in a fury over some pending legal matter. She'd dragged Merenda to talk to Lucius about it. As Merenda was leaving, Salvia was overheard saying that Merenda had already disgraced the family once and he mustn't be allowed to do so again."

That confirmed Avitus's suspicions. "I think Gracchus and Lucius both want Merenda to use his influence in an upcoming case, but they're on opposing sides of the issue."

"I agree," Rutilia said. "Merenda is being pressured by two powerful men. He can't please them both, so in desperation he tried to solve his dilemma by eliminating Gracchus."

Avitus nodded. It was a neat theory, both logical and probable.

"Any idea what case is causing the dilemma?"

Rutilia shook her head. "But I think we can assume it hasn't yet come to trial. Which means Merenda will be desperate to kill

Gracchus before it does. And that worries me. Gracchus ordered Dioges to concoct him a jar of *theriac*, which the doctor delivered this morning. When Merenda learns about the theriac—and he will—I shudder to think what he'll try next."

She clenched her fists and dropped her voice to a fierce whisper. "We must stop Merenda before he harms my children!"

Avitus held her gaze. "Do I need to confront Merenda?"

Rutilia shook her head. "A direct confrontation will only make him deny everything. Instead, we prey on his conscience. Salvia died a horrible death. The guilt must be eating at him, and we can use it to our advantage. I'll arrange a dinner party and invite both Merenda and Lucius. As entertainment, I'll hire a storyteller who will spin a tale that describes Salvia's murder. Merenda is a coward. When he hears his crimes uncovered in minute detail, he'll be too scared of discovery to make another attempt."

CHAPTER THIRTY-TWO

Livia ground her teeth.

Rampaging animals, smashed crockery, a ruined dinner, and a cat having kittens in her bedroom. Not to mention slaves ready to tear each other's eyes out. Nissa stood guard at the bedroom door glaring at Brisa, who was sweeping the colonnades with enough force to wear through the floor tiles.

Please, Lord Jesus, help me!

Livia took a deep breath to settle her anger. The best way to tackle any disaster was one problem at a time.

And the biggest problem was Brisa. If she'd minded her own business, the kitchen wouldn't be a mess, and tonight's dinner wouldn't have landed on the floor. Livia beckoned her.

"The kitchen is a wreck thanks to your broom. You can clean up the mess. Then you can salvage what's left of that fish to make your master something for dinner."

"Cooking is Nissa's job now."

Livia clamped her jaw on a sharp reply. What was Tirzah always reminding her? *Kindness works better than harsh words even when others don't deserve it.*

"Don't argue. Please go clean the kitchen and make dinner."

Brisa grabbed her broom and stomped to the kitchen.

Good riddance!

Er, sorry Lord. I mean, please bless Brisa and forgive my temper. Thank you that Avitus wasn't home to witness this disaster. And thank you for protecting the kittens.

Because a miracle was the only explanation for the way Fumo had blocked Brisa from thwacking the helpless kittens. Brother Titus had read them something one of the Jewish prophets had written about wolves lying down with lambs and lions lying down with calves. He'd used the passage to teach them that God rules over the animals just as he rules over mankind.

So it was possible God had used Fumo to protect the kittens and forestall a war. Because if Brisa had killed a kitten, there would be no hope whatsoever of peace in the house.

Livia said another prayer of thanks, then slipped into the bedroom to check on the kittens. Roxana was stroking one tiny beast while Nemesis licked another.

"How are they? Is everyone healthy?"

"I think so, Mistress. There are four kittens, and Nemesis seems to be finished bearing."

"I'm glad to hear it because you need to move them out of here before Avitus returns home."

Roxana looked shocked. "You aren't going to send them out into the street?"

"They can stay in the house until morning. Find a place out of sight where Avitus won't hear their mewling."

"Yes, mistress."

After shooting an irritated glare at the cat for her part in the chaos, Livia returned to the peristyle, where she found Momus.

"I told you to stay in the atrium and keep that dog out of trouble."

"Grim is tending Fumo, my lady. A message has come for you."

"Give it here." Livia held out her hand.

"The girl says she has to speak to you herself."

A girl? Interesting.

Livia followed Momus to the atrium, where a girl of perhaps twelve giggled as she rubbed the belly of an ecstatic Fumo. The girl got to her feet and dipped her head when Livia appeared.

"Good afternoon, my lady. My mistress Nerilla says she will meet you at the perfume shop. She's there now, and she begs you to hurry for she has a patient who needs her."

"I'll come at once."

Avitus headed to his brother's house to report the latest developments and enlist Publius's help writing a story to trap a murderer.

Except Publius wasn't home.

"I'm sorry, sir," the doorkeeper said. "He has a trial today."

Beard of Hercules. How had Avitus forgotten that? He turned around, heading for the forum of Augustus. The vast rectangular space surrounded by colonnades had been built by Emperor Augustus to handle the overflow of legal business. On days when the courts were in session, the forum was a hive of activity.

Most cases were held in the open where anyone could stop to listen. Avitus wandered one long side of the forum until he heard his brother's voice above the rumble of the crowds. He joined the small throng of onlookers listening to the case.

The senator representing the prosecution finished speaking, and Publius stood to give his final speech. Based on his body language and the timbre of his voice, Publius was confident his client would be found not guilty.

As Publius spoke, two men took up positions on either side of Avitus. Minions of Gracchus who had ambushed him at the Temple of Neptune.

Uh oh!

Avitus turned around and found himself facing his enemy. He spread his feet and straightened his shoulders to prove he wasn't intimidated. "What do you want?"

"I want you to relay a message to your brother," Gracchus said.

"I'm not your messenger boy."

The men surrounding Avitus bristled. Gracchus's eyes flashed. "You'll listen if you know what's good for you. Tell Publius I'll see him publicly humiliated for what he's done to my wife, and I'll make sure Hortensia suffers, too. If he thinks he can keep his wife safe by sending her out of town, he's more fool than I thought." Gracchus paused, eyes flaming with a hatred that raised goosebumps on Avitus's neck.

"And tell him I'm taking him before the praetor to face his crimes. He must meet me tomorrow. The third hour. I'll be waiting for him at the northwest corner of the Temple of Mars Ultor."

Gracchus was referring to the preliminary stage of a trial where accuser and accused met with the presiding magistrate, who would dictate the terms of the case and set a date for the main trial.

Gracchus locked eyes with Avitus. "Once I'm finished with him, I haven't forgotten you and your troublesome wife. You'll be the next to suffer."

Avitus kept his face like stone. He would not flinch. He would not let this man frighten him. After an eternity, Gracchus snapped his fingers and strode off. His entourage of glowering slaves and brawny clientes followed in his wake.

The trial concluded, but Avitus remained rooted to the spot. His stomach churned with Gracchus's threats. How had Gracchus known Hortensia wasn't in the city? Did the snake have spies in Publius's house? If so, what else did he know? What if he'd been informed about Livia donning a disguise and sneaking into his house? How might Gracchus retaliate for that?

"Avitus?"

"Huh?" Avitus dragged his attention to his approaching brother.

"I saw Gracchus and his minions surrounding you. What did he want?"

"He knows you've sent Hortensia from the city." Avitus pulled Publius away from his attendants and dropped his voice. "He must have a spy in your household. You can't trust anyone."

Publius patted Avitus's shoulder. "Of course Gracchus knows Hortensia left the city. You could hardly miss it. She took half the household with her plus enough trunks to fill a wagon."

Right.

Like a fool, Avitus had allowed his fears to get the better of him. Again. He forced all emotion from his head. Time to focus on the matter at hand.

"Gracchus demands you meet him tomorrow at the third hour to come before the praetor."

Their enemy was wasting no time, and he'd no doubt push the praetor to schedule the main trial as quickly as possible, forcing Publius to scramble in preparing a defense.

"We can't let him win!" Publius muttered.

"We won't," Avitus said grimly. "I've just had a productive conversation with Rutilia."

Avitus explained their theory about Merenda feeling caught between Gracchus and Lucius Calidius, who both wanted him to promote their side in an important case. "We think that's what forced Merenda to attempt murder. Rutilia has proposed a creative means of persuading him to stop."

Avitus described Rutilia's idea to spin a story that would prey on Merenda's guilty conscience and scare him out of making another murder attempt.

"That might work," Publius said. "But how will it help me in my defense?"

"It's the first step," Avitus said, slapping Publius on the shoulder. "Once we confirm Merenda is our killer, we'll know how to proceed. Let's go craft a story to trap him into revealing his guilt."

The brothers headed to Publius's house, where they enjoyed several uninterrupted hours concocting a story that would prey on Merenda's guilt and frighten him into inaction.

CHAPTER THIRTY-THREE

Livia headed for the perfume shop immediately. She found Elpis and Nerilla in the back of the shop comparing vials of scents.

Nerilla stood straight-backed and confident, her chestnut hair primly twisted into a no-nonsense bun. She wore a tunic of fine wool embellished by subtle embroidery at the hem and neck. In her left hand, she held a walking stick that had been polished to a glossy sheen. The woman's deep brown eyes exuded a keen intelligence, but the wrinkles around them spoke of pain as well as laughter.

"Thank you for agreeing to see me," Livia told Nerilla after Elpis made the introductions.

"I'm always ready to serve a woman in need." Nerilla studied Livia with concern. "Since we're meeting here, I assume you're not free to talk at home. Do you fear for your safety?"

Livia shook her head. "I'm fine. I sought you out because I'm helping Calida figure out who killed her sister Salvia."

Nerilla fixed Livia with a hard stare. "Everyone knows who killed Salvia. Gracchus has announced it all over the forum."

"It's not true. Publius is too honorable to stoop to murder."

"A man may act out of character when pressed by difficult circumstances."

"We have evidence that Salvia wasn't the intended victim."

Nerilla's brows rose. "The poison was intended for someone else? Who?"

Livia bit her lip, cursing her promise to Avitus. "I can't say."

"But you suspect?"

Livia nodded.

"The killer was after Gracchus." Nerilla quirked an eyebrow. "Am I right?"

Interesting that Nerilla would so quickly surmise the truth. Why? Could she have been involved in the crime? Perhaps she provided the killer with the poison?

But no, Nerilla had no connections to Merenda or Gracchus.

"We believe so," Livia said. "I thought you might know something that could help us."

The woman pursed her lips. "I know nothing about Gracchus's enemies, but I can say this. A man will do almost anything to defend his wife or daughter."

What was Nerilla implying? That Gracchus was abusing women?

"I'm not sure I understand."

Nerilla's face hardened and her eyes sparked with anger. "Gracchus sows his seed far wider than he should. I had a patient a few years back who confided to me that Gracchus had forced himself on her. She was terrified the coming child would look like

Gracchus and her husband would divorce her. The gods were kind to my patient. The baby was a daughter who looked like her mother. But if Gracchus has forced himself on one woman, he's done it to others."

Livia's stomach lurched. It hadn't occurred to her that Gracchus might have abused others as he had Fausta.

Nerilla slammed her walking stick on the floor. "Men like Gracchus are an abomination! They prey on the weak and abuse the laws of patronage our society is founded on."

"I agree," Livia said. "Both my husband and I oppose those who trample others in their blind ambition. Like Brother Titus, I believe in a life of honesty, compassion, and kindness to those who are weak and vulnerable. I hear you've also chosen to serve women who have little else in this world."

"A decision I've not regretted." Nerilla gave Livia a fierce smile. "My brother thought he'd defeated me when he turned my wealthy customers against me with his cruel lies. He was wrong. My patients for the last twenty years have been grateful for my care. I don't regret my decision to turn my back on my brother and my inheritance. My only regret is leaving my sister, Leto. I would have liked to have had her at my side all these years, but Leto was too timid to stand up to our brother as I did."

Pain flickered across her eyes. Then it vanished. Her jaw tightened.

"But that's in the past. You were asking about Gracchus. If you want to find who tried to kill him, look for a man whose honor has been destroyed to the core because Gracchus has abused the women under his protection."

"I will. Thank you."

Nerilla took her leave.

"Well, that was interesting," Elpis said. "Who would have guessed Nerilla was Leto's sister? Once she mentioned it, I could see a resemblance between the two. Leto was one of our favorite customers. A sweet lady although she often seemed a little sad. Perfumes cheered her up. She even helped us invent one or two."

Elpis plucked a clear glass bottle from the shelf and unstoppered it. "What do you think?"

Livia took the bottle from Elpis and held it to her nose. "Herbal and earthy. It smells like a garden in springtime, moist and alive."

"Exactly!" Elpis replaced the perfume bottle on the shelf. "Leto liked herbal scents best. Her brother being a doctor, she knew more about plants than most people. She and Father would get into discussions about the best method for boiling down the essence of flowers or herbs. I miss her."

Elpis gave Livia a thoughtful look. "Actually, there's something about her death that's always bothered me. Maybe you can help me figure out the truth?"

Why not? Livia had nothing better to do, and she owed Elpis for hosting Nerilla.

"Sure. Tell me the story."

"We were told Leto died of ague, but from what I saw, the symptoms didn't add up. She was here a few days before she died, and she wasn't acting sick at all. In fact, I'd say she looked healthier than she had in a while, pink-cheeked and bright-eyed instead of wan and hollow-eyed from fretting over her brother.

"He'd made a bad investment and owed money to his patronus. Leto worried about it. She was a widow and childless, so her brother was all she had to take care of her. I asked her once why she'd never asked her brother to find her a new husband. She said Dioges needed her. They were both widowed and content taking care of each other."

"Did you say Dioges?"

"That's right. Since Dioges was a doctor, he ought to have known how Leto died. That's why it puzzled me. He claimed it was the ague, but she died so suddenly, and as I said, she didn't seem sick…"

Livia was only half listening. If Dioges was Leto's brother, then he was also Nerilla's brother. No wonder Nerilla had rebelled. A woman as capable, intelligent, and fiercely independent as Nerilla couldn't stand to live under Dioges's constant criticism and belittlement.

"So what should I do?" Elpis asked.

Livia blinked and returned her attention to her friend. "I suggest you talk with some of Leto's neighbors and find out all you can about her symptoms. With ague, the fever comes and goes. Maybe you happened to see Leto on the better days, or maybe her red cheeks were due to fever rather than health."

Elpis didn't look convinced. "I'll talk to her neighbors, but what if I'm correct?"

"Then you need to ask why Dioges lied to you."

Elpis gaped at her. "You mean like, maybe he poisoned her and lied to cover up his crime?"

Livia rolled her eyes. "I was thinking about his reputation. He's arrogant and ambitious. Maybe Leto died of something he ought to have been able to cure, and he didn't want her death to look like a failure."

"That I'd believe!" Elpis said with a sniff.

So would Livia.

While the mistress talked with the midwife in the back of the perfume shop, Roxana waited at the front with the midwife's servant girl. She was a skinny waif with black hair and large, sad eyes. Every few seconds, she darted a nervous glance at Grim, standing at attention outside the shop doorway.

"Don't mind Grim," Roxana said. "He glowers at everyone. If he tried to smile, his cheeks would crack from the strain."

The girl's lips twitched into a shy smile—exactly as Roxana had hoped.

"My name is Roxana. Have you worked for Nerilla long?"

The girl nodded. "I've been with her for three years. She took me in when my parents died. She's training me to be a midwife. She knows so much! Her father was a brilliant physician, and he taught her everything he knew. He studied at important medical schools like Tarsus and Laodicea."

Roxana didn't know where Tarsus or Lay-do-whatsit were, but she murmured in admiration. "So, your mistress is really smart?"

"Uh huh. She knows more than half the doctors in the city."

"She sounds like a wonderful mistress."

A nod. "She makes me work hard, but she's never mean. My life is nicer working for her than it was when I lived at home."

The girl chattered on, sharing stories of Nerilla curing woefully sick children and bringing women through difficult births. By the time the midwife collected her assistant and left, Roxana had made a firm decision. When it came time for her Mistress Livia to deliver a baby, Nerilla would be the midwife at her side.

Wouldn't it be lovely with a precious little one to hold? The master would be so proud, and—

"When will the poisoner strike again?"

Roxana gave Grim a confused look. "Did you say something?"

"While you were chattering with the girl, I was thinking about the poisoner. If I was him, I'd be eager to try again. It's been four days since Salvia died. Soon, Gracchus's household will begin preparing for the ninth-day feast."

Grim was referring to the traditional feast that marked the end of the funerary rites when the shade of the departed supposedly left the earth for good. "The feast seems an ideal time to slip poison into Gracchus's food."

"Why not simply put the poisoned love tonic back in the chest?" Roxana asked.

"Has it occurred to you that the killer likely tossed the poisoned tonic down the sewer to keep it from being discovered?"

"Has it occurred to you that maybe he didn't? Humph."

But old poison or new, Grim was right. Gracchus was still alive, which meant the poisoner would try again. Could they figure out who it was and stop him before anyone else died?

Livia returned home to find Avitus playing fetch with the dog. Nissa stood, arms crossed, on the opposite side of the peristyle, guarding the doorway to the small room where they'd installed the cat and her babies.

Ugh. Livia would have to tell Avitus about that.

Later.

"You're home." Avitus studied her with concern. "Momus said you'd gone to see a midwife. Is everything alright?"

Fish pickle! She'd expressly told Momus not to mention the midwife.

"I'm fine. I wanted to talk to the woman because she provided certain medicines for Salvia. The healer didn't know anything useful about Salvia, but she told me about a patient of hers who suffered at Gracchus's hands much as Fausta had. If Gracchus has abused two women, he might have abused others. What if an angry husband tried to poison Gracchus rather than Merenda?"

Avitus didn't answer, his eyes still probing hers. "You didn't seek out the midwife for any other reason?"

"No." Livia held his gaze, letting him see the truth of her statement. "Now please answer my question. What if we're wrong about the poisoner?"

"We'll find out tomorrow." Avitus told her about the story he and his brother had concocted and Rutilia's plan to use it to scare Merenda during a dinner party.

"Rutilia is confident she'll be able to detect whether Merenda is guilty or not."

"It's a clever plan," Livia said. "I hope it works."

"We're hoping it will," Avitus said. "In the meantime, Dioges should have delivered a jar of his love tonic for you to compare with Drash's mixture. Do you want to do that now?"

Blech! "I'd rather wait until after dinner. Shall we eat?"

They took their places in the dining room. Livia sent Roxana to inform Brisa they were ready to eat.

Avitus wrinkled his brow. "I thought Brisa had been banned from the kitchen. Have you changed your mind?"

"Only for today. There was an incident with the cat."

He made a noise of disgust in the back of his throat. "Forget I asked."

Brisa arrived. She set three dishes on the table and left with a parting scowl at Livia. A watery fish stew. Hardboiled eggs in a pool of congealed sauce. A dish of fava beans, cooked to mush. Brisa had attempted to dress up her offerings with some minced herbs sprinkled on top. A futile effort which failed to conceal how long the beans and eggs had been sitting.

Livia took a bite of beans. Mealy and unpleasant. Had Brisa scorched them? No, must be the sauce. Livia took another bite, trying to identify the flavors. Garum and vinegar with traces of cumin and something sharply bitter. She took another bite. A familiar flavor, but what was it? Not parsley. Not lovage. Not rue. Not coriander.

She selected a slice of egg liberally sprinkled with herbs. A nibble confirmed it was the same herb—one that did not go well with egg. Brisa didn't know the difference between parsley and pine needles. Who knew what she'd sprinkled on their food?

Whatever it was, the mystery herb was making Livia's lips tingle. Hmm. Had Brisa been overzealous with black pepper? Livia took another nibble. No, this wasn't the sharp heat of black pepper, just the unpleasant bitterness of …

With a rush, she remembered where she'd tasted that bitter flavor before.

Lord, no! Please let it not be.

But it was.

Livia tossed the remainder of the egg to the floor. "Don't eat another bite."

Avitus stared at her, a slice of egg halfway to his mouth. "Hades! What's wrong?"

She pointed to the platter. "The food has been poisoned."

He dropped the egg like a hot coal. "You're sure?"

"Absolutely. I recognize the bitter taste, and my lips are tingling."

CHAPTER THIRTY-FOUR

This could not be happening. Not in his house. Not to his wife. But the evidence was staring him in the face. Avitus clenched his fists against the fear jangling his limbs. "Sorex! Send Grim to fetch Brother Titus immediately."

"Yes, sir."

"Roxana, bring your mistress a feather."

A wide-eyed Roxana hurried to obey.

Livia pushed to her feet.

Avitus grabbed her arm. "Where are you going?"

"I'm getting to the bottom of this! Someone tried to kill me."

"I know." Avitus took Livia's cheeks in his hands. "We'll find who did this, but you must remain calm. Agitation will spread the poison faster."

Livia huffed in frustration, but she complied.

Roxana hurried back with a feather and an empty basin. Once the contents of his wife's stomach glistened in the basin, the tightness in his chest began to ease.

Slightly.

Had he reacted in time? How much poison had she ingested? Should he make her drink a glass of wine with—what had Brother Titus said he ought to use?

"Sir?" Roxana held out the feather. "Hadn't you better vomit as well? Just in case."

He blinked at the maid. Saw the fear in her eyes. Only then did her words sink in. Dear gods, had he ingested poison as well?

He hadn't eaten any egg, and his lips weren't tingling, but to be safe he took the feather and tickled the back of his throat until the heaving started. When it was over, he reached for his cup to clear the foul taste from his mouth.

"Don't!" Livia snatched the cup from him. "Brisa might have poisoned the wine too."

"Why would you blame Brisa?"

Livia crossed her arms. "Who else can have done it? Brisa was the only person in the kitchen this afternoon."

That couldn't be true. He must find the real culprit. And he would do it calmly and logically.

"Roxana, gather the household."

When the servants were standing before them, Avitus studied each one in turn. Timon and Sorex had been with him all day, and they would never harm him in any case. Roxana had been with Livia all afternoon (as had Grim).

That left Momus, Brisa, and Nissa. Avitus gave each a probing stare. All he saw was confusion and fear. No murderous resentment. No guilt. No surreptitious glances at the poisoned food.

But one of them must be guilty.

"One of you attempted to poison your master and mistress. I will find who is responsible, so don't try to hide your guilt."

There was a collective gasp, followed by blanched faces and darting eyes. Suddenly, a strange ululating noise filled the room. Brisa fell to her knees, arms wrapped around her head. "O-o-o-oh. We've been poisoned …"

The hair-raising sound was more than his frayed nerves could handle. Avitus slammed his fist on the table so hard a slice of egg bounced off the plate. "Silence!"

The moaning stopped.

"I don't want a word out of anyone except to answer my questions. Is that clear?"

Heads nodded.

"Who cooked this meal?"

"I did," Brisa said.

"All of it?"

"Yes, sir, although Nissa shelled the beans, so if you found bits of pod, it wasn't my fault."

Avitus pointed to the platter of eggs with their garnish of poison. "Did you cook these and place them on this platter?"

"Yes, sir."

"Told you," muttered Livia.

He ignored her.

"Did anyone else enter the kitchen at any time even for a moment?"

"No, sir," Brisa replied.

"You're sure?"

A nod.

Avitus stared at his housekeeper. She wouldn't admit the facts so readily if she were guilty. Therefore, there must be another explanation. "Did you purchase these ingredients?"

"No sir. I made do with what Nissa bought this morning."

Aha! Avitus turned to Nissa. "Did you shop for today's meal?"

"Yes, sir."

"What did your purchase?"

"The fish, the eggs, the beans, a string of onions, and a bunch of rosemary."

Rosemary. That was an herb! He pointed to the green stuff on top of the eggs. "Is this rosemary?"

Nissa shook her head.

"Then what is it?

She shrugged. "I don't know, sir. The only fresh herb I had in the kitchen was rosemary. I don't recognize this leafy stuff. It wasn't anything I purchased."

Avitus reluctantly turned back to Brisa. "Where did this herb come from?"

She frowned at the platter. "I don't know, my lord. I didn't put it there."

"Somebody did," Livia snapped.

"It wasn't me."

"Then it must have been someone else. Who else was in the kitchen?"

"Nobody."

"You're absolutely sure?" Avitus demanded.

Momus cleared his throat. "Are you forgetting the doctor?"

Livia frowned at Brisa. "What doctor? Are you sick?"

Brisa clamped her mouth shut and stared doggedly at the floor.

Avitus slammed his fist on the table again. "Answer us!"

"The doctor said you'd asked him for—" Brisa's eyes slid to Livia, and she pressed her lips together.

"Tell me," Avitus said sternly. "Every word."

"He said you'd asked him for a tonic and you didn't want the mistress to know about it. He made me promise not to tell. He gave me directions for mixing it properly. Then he asked me what I was cooking and left."

"Were the eggs on the platter when the doctor was in the kitchen?"

Brisa nodded.

Her answer sent prickles of fear up Avitus's spine.

"What doctor are you talking about?" Livia asked, "Do you mean Dioges?"

"No, my lady," Momus said. "Alexander of Tarsus was his name."

Avitus shook his head. "That's not right. I don't know a doctor named Alexander. What did this man look like?"

Momus shrugged. "Old and hunched."

"I need more than that to identify him."

"Over forty. Thin face. Balding."

Avitus ground his teeth. Hundreds of men could fit that description.

"Would you recognize the doctor if you saw him again?" Livia asked Momus.

"Yes, my lady."

"Then I have an idea." Livia sent Roxana for her drawing board. She sketched a thin face with a beak of a nose and angry eyes over a long neck and hunched shoulders. An excellent likeness of Dioges. She held her board for them to see. "Is this the man?"

Both Brisa and Momus nodded.

Livia stared at the sketch. "But why did he try to kill us?"

"I must have frightened him, asking him about the love tonic this morning."

Avitus closed his eyes and thought back over the interview with the doctor. (Amazing how a scene could have a drastically different interpretation when looked at from a different angle.) Avitus's request for the love potion would have made Dioges instantly suspicious. When Avitus persisted in trying to purchase some, Dioges must have decided to silence him. But why would Dioges risk killing Avitus so blatantly? Unless…!

He opened his eyes. "You've seen Dioges's shop. How would you describe it?"

Livia wrinkled her brow. "It's cramped but tidy, and it reeks of the vile medicines he brews."

"Tidy? You're sure?"

She nodded. "Tidy to the point of fussy. Every jar and sack arranged just so on the shelves. Why?"

"Because this morning his shop was in disarray, and there were two open traveling chests on the floor."

Livia sucked in a breath. "You think he's planning to flee the city?"

The killer had been under their noses the entire time, and Livia had missed it. How could she have been so blind?

Dioges had made the love tonic. Dioges knew it was meant for no one besides Gracchus. And Dioges had been in the kitchen that night, handling the medicines. It would have been a simple thing to switch jars when the cook wasn't looking.

And now the devious doctor planned to escape before his latest poisonous deeds were discovered.

Livia grabbed her husband's arm. "We can't let him get away with this! You must have him apprehended at once."

Avitus shook his head. "I'm not leaving you."

"But—"

"Shh." He laid a finger on her lips. "We'll find him. Trust me."

Avitus beckoned Timon. "Go to Publius. Tell him Dioges is the murderer and we fear he's trying to flee. He'll probably head for the harbor to find passage on a ship. And since he was packing two large chests this morning, I'd guess he'll either travel by ox cart or barge. Tell Publius to send men on horseback to Ostia right away. They should search every oxcart they pass. If they don't find Dioges on the Ostian Road, Publius's men can search the barges coming downstream from Rome."

An excellent plan. Despite Avitus's annoying tendency to caution, he could act quickly when he needed to. Men on horseback could easily catch up to a slow-moving ox cart before it reached the busy port of Ostia.

"After you've talked with Publius," Avitus said to Timon, "go to Dioges's apartment. If Dioges is still there, keep watch. If not, return home."

"Yes sir." Timon headed for the door.

"Wait!" Livia called.

Timon turned. "My lady?"

She held up her drawing board. "Take this sketch of Dioges to show Publius's men."

Timon hurried off. Avitus ordered the servants not to touch any food or drink until Brother Titus checked it for poison. Then he slumped wearily in his seat and rubbed his temple.

How could he feel tired at a moment like this? Livia's mind swirled. If Dioges had attempted to poison them, who else was in danger? Calida? Publius?

Gracchus!

Livia bolted up straight. "You must warn him!"

Avitus blinked at her. "Warn who?"

"Gracchus. Dioges wouldn't leave Rome unless he was sure Gracchus was going to die."

"Humph. Good riddance."

"No, Avitus! Don't talk like that! Consider how many in Gracchus's house are at risk. Think of the children! You don't want their deaths on your head."

Avitus's jaw twitched. "No one can blame me. I'm not the poisoner."

"But you can stop him."

"We're probably too late. Dioges was at Gracchus's house this morning to deliver a jar of theriac—Oh!" her husband's eyebrows rose. "I bet he's poisoned the theriac. How deliciously ironic, killing Gracchus with the medicine he believes is an antidote."

Livia could strangle him! "How can you smile about something so horrible? You must warn Gracchus before he and his sons succumb."

"I will do no such thing. Gracchus would laugh in my face."

Please, Lord Jesus! How do I convince him when he sees mercy as weakness and forgiveness as a loss of dignitas?

Hmm, could she appeal to his honor?

"My dear husband, you value the legal rights of all citizens. Doesn't Gracchus deserve the full protection of the law as much as anyone?"

"No! There is no law that compels me to warn Gracchus that his doctor may have poisoned his theriac."

"But by keeping silent when you know a murder will happen, you are abetting the killer. You don't want to live the rest of your life knowing you *could* have prevented murder and failed to act, do you?"

CHAPTER THIRTY-FIVE

How could his wife worry about Gracchus's welfare at a time like this? It was illogical and infuriating. But he mustn't allow Livia to become agitated with poison in her veins. Avitus banished his annoyance and softened his voice.

"You're right. I don't want murder on my conscience. I promise I'll do everything reasonable to prevent it." (Obviously, knocking on the door of his bitterest enemy to tell him his physician may have tried to poison him fell outside what was reasonable.)

Fortunately, Brother Titus arrived before Livia could probe his motives. While the physician tended Livia, Avitus paced the peristyle. Anger surged through his limbs. The sanctity of his home had been breached.

Now, they must prevent the deadly doctor from fleeing Rome because they needed his testimony to prove Publius innocent. Avitus yearned to join the chase and ensure Dioges was found, yet he couldn't abandon his wife to face a painful death alone.

The physician emerged from the bedroom. "Thanks to your quick action, I think she'll live. I've administered an antidote and a calming tonic. If she lives past midnight, I'm confident she'll make a full recovery. However, there's a complication. She wants to tell you herself."

Livia was sitting up in bed. Avitus kissed her, not caring if poison lingered on her lips. "Brother Titus says you'll live."

"I believe him. But there's something I haven't told you. I was waiting until I was sure, but now you must know. I might be with child. Oh, Avitus, what if the poison harms the baby?"

Avitus was too stunned to answer. A baby? His baby?

"I could be wrong, but my cycle is late, and I'm terrified that …what if the poison…?" Livia crumpled, sobbing. Avitus gathered her into his arms and held her against his chest.

"Shh." He rocked her gently as his mind raced. His wife was—could be—expecting. What if they both died?

No! He wouldn't think that way.

"You're not going to die, and neither is the baby. I'll ask Brother Titus to pray for you. If your God is as good as you say he is, he'll protect you both."

Livia nodded. Wiped the tears from her cheeks. "Yes. God is with us. And he'll be with you too, helping you find Dioges."

"I'm not leaving you."

"Yes, you are." Livia sat up and grabbed his arm. "There's nothing you can do to help me. There's a killer on the loose. You must stop Dioges and save innocent lives. Promise me you'll do it."

"I'll do everything in my power. But while I'm gone, you must promise to rest quietly and obey the doctor's orders."

"I will." She smiled and lay back on her pillow. "May God protect you and give you success."

Avitus kissed her forehead, pleading with all the gods who were listening to keep her alive. Then he went out to talk with Brother Titus, who agreed to stay but insisted on praying over Avitus first.

"Dear Lord Jesus, I ask your favor over my friend, Avitus. Protect and guide him. May you provide a lamp for his feet and a light for his way. Amen"

Duly blessed, Avitus and Sorex set out for the *vigiles* barracks located near Dioges's apartment. In addition to serving as the city's firefighters, the vigiles were tasked with apprehending criminals and keeping the peace after dark. The barracks was humming with activity as men prepared rope buckets, axes, and other firefighting equipment before heading out on their nightly rounds. Avitus hailed one of the men. "I'm Avitus, brother of Senator Publius. I need to speak with your commanding officer."

"Yes, sir. About what, sir?"

"My wife's been poisoned."

"I'll take you to the tribune right away. Follow me."

The young man led Avitus to a cluster of men standing around a siphon cart. The heavy, water-filled cart contained a powerful pump that could spray water dozens of feet into the air, an important tool for fighting fires in the four- and five-story apartment buildings that filled the crowded city.

"That's the tribune there, sir." The young man pointed to a tall man who was glaring at the others, arms akimbo.

"I don't want excuses!" the tribune shouted at parade-ground volume. "Get this pump fixed immediately. I'm not going before the Prefect to explain why we didn't have our equipment working and let half the city burn down."

"Yes, sir!" the other men chorused.

They sprang into action. The tribune turned to go. Avitus's escort waved him over. "Sir, a gentleman to see you. Says his wife's been poisoned."

The tribune muttered a curse. "Another poison case. That's all we need tonight. Come with me." He led Avitus to a small room furnished with a bare table and three stools. "You've come at a busy time. Make it quick."

Avitus gave a brief account of how Dioges had tried to poison them. "We suspect him of several other deaths as well."

"Dioges, you say?" The tribune shook his head in disgust. "I wondered if he was quite right in the head. He hasn't acted normal since his sister died. I'll dispatch a squad to arrest him at once."

"We think he may have fled his apartment."

"If he's not home, we'll search the area. I'll send word to the other units, requesting they search for him as well. Though I can't guarantee the other cohorts will see this as a priority." The tribune shrugged. "I wish I could do more, but I have to work through official channels."

Avitus clenched his jaw in frustration. There were cohorts of vigiles spread throughout the city's fourteen regions, and they didn't always cooperate with each other. If he wanted Dioges caught, he'd need to find him on his own.

"Perhaps you can do me favor," Avitus said to the tribune. "My guess is Dioges will head for the river to take a barge down to Ostia. Can you give me a letter asking for the support of the vigiles in that region?"

The officer shook his head. "I have a better suggestion. What you really want is assistance from barge captains who know the river."

The tribune scratched a hasty message into a blank tablet. "Take this to Big Marcus. Anybody along the river can tell you where to find him. Make it worth his while, and he'll be your best resource."

Avitus stuffed the tablet into his belt. "Thank you. If you find Dioges or any hint of where he's gone, send word to Senator Publius."

"Will do. Good hunting."

Within a quarter-hour of reaching the river, Avitus and Sorex had located Big Marcus—who lived up to the name and then some. He was as broad as Sorex, almost as tall, and significantly wider about the waist. His girth was augmented by a booming voice, which he was using to chivvy a line of porters loading a barge.

"It's almost sundown, you flea-infested, no-good varmints. No rest for any of you 'til every crate is loaded and properly stowed. Hey, granite-for-brains! Where do you think you're going with that amphora?"

Avitus waited until the big man's tirade came to an end. "Big Marcus?"

"Yeah?" He turned and looked Avitus up and down. "If you're wanting to hire barge passage, come back tomorrow."

"I was told you could help me." Avitus handed him the tribune's message. Big Marcus scanned it quickly and grunted. "I can spare you a moment. What's the problem?"

"We're hunting a murderer who tried to poison my wife. A doctor named Dioges. Graying hair, small and hunched, with a narrow face and a beaked nose. Probably traveling with two large wooden chests."

"He's a murderer, eh? No wonder I took against him."

Avitus's heart drummed in his chest. "You've seen him?"

"Think so. A man matching your description was here this afternoon, 'cept he only had one chest with him. Arrived just after my final barge of the day headed downriver. The idiot demanded I call the barge back for him. When I refused, he wanted to buy passage on another barge and leave immediately."

Big Marcus made a noise of disgust in the back of his throat. "If he thought I was going to send an empty barge downriver to transport one man, he was a bigger fool than he looked. I told him he'd have to wait until morning. That got him bug-eyed and spluttering—er, hold on."

Big Marcus bellowed at the line of porters, "That's quality merchandise you're handling, you ham-fisted baboons! Watch what you're doing! I'll take it out of your sorry hides if I find any damage!"

After shaking a fist, Big Marcus turned back to Avitus. "Sorry. Got to keep an eye on those brutes. Where was I?"

"Refusing to send Dioges on an empty barge."

"Right. Next, he demanded I hurry up and load another barge. I told him it was too close to sundown and there's the tide to consider. Have to respect the currents if you want to survive on the river. When the idiot finally realized I wasn't going to change my mind, he marched off. Good riddance, I say."

"Where did he go?"

"Off to hire passage with someone else, I assume. But I doubt he'll find anyone to take him downstream to Ostia tonight. Not for the paltry sum he was offering."

Avitus's heart lifted. They still had a chance. "Which way did he go?"

Instead of answering, Big Marcus crossed his arms and tilted his head. "The river is a busy place, and you two don't know your way around. I can round up a few lads to help you search. How much is it worth to you?"

They haggled over the price. Avitus was in too much of hurry to bargain long, and Big Marcus knew it. He pocketed the coins with a smile. "Good doing business with you. Tell anyone you talk to that Big Marcus sent you, and they'll cooperate."

"Thank you."

Avitus assigned one team of Big Marcus's men to go upstream and the other team to search farther downstream. That left the closest section of riverbank for Avitus and Sorex.

At first, every person they questioned remembered seeing Dioges. "You'd think the idiot would have figured out he wasn't going downstream tonight without offering to pay more," one bargeman commented.

"Guess he couldn't afford to," said his mate.

"Sure, he could," the first man said. "Must've had something valuable in that heavy chest of his. Too greedy to part with any of it, I'd guess."

The doctor's frugality was a boon to Avitus, but they still had to find the man. Dusk was fast approaching. The shouts of porters and foremen died out, replaced by the creaking of mooring ropes and the flickering light of torches. The sun sank below the horizon, and the riverside was becoming a shadowy, treacherous place. Avitus and Sorex were forced to move slower lest they pass a boat unawares.

Avitus was beginning to fear their quarry had escaped when a squint-eyed bargeman told them he'd seen Dioges.

Finally!

"The man you're looking for said he was a doctor, and it was urgent he get to Ostia to see a patient. Insisted it was life and death and he had to go tonight." Squinty huffed in indignation. "How stupid does he think I am? If someone's dying in Ostia, how does he know about it up here in Rome, huh? We see that a lot, you know. People desperate to get away from the city for one reason or another. You say this one was an escaped criminal? What's he done, then? Filled his big chest with stolen silver?"

"Poisoned a senator's wife," Avitus replied.

"Ooh, that's bad. Glad I sent him on his way."

"Which way did he go?"

"Downstream."

"Thanks."

Avitus and Sorex trudged to the next barge, but the gruff man standing guard claimed he hadn't seen the doctor. Nor had the one after that. Another few minutes of fruitless searching brought them to the end of their stretch of river. The team of Big Marcus's men who'd been downstream were waiting for him.

"We've lost his trail," Avitus told his allies.

"Probably holed up on a barge overnight, sir. Nothing we can do but wait until morning and start the search again."

"We can't quit," Avitus said. "He must be close by somewhere."

"The river is dangerous at night, sir. You don't want to risk a stumble in the dark, or the next thing anybody knows, your body will be found a mile downstream. Come back at first light, and we'll help you find your criminal."

They started upstream. With every step, Avitus's heart grew heavier. If they gave up now, Dioges would get away. He was certain of it.

In desperation, he muttered a prayer. "Are you there, God of Livia? If you are, show me the light Brother Titus said would guide my path."

The next instant, a torch flared to life along a stretch of riverbank he'd thought was empty. A second torch followed.

It was a sign.

"I see a barge we missed. Follow me."

CHAPTER THIRTY-SIX

Roxana sat on a stool, holding Mistress Livia's hand while Brother Titus led them in prayers. The mistress lay in bed, pale and in pain, moaning at the burning in her throat. Despite all their efforts, the mistress had gotten slowly worse over the last hour. Between prayers, Brother Titus recited psalms to comfort the mistress and remind her that God was able to heal all diseases. That God was their strong tower and his love for them was higher than the heavens.

After a while, the mistress grew agitated. Brother Titus laid a hand on her forehead. "Be at peace, my sister. Rest now."

"I can't," the mistress whispered, her voice raspy. "My heart is troubled. I tried to convince Avitus to send a warning to Gracchus, but he refused. I can't rest until I take care of it. Roxana, bring Grim to me."

Roxana turned to obey, but Brother Titus stopped her. "This is not your responsibility."

The mistress huffed a frustrated sigh. "Yes, it is. Avitus won't act, so I must."

Brother Titus shook his head. "This matter is between God and your husband. Remember how God changed Avitus's heart two days ago? We will ask God to do so again. Therefore, be at peace."

"I can't until I talk to Brisa. I want peace between us in case I ... don't survive."

"Don't talk that way, Mistress! You'll live!"

"I'll fight for life with every breath, but I need to talk with Brisa. Now, please."

"Yes, my lady."

Stepping out of the bedroom, Roxana found everyone huddled outside the door. Even Fumo was there leaning forlornly against Momus.

"How is she?" Grim asked.

"Weak but fighting. Brother Titus is hopeful."

"Thank the gods," Momus said. "What can we do to help?"

Good question. Roxana could see everyone needed a task to occupy their minds and channel their restless energy.

"Momus, you and Fumo keep watch at the door and bring us word of any developments. Grim, tell Tirzah that Brother Titus is staying with Livia and ask her to pray for us."

The men nodded and left. That left Nissa and Brisa. Even the old sourpuss looked concerned, her hands worrying the end of her belt.

"Nissa, please fix the mistress a cup of honeyed wine. Then check on Nemesis and the kittens."

Nissa scuttled to obey. Roxana turned to Brisa.

"The mistress is asking for you."

Brisa paled. She followed Roxana into the room, head hanging. "Forgive me mistress! It's my fault. I should have noticed the deadly leaves. I should have kept a better eye on the doctor—"

"Stop! No excuses," the mistress whispered. "Come closer."

Brisa approached the bed. Mistress Livia took her hand. "I don't hold you responsible for what happened. I forgive you."

Brisa dropped to her knees. Tears streaming down her cheeks, she kissed the mistress' hand. "Thank you, my lady. May all the gods bless you."

The mistress lay back and closed her eyes.

"Come, Roxana." Brother Titus whispered after Brisa was gone. "Our prayer vigil isn't over."

Avitus strode toward the torches, followed by Sorex and the two allies. As they neared the barge, Avitus could make out shadowy forms of tarp-draped piles filling the barge's interior.

Was Dioges hiding on that boat? Avitus's gut told him the answer was yes.

A man stepped into their path, arms crossed and feet spread. "Halt! Who are you and what do you want?"

"We're looking for a man called Dioges. Gray hair, thin face, hooked nose, hunched shoulders, traveling with a large chest. Have you seen him?"

"No, so you can move along."

The guard was lying. Avitus could read it in his voice and tautness of his body. What would be the quickest way to win the man's cooperation? A bribe? Threats? Logic?

The guard drew a stout cudgel from his belt. "I don't trust strangers after dark. Scram, or I'll whistle for my mates."

Avitus could see at least two more men standing guard on the barge. All three oozed hostility. They were clearly hiding something.

Which gave Avitus an idea.

"The man we're searching for is a murderer. Either you hand him over to us quietly and we'll be on our way, or else I'll fetch a company of vigiles to search your boat. If you don't want the authorities looking closely at your cargo, I'd suggest you cooperate."

"This man you're looking for. What's he guilty of?"

"Killing a senator's wife. With poison."

The guard swore. "I knew that man was trouble. Let me talk to my mates."

Avitus's heart soared. He'd guessed correctly!

After a whispered conference, the shore guard returned to Avitus. "The man you want is sleeping near the bow."

Clambering into the barge, Avitus and his fellow searchers silently surrounded a shoulder-high pile of cargo draped with a tarp. When all four men were in place, Sorex yanked the tarp up and over the crates.

Dioges sat up, blinking in sleepy surprise. Then he scrambled to his feet. "What's the meaning of this? I paid you to leave me alone."

Avitus stepped into the torchlight. "Good evening, Dioges. I hereby arrest you for attempting to murder me and my wife.

You are also answerable for the death of Salvia, wife of Senator Gracchus."

"Lies!" Dioges pressed his back against the pile of crates, eyes darting wildly from one attacker to the next. A cornered rat with no place to run.

"There's no point trying to escape, Dioges. Give yourself up."

"You'll never take me alive." Dioges scrambled up the pile of crates. He pulled something from his belt and held it aloft with a maniacal laugh. A glass vial. Before Avitus could react, Dioges yanked a cork from the tiny vial and tipped the contents into his mouth.

"Stop him!"

Sorex grabbed the man and tossed him over his shoulder. Avitus snatched the vial. It still held a few drops of acrid-smelling liquid. Poison?

"Too late. I'll be dead in minutes." Dioges cackled, eyes feverish in the wavering torchlight.

No! Avitus would not let this murderous weasel defeat him. "Make him vomit."

Sorex obliged.

When Dioges finished heaving, he stood and sneered at Avitus. "It won't do any good. I took enough hemlock to kill an elephant."

Was he telling the truth? Hades! They must get a confession out of him immediately. Avitus fought the panic tightening his chest. He took two deep breaths and stilled his thoughts. This would require finesse.

Letting his shoulders droop, Avitus added a hint of despair to his voice. "Curses, you've outsmarted us all."

"Yes, I have," the dying man said.

"But why did you want to kill me? What have I done to harm you?"

"You knew about the love potion. I couldn't let you tell Gracchus before I'd had a chance to kill him."

Avitus wrinkled his brow and shook his head. "I thought you were trying to kill Salvia."

"That was the maid's fault!" Dioges hissed. "That stupid cow gave her mistress the wrong medicine and ruined my perfect plan. The poison was meant for Gracchus, curse him."

Got you!

Avitus checked to see that his allies had heard the confession. Good. Then he pretended shock. "You were trying to kill Gracchus? Why?"

The doctor's eyes flamed with hatred. "He killed my sister. She'd still be alive if it wasn't for his black lustful heart." Dioges drew a ragged breath. "I found her writhing in pain on the floor. I couldn't save her. As I wept over her lifeless body, I vowed I would have my revenge. This time I've made sure Gracchus will die a painful death."

The man was diabolical. But he'd given Avitus the confession he needed. "Bring him and let's be gone."

CHAPTER THIRTY-SEVEN

According to Plato's account of Socrates's death by hemlock, the great teacher had continued to walk and talk until his legs had ceased to function. In similar fashion, by the time they marched Dioges to the nearest vigiles barracks, his arms and legs were going limp. But his mouth still functioned, and the vigiles recorded a full confession of his crimes.

Avitus had accomplished all he'd set out to do. He should be elated. But instead on his trek back across the city, a debate raged in his head.

Should he warn Gracchus of the poisoned theriac? Or not?

For once, Avitus held the power of death over his enemy. He could keep silent and allow the mad doctor's poison to do its evil work. Then Gracchus's threats would be eliminated. Forever.

But what came after? Did Avitus want Gracchus's death on his conscience? Would the guilt of it fill his soul with shame each time he looked into his wife's eyes?

A voice deep in his soul cried, *No*.

Unlike Gracchus, Avitus respected the law. It was the law that made Rome a civilized society by guaranteeing every man's right to a fair trial. It was the law that protected free men from being unjustly preyed upon by cruel tyrants and unscrupulous liars. Without the due process of law, any man could kill his neighbor and get away with it. Was that the society Avitus championed?

Absolutely not.

And yet, only a fool would rush to the protection of his enemy.

Jupiter, Best and Greatest! He would drive himself insane thinking in circles. Which choice was the right one?

"You're upset," Sorex said as they crossed the wide and empty forum.

"I face a dilemma. Warn Gracchus of Dioges's treachery or keep silent and let him die."

"A difficult choice."

"It shouldn't be. He deserves death for his many crimes."

"What Gracchus deserves is a matter for the gods."

"Then you counsel me to proceed with this fool's errand?"

"When I was a gladiator, there were many fighters who were fueled by hatred. They wanted only to make their opponent suffer. Others strove to fight well and honorably. These men I respected. A small-minded bully lives for vengeance. An honorable man extends mercy to his enemy. In so doing, he shows he is the stronger of the two."

"So be it."

Avitus set his jaw and turned toward his enemy's house. Each step was like wading through waist-deep water. The closer he got, the louder the voices in his head screamed at him to stop. *He'll find a way to use this against you. He'll make a fool of you before you get a chance to explain the danger. He'll make you the laughingstock of Rome.*

Avitus stopped walking. This was pointless. Gracchus wouldn't trust a word he said, so why bother?

Ahead, a torch in a wall bracket flared brightly. It drew his attention, and as he looked at the flame, his fears quieted, replaced by Brother Titus's voice praying that God's light would guide him. Was this another sign?

Can you protect me from Gracchus? Can you convince him to listen?

As if in reply, more torches flared farther up the street. Taking another step, Avitus found the force resisting him had lessened.

He kept going.

Gracchus's doorkeeper met them in the street, his arms crossed over his broad chest and his hard eyes glittering with malice. "What do you want?"

"I've come to speak with Gracchus," Avitus said.

"He doesn't want to speak with you."

"I've come to save his life."

"Sure you have. And I'm the king of Parthia."

"Tell your master I've discovered a plot to murder him. If he wants to know more, he can invite me in."

A flicker of concern crossed the big slave's lumpy face. "Wait here."

The doorkeeper was back almost immediately. He led Avitus to a formal study where silver lampstands illuminated a table strewn with scrolls.

Gracchus didn't bother to rise from his chair. He leaned back and regarded Avitus with a scowl. "I thought my doorkeeper was seeing visions when he reported you were at my door. He may have believed your feeble story, but I don't."

And yet he'd admitted Avitus to his study. More proof of Livia's God and his power? Perhaps. Avitus pressed on. "I'm here to warn you. The man who poisoned Salvia was in your house today."

Avitus pointed a finger at Gracchus's head. "You're the one he wants to murder."

"Why should I believe you?"

"Because you almost died the night your wife was poisoned. You're only alive because you forced Fausta to drink your cup of love tonic after hers spilled. She died later that night, poisoned by the wine that was meant to kill you. Even the small amount you sipped made you sick. Did you notice your lips burning?"

Gracchus pushed to his feet, eyes glittering with malice. "Do you think you can scare me? What do you hope to accomplish with your pitiful lies?"

"Not lies. Truth. Fausta wasn't your first unwilling victim. There was also Dioges's sister Leto." Avitus pulled a tablet from his belt. "I have a signed copy of Dioges's confession. He poisoned the tonic that almost killed you. He was in your house this morning, and he's confident you'll die this time. Do you know what he tampered with?"

"I didn't send for Dioges today. Get out of my house."

Avitus placed his hands on the table and leaned down to stare into Gracchus's face. "I'd be happy if you ignored me and died a painful death, but it would be a pity for your sons to die. If I were you, I'd talk to your steward about the theriac Dioges made for you. You've been warned."

Spinning on his heel, Avitus left without a backward glance.

Avitus arrived home steeling himself for the worst. He found his wife sitting up in bed. She was pale but her eyes were clear—not bright with fever or clouded in pain. He rushed to her side, relief buckling his legs. Dropping onto the bed, he pulled her into his arms.

"You're alive." Avitus buried his face in her hair and breathed the scent of her.

Livia pulled away, smiling at him. "Brother Titus says my breathing and pulse are normal, and my throat no longer burns so painfully. Did you find Dioges?"

"Yes." Avitus gave her the full story of Big Marcus and the search along the riverbank. "It was getting dark, and my allies wanted to quit. In desperation, I asked your God to guide me. And he did. Torches appeared in the dark and led us to where Dioges was hiding."

"Hallelujah, our prayers were answered. Where is Dioges now?"

"When he saw he was surrounded, Dioges poisoned himself. But your God must have been listening to your prayers because we got Dioges to the vigiles, where he confessed the whole story before it was too late. It was his sister's death that pushed him to murder. She'd been abused by Gracchus just like Fausta had. When she became pregnant, she was afraid Dioges would cast her out, so she attempted to end the pregnancy. Dioges found her dying of the drugs she'd taken and vowed to kill Gracchus to avenge her death. I have a copy of his confession signed by a vigiles centurion. I'm confident that with this confession, Publius and I can convince Gracchus that Publius isn't guilty of murdering Salvia."

"One more question," Livia whispered. "Did you warn Gracchus?"

"I did."

Livia laid her hands on Avitus's cheeks and looked him in the eyes. Her own shimmered with tears. "You, my love, are the bravest, most honorable man I have ever met."

Her words spread warmth through his whole body, loosening the knot of fear in his stomach. Avitus pulled Livia to him and closed his eyes, feeling the steady rise and fall of her breathing.

This was all he wanted. For this night, all was well with his soul.

CHAPTER THIRTY-EIGHT

The two-week-old kitten tottered across the peristyle, heading for Fumo, who lay with his chin resting on his paws, watching the tiny beast approach.

Livia's guest Tirzah drew a nervous breath.

Don't worry," Livia whispered. "Watch what happens."

The kitten clambered over Fumo's outstretched paws and raised its head. A tiny pink tongue flicked out and licked the dog on the nose. Fumo didn't move.

"Amazing, isn't it?" Livia murmured.

"Yes," Tirzah said, eyes shining in wonder. "I've never seen a dog behave so calmly with a cat."

"Neither have I," Livia said. "Good dog, Fumo. Thank you for being patient with the little pests."

Fumo's tail thumped, drawing the kitten's interest. It toddled around the dog and pounced on the tail. Fumo swished his tail away. The kitten chased after it.

"That's enough, little adventurer," Roxana said, coming to the dog's rescue. "You mustn't outstay your welcome."

She returned the kitten to its litter mates on the opposite side of the peristyle. Tirzah shook her head, an amused smile on her lips. "What does Avitus think about this little miracle of domestic peace?"

"Since the night I was poisoned, he's a changed man. Avitus credits our Lord for keeping me alive. And for guiding him to Dioges and giving him the courage to warn Gracchus."

"Thank you, Lord Jesus," Tirzah said, gripping Livia's hand. "We've been praying Avitus will be drawn to our faith."

And Livia was watching it happen. Her reserved husband didn't trust others easily and had few friends. But in the last week, he'd enjoyed several long talks with Brother Titus. Today the two men had gone to watch the races. While they enjoyed the drama of galloping horses and careening chariots, Livia and Tirzah enjoyed a peaceful day of women's talk and kitten antics.

Smiling widely, Nissa trotted into the peristyle with a loaded tray. "Good afternoon, ladies. I've prepared refreshments."

She set out sesame biscuits, olive and pine nut spread, and a platter of cheese and fruit artfully arranged to look like a flower.

"That looks delicious." Tirzah took a bite of sesame biscuit. "Mm, these are excellent."

"Everything Nissa makes is delicious. Auntie's cook says she's a natural in the kitchen."

Nissa beamed at Livia's compliment. "Thank you, Mistress."

"That young woman has bloomed under your care," Tirzah said when Nissa was gone.

"I thank God at every meal for her transformation."

The conversation moved on to other topics. Tirzah was finishing an amusing anecdote about a neighbor who'd sprained her arm chasing a magpie that had stolen her hair ribbon when Momus entered.

"Forgive me for interrupting, Mistress. This came for the master." He handed her a scroll.

"Thank you, Momus."

Anger tightened Livia's stomach as she saw Gracchus's emblem stamped into the seal. Could this finally be a word of thanks for warning him of Dioges's poisons? Or was Gracchus up to his usual tricks, breathing threats and retribution?

She wanted to crush the scroll, but that would solve nothing. "I know it's wrong, but there are moments when I regret pleading with Avitus to warn Gracchus. If we'd kept our mouths shut, he would most likely be dead, and we wouldn't have to fear him any longer. Sometimes I get angry at God for allowing evil men like Gracchus to prosper."

"I understand how you feel," Tirzah said. "But hating evil men won't solve anything. It only burdens our hearts. That's why our Lord asks us to forgive others, even our enemies. We conquer evil with love and mercy. One heart at a time."

Gracchus's selfish heart was far from being conquered, but brooding over him would only ruin their pleasant afternoon. Livia took the scroll to Avitus's study and turned her attention to happier topics.

"You can help me choose which room to redo next. I can't decide between our bedroom and Avitus's study. He doesn't see what's wrong with either room, but the frescoes are faded and out of date."

Tirzah tksed and nodded as Livia showed her the tired decor in both rooms. "I agree with you the rooms could use a makeover, but I think you might want to consider tackling the nursery first."

Livia felt her face grow red. "We have no need of a nursery yet."

"You will soon enough."

Bouts of nausea had confirmed Livia was with child. She'd confided her fears to Tirzah, who had pledged to mentor Livia through every step of the journey. Perhaps planning a nursery would help prepare her heart for motherhood. Livia brought out her sketching board. She and Tirzah discussed possible artwork for the nursery until the men returned.

Avitus and Brother Titus walked in together like old friends. They both seemed happy and relaxed. Wonderful!

"Did you have a pleasant afternoon?" Livia asked them.

"Most satisfying," Avitus said. "The Blues won more races than any other team, and the Reds suffered a spectacular crash in the second-to-last race."

Since Livia was a fan of the Reds, she scrunched her face at him.

He grinned back. "To celebrate the Blues' superiority, Brother Titus has invited us to dinner tomorrow night. I've accepted."

"That sounds lovely." Livia would happily sit through an evening of the men crowing over their favorite team if it cemented their relationship. The more opportunities her husband had to probe Brother Titus on their faith, the closer he would come to the kingdom.

After thanking their friends for the invitation and bidding them cheerful goodbyes, Livia and Avitus settled onto their favorite bench.

They traded tidbits from their day. Livia told Avitus about Tirzah's neighbor and the magpie. Avitus said he'd bumped into Rutilia, who had thanked him profusely for warning Gracchus about the poisoned theriac. "I told her you deserved credit too. I wouldn't have found the courage to face him without your urging. Or your prayers."

"Thank you."

Sadly, Livia's joy over her husband's change of heart was soured by Gracchus's ingratitude. "Speaking of Gracchus, he sent you a scroll this afternoon. It's in your study."

Avitus retrieved it. He glowered at it for twenty heartbeats. Sighed heavily. Broke the seal and unrolled the short length of papyrus. He mouthed the words to himself. Frowned. Shook his head and read them again.

Then he looked up, wonder in his eyes.

"What does it say?"

He thrust the scroll into her hands. It bore a single line of text:

You were right. I am in your debt. G.

EPILOGUE

An Ode to Motherhood

O motherhood, that wondrous state.
A new life begun, a heart forever changed.
Who am I now
As this chapter of my life unfolds?

With maid and midwife at my side,
I face the future with hope and faith.
I will not fear.
Whate'er may come, I will not be alone.

Mother and sleuth, can I be both,
Pursuing justice while I raise a child?
A mystery
As yet unsolved. A tale for another day.

By Livia Aemilia (who still doesn't pretend to be a poet).

GLOSSARY

Ague: An archaic term for an illness such as malaria involving intermittent periods of fevers, chills, and flu-like symptoms.

Aesculapius: (also spelled Asclepius). A god of healing and medicine. His snake-entwined staff remains a symbol of medicine today.

Brigands (game): A two-person strategy game similar to chess and played on a square grid.

Cliens: plural *clientes*. Roman society functioned on a system of patronage—a mutually beneficial system where a powerful man (*patronus*) collected a group of less-influential men (*clientes*). The *patronus* used his influence to aid his *clientes*. The *clientes* enhanced the prestige of their *patronus* and supported his public endeavors.

Cloaca Maxima: The "great sewer" of ancient Rome. The central section was large enough to drive a wagon through. It still drains water from the old forums today.

Erato: One of the nine muses of Roman mythology. Erato was the goddess who inspired lyrical poetry (also erotic poetry, but respectable Roman women don't mention this fact). See *muses*.

Gorgon: A mythological monster who could turn people to stone by looking at them. Medusa is the most well-known gorgon.

Majestas: The crime of treason, including sedition, falsifying documents, or dishonoring the emperor. Those accused were killed, and their property was forfeit to the state.

Medicus: A trained physician serving in the army.

Money: Common Roman coins include the *denarius*, *sestertius*, *as*, and *quadrans*. A denarius was roughly equivalent to the daily wage of a common laborer. A denarius equaled four sestertii. A sestertius equaled four asses or sixteen quadrans.

Muses: In Greek and Roman mythology, the nine muses were goddesses who gave humans inspiration for the arts, literature, and the sciences. Ancient writers often invoked the muses at the start of a poem or work of literature.

Paterfamilias: The male head of household. He had legal authority over everyone in the household, including his wife, adult children, and slaves.

Patronus: A Roman man of influence. The benefactor mentioned in Luke 22:25 probably refers to a patronus. See *cliens*.

Praetor: An elected Roman magistrate who presided over one of the standing courts.

Peristyle: A private interior garden often surrounded by colonnades. The *peristyle* was the central living area of many wealthy Roman houses.

Quadrans: A small copper coin worth 1/64 of a denarius. Mentioned in Mark 12:42 (typically translated mite, penny, or a few cents). See *Money*.

Shade: In Greek or Roman mythology, the spirit of a deceased person, now residing in the underworld. Derived from the word for shadow.

Siren: A mythological being with a seductive voice who lured sailors to their deaths. Mentioned in Homer's Odyssey. Mermaids may have evolved from *Sirens*.

Sylphium: A plant native to northern Africa that was highly valued for both culinary and medicinal purposes. It was overharvested to the point of extinction, making it rare and very expensive in the early first century. Based on descriptions, scientists guess it was related to fennel.

Theriac: A legendary antidote for poisons and various diseases. The mixture was first developed by King Mithrades IV of Pontus and later refined by Roman physicians. In the second century AD, the physician Galen wrote an entire treatise on *theriac*. Emperor Marcus Aurelius took *theriac* regularly.

Tribune: This title was (confusingly) used for various Roman offices, both governmental and military. For the purposes of this story, tribune refers to a legionary officer above a centurion or the officer in charge of a *vigiles* cohort (which were organized like military units).

Urban Praetor: The magistrate who presided over all civil cases involving Roman citizens.

Vigiles: The night watchmen and fire brigade for the city of Rome. Their main duty was to put out fires, but they also caught petty criminals and runaway slaves. The *vigiles* were assigned to patrol different regions of the city. Each of the seven *vigiles* cohorts consisted of one thousand men.

ACKNOWLEDGMENTS

I'm thankful for all the people who have mentored and encouraged me along my writing journey. From writer's conference instructors to chance encounters with fellow authors, many generous people have helped me become the author and speaker I am today.

I especially want to thank the people who have been instrumental in bringing this book to life. My mentor and brilliant editor, Jeanette Windle. My Sisters in Crime critique partner, Kym Brunner. The ever-encouraging women in my AWSA Mastermind group. Virginia Grounds, who guided me through the publishing journey. My team at Christian Speaker's Bootcamp, especially Robyn Dykstra. And finally, my family, who have supported me every step of the way.

IF YOU'RE A FAN OF THIS BOOK, WILL YOU HELP ME SPREAD THE WORD?

There are several ways you can help me get the word out about the message of this book…

- Post a 5-Star review on Amazon.
- Write about the book on your Facebook, Twitter, Instagram, LinkedIn, – any social media you regularly use!
- If you blog, consider referencing the book, or publishing an excerpt from the book with a link back to my website. You have my permission to do this if you provide proper credit and backlinks.
- Recommend the book to friends – word-of-mouth is still the most effective form of advertising.

OTHER BOOKS BY LISA E. BETZ

https://www.amazon.com/stores/Lisa-Betz/author/B00LMO3MN0
or https://lisaebetz.com/books/

Death and a Crocodile – Livia Aemilia Mysteries, Book One.

Fountains and Secrets – Livia Aemilia Mysteries, Book Two.

You can reach me through my website:
https://lisaebetz.com/contact/

Printed in the USA
CPSIA information can be obtained
at www.ICGtesting.com
CBHW031618131124
17315CB00024B/543